Praise for the writing of Cherise Sinclair

Club Shadowlands

"If you're looking for a fast-paced, intelligent, character driven BDSM story, you need to pick up Cherise Sinclair's *Club Shadowlands.*"

– Victoria, *Two Lips Reviews*

Dark Citadel

"*Dark Citadel* takes the reader on one hell of a ride."

– Fern, *Whipped Cream Reviews*

Breaking Free

"*Breaking Free* is one of the most spell-binding and intimate books I have ever read."

– Natalie, *Romance Junkies*

Lean on Me

"...Ms. Sinclair seems to paint each scene brightly, making the reader feel as if they are sitting directly in front of the action..."

– Shannon, *Studio*

"Congratulations to Ms Sinclair for an e   ion to this series."

– Anya, *Coffee Tim*   *views*

"Ms. Sinclair's stories are rare gems that   haunt the reader even as the last page is read."

– Dawn, *Love Romances and More*

LooseId®

ISBN 13: 978-1-60737-744-3
LEAN ON ME
Copyright © September 2010 by Cherise Sinclair
Originally released in e-book format in March 2010

Cover Art by Christine M. Griffin
Cover Layout and Design by April Martinez

DISCLAIMER: Many of the acts described in our BDSM/fetish titles can be dangerous. Please do not try any new sexual practice, whether it be fire, rope, or whip play, without the guidance of an experienced practitioner. Neither Loose Id nor its authors will be responsible for any loss, harm, injury or death resulting from use of the information contained in any of its titles.

This book is an original publication of Loose Id. Each individual story herein was previously published in e-book format only by Loose Id and is a work of fiction. Any similarity to actual persons, events or existing locations is entirely coincidental.

Printed in the U.S.A. by
Lightning Source, Inc.
1246 Heil Quaker Blvd
La Vergne TN 37086
www.lightningsource.com

LEAN ON ME

Cherise Sinclair

Acknowledgements

I'd like to express my deep appreciation and gratitude to the following people without whom this book would not have been possible:

To Maestro Stephanos who ran the Master's Den auction at The Citadel with verve and style...and who demonstrated how to keep the bidding going;

To my fantastic editor, GG Royale, who kept shoving the plot back onto the right path despite all the detours I wanted to take. I cannot express how much I appreciate your enthusiasm, your honesty, and your skill;

To the Erotic Romance Authors (ERAuthors), the courageous people who patiently critiqued the seemingly endless beginnings of this book;

To Chelle Hicks, beta reader extraordinaire, who whipped this manuscript (sorry, couldn't resist) into a coherent shape;

To the Loose Id Quad for their unfailing support and their permission—no, their encouragement!—to push the boundaries;

And to you, my wonderful, soft-hearted readers—you truly make it all worthwhile.

Bless you all.

Chapter One

Not an empty bar stool in sight. Suppressing a groan, Andrea Eriksson shifted her weight to the other foot and wiggled her cramped toes. Whatever demon invented stiletto-heeled boots should roast in hell.

Then again, some people would probably think the Tampa BDSM club was hell. A trickle of sweat ran down her back under the biker jacket. It was definitely hot enough for hell.

She should have stayed home, taken a long bubble bath with music, turned on some Enya, and enjoyed her cozy apartment. Her haven, far away from the slums, and rented with her own money.

But no. She wanted to be here at this downtown BDSM club. *Kind of.* Unfortunately, she'd already walked through the place twice, checking out the possible Doms. Only two had that ultimately confident look of authentic Doms, and both had submissives with them already.

Sipping her Diet Coke, she gazed at the nearby scene where a gray-haired man in a suit stood in front of a slender woman restrained on a St. Andrew's cross. He tapped a cane on his leg, just standing and waiting while his sub quivered in expectation. The sub's eyes never left the Dom.

A tremor ran through Andrea. He controlled the scene, himself, and his sub completely. She wanted to be that sub, to be the one who'd given up control, who trusted someone enough to do that.

"You like the scene?"

Andrea startled, and her drink sloshed over her hand. Shaking her fingers dry, she took a step back from a Dom who'd eyed her earlier. "Uh. Hi. What did you ask?"

"Do you like to be spanked?"

Spanked. Held down. A big hand swatting her bare bottom. A heady anticipation ran up her body, followed by caution. Over the past month, none of the scenes she'd done with Doms had worked out. *Please let this guy be better.*

A few years younger than she, maybe early twenties, the Dom wore latex jeans and a black T-shirt. He looked confident, but she didn't get any sense of the kind of absolute authority that would demand her submission.

Is it really too much to ask for instant domination?

"Well..." she hedged. If she said yes, and he tried to order her around without being able to pull it off, then she'd end up smarting off and defying him. She knew all too well how embarrassing that got.

"Let's talk a bit." He grasped her forearm.

She knocked his hand away and winced at his annoyed expression. "Sorry," she said. "Too much karate when I was young." Why couldn't she get over these reactions? She wanted to submit, wanted someone to just take her over. The thought made her needy and hot, but this kind of place—filled with guys on the make—brought back too many memories and brought out all her defenses. Papa had trained her too well. *Don't let them grab you. Don't let them corner you. The best defense is a good offense.*

"No problem. I make a lot of submissives nervous." His chest puffed out.

Oh, Dios. *Stuck on yourself a little?*

Ignoring the way the Dom tried to hold her eyes, she glanced around the club. Tampa's Goth contingent was well represented with heavy-handed makeup and bizarrely spiked hair. Piercings and tattoos decorated the most unlikely and intimate places. *Ouch.* Farther toward the back, people crowded around a flogging scene.

"I'd like to put you on a spanking bench," he said. "I think you'll get off on it."

She turned to him, hoping, wanting, to feel a sinking feeling inside, the funny something that made her want to just say *yes,* and nothing happened. He wasn't the one for her. "Thank you, but no."

How did anyone ever find a good match in a place like this?

She gave the Dom a polite smile and walked out of the club. Antonio should show soon; she might as well meet him outside.

Pulling her leather jacket closer against the depression creeping through her, she trudged to her van in the nearby parking lot. A stone blocked her path, and she kicked it out of the way with her stupid, painful boots. It just wasn't fair. Other women didn't have so much trouble finding a Dom. And she'd watched some Doms that she'd turned down, and they handled other submissives easily.

Maybe the problem is me.

The moist March air brushed against her face, bringing a tang of the sea with the usual Tampa rush-hour fumes. Pacing back and forth, she watched two women enter the club. A couple holding hands walked out. And finally, Antonio's red Camaro hummed into the parking lot and slid into an empty space. Antonio popped out. "Hey, you. Why aren't you inside?"

A piece of trash caught her eye. She picked the paper up, crumpled it viciously, and threw it in a nearby garbage can. "I didn't find anybody who"— *who I would bow my head to*— "who I wanted to play with."

"Fussy, fussy." He frowned at her. A streetlight flickered indecisively, highlighting his face like a strobe. "Poor *chiquita*. Why aren't you into an easier kink, maybe ménages or public sex?"

"Darned if I know." The night air had chilled, and Andrea hugged herself. "Why aren't you all dominant so I wouldn't have to jump through hoops to meet someone? And you might be straight too. Straight would be good."

She leaned beside him on the car, her arm brushing his companionably. Her best friend since she could remember. At five, they'd gone on crusades with sticks as their swords, and a battered tricycle from a dumpster as their horse. At fifteen, when he came out, she had wiped the pavement with anyone who gave him grief. After he finished college, he'd moved here from Miami, becoming an unofficial member of her huge family.

"I am who I am." He grinned and tugged one of her curls. "But I still have trouble believing you're submissive. You've never let *anyone* boss you around. Are you sure?"

"'Fraid so." After reading a romance with BDSM in it, she'd talked a boyfriend into trying it. "Submitting is different in"—her face heated—"in…with sex. Going to bed with most guys is as exciting as making love with—well, a brother or something. Blah, you know? Remember when you realized you were gay? You said, '*This is why nothing worked for me before. I need this.*' Well, that's what it was like for me with BDSM. When someone tells me to do something and can make it stick, I go all melty inside."

He snorted. "And if they don't make it stick, you probably take them apart, Rambolita."

"I just—"*I just want to meet the right man, one who can give me that shiver deep down inside. How can I ever fall in love with someone who doesn't make me feel that?* "I… Well, it doesn't matter, does it? I've tried everything—clubs and groups, and haven't found anyone. Not even close."

"Oh, don't give up yet." Antonio lit a cigarette and studied the glowing end for a second. "On that list of clubs you made, you eliminated one. The private club outside of town."

"The Shadowlands, where the membership fee would require an entire year's salary and my firstborn child? I can't do that." The momentary hope died.

"Maybe you can."

"Earth to Antonio… I own a cleaning business, not a Fortune 500 company."

"I'm not senile." He drew on his cigarette before explaining. "A guy there owes me a favor."

"Really?" A private club. More experienced people, more protection. She stared at Antonio.

He stared back, lifting his eyebrows.

Dios, she hated needing others to have to help her, even Antonio. "He'd overlook a membership fee?"

Antonio tossed the cigarette on the ground and stepped on it. "Not exactly. The guy is in charge of the trainees, and they don't pay the fees. I'll try to have him to take you as one." He frowned at her. "But being a trainee might be a hell of a lot more intense than you want."

It meant she would really be under orders and not able to pick and choose. Her mouth went dry, but her chin went up. "Do it."

Chapter Two

In the middle of setting up the bar, Cullen looked up at the sound of the clubroom door opening. *Right on time.* Two points for her, he thought sourly.

Annoyance burned in his gut at Antonio calling in his favor in this manner. True, the reporter had provided enough information to nail the arsonist Cullen had investigated, and they'd put the bastard behind bars, but he didn't like his job as an arson investigator touching the Shadowlands.

Or someone screwing with the trainee program. Normally he and Z selected trainees from long-standing members of the club, submissives who wanted to immerse themselves deeper into the lifestyle as well as meet unattached Doms. Newbies didn't get chosen.

Z hadn't been pleased. *Understatement.* He'd been fucking pissed off.

That left Cullen's ass hanging out now. So this friend of Antonio's better be the best trainee he'd ever seen—and fit well into the Shadowlands—or she'd better cry off quickly. *I know which I'd prefer.* In fact, he might just help her along a bit. With a little work on his part, she might decide the club didn't suit her.

The woman stepped into the clubroom and stopped, probably letting her eyes adjust to the dim, candlelike light cast by the wrought-iron sconces. After a second, she strode forward.

Tall, muscular woman. She reminded him of a pain-slut sub he'd partied with; the memory wasn't a fond one. He leaned an arm on his bartop and watched her approach. Tight latex pants—very nice over those long legs. Light brown hair coiled tightly on top of her head in a don't-touch-me style. Subtle makeup. Only a small crucifix for jewelry. The calf-high stiletto boots shouted "Domme," as did the long-sleeved biker jacket. Arrogant posture, chin up.

What the hell kind of sub had Antonio coerced him into taking? Just on first sight, he felt like kicking her out.

"Hello." Her smooth, low voice with a hint of a Spanish accent went easy on the ears. "I'm Andrea Eriksson."

Testing her, he didn't speak, simply watched her face. Most subs would lower their eyes but not this one. Instead her lips tightened slightly, and her chin raised another notch.

"You may call me Master Cullen or Sir. I'm in charge of the trainees at the Shadowlands." He pointed to a bar stool. "Sit."

A hesitation. A sub who didn't like obeying orders? She slid onto the bar stool and leaned her forearms on the counter. Another aggressive posture.

Domme or sub? Easy enough to find out. Taking his time, he walked out from the bar to stand in front of her—to loom over her. The flash in her eyes said she wanted to rise and put them on a more equal level.

He put a finger under her chin and tilted her face up.

Her muscles tightened, and she tried to pull away.

"Be still."

At his hard command, she froze, and then he saw it—her eyes dilated and a flush washed over her cheeks.

Pleasure ran through him. Nothing appealed to a Dom more than that instinctive surrender of a body under his hands.

"So there's a submissive buried in there after all," he murmured. He gripped her hair and held her in place as he stroked one finger over a high cheekbone, across a velvety lip, and down her vulnerable throat...and felt the telling quiver that ran through her.

Very nice. He ran his fingers down to the zipper of her biker jacket. Now what might she hide under it?

She didn't move. The big, golden brown eyes held trepidation, and her hands clenched despite the papers she held. She was trying. It took guts to face a strange club and a strange Dom all at once.

He felt a twinge of pity, so now half of him wanted to boot her ass out the door, and the other half wanted to cuddle and reassure her. Dammit. But neither side would get what it wanted. With a sigh, he released her hair and stepped back. "Give me your paperwork."

As she handed the papers over, her lightly tanned cheeks flushed at the crumpled mess she'd made.

He flattened everything out and started with the medical form—disease free, healthy, on birth control. No problems there. He turned to the next page. She'd filled out and signed the basic Shadowlands' membership and rules. Then the trainee rules. Last year, a novice had signed the papers unread; when she'd broken a rule, the ensuing punishment had shocked her silly. "Did you read these?"

She nodded.

"In this club, a submissive answers with, 'Yes, Sir or Ma'am.'"

"Yes, Sir."

Better. He gave her a nod of approval. Although she displayed none of a normal sub's eagerness to please, the tiny lines beside her eyes eased slightly. His good opinion did matter, even if she refused to show it. And why not?

He studied her for a moment. Stiff posture, chin up, hands clamped together. Yet he'd felt her melt beneath his touch. Intriguing puzzle, wasn't she? In spite of his annoyance, he couldn't stop thinking she'd be just the sort of challenge he liked.

When he reached the negotiation checklist, she stiffened, and her cheeks flushed with obvious embarrassment. Amusement trickled through him, lightening his mood. He might enjoy getting her past that bashfulness. Maybe assign her a different Dom for each item where she'd indicated interest: oral sex, spanking, stocks, dildo....

When he met her big eyes, she swallowed. Perceptive little sub to pick up on a Dom's nefarious intentions.

He kept his gaze on hers for a minute. What would those eyes look like glazed with passion, mindless with need? Hell, he wouldn't mind bending her over and securing her in the stocks and… He glanced at the anal section on the form. No prior experience, but she'd checked the box for "Willing to try at least once." Yes, he'd enjoy teaching her the joys of anal play.

If she stayed. The votes weren't in on that one yet.

Male Doms only. So she wasn't bisexual. That would disappoint Olivia. Next he ran a finger down the questions that focused on pain. Apparently the girl wasn't a pain slut like Deborah. "You absolutely don't want to be whipped, pierced, cut, or beaten."

She tensed at just the words and shook her head.

"I didn't hear you."

She cleared her throat. "No, Sir."

"You're not sure about spanking, light floggings, paddles." Those long legs seemed designed for a flogging. Would she whimper or moan? If he had her under his command, he wouldn't allow her the chance to hide her responses. He studied her face. "You'll get to try some during your time with us."

A quiver of her lips. "Yes, Sir." Her voice came out a whisper.

He smothered a smile. *Having more and more trouble staying detached, little sub?* "You're fine with bondage, it appears. And you haven't ruled out sex, is that right?"

Her cheeks flared, and her back straightened. "Right," she said in a voice so sharp it could have sliced him in half.

Aggressive. Interesting. But unacceptable. He gave her a level look.

Her gaze dropped instantly. "Yes, Sir. That's right."

A sub with an attitude to match her size. Damn, she was cute. He pulled out a set of trainee cuffs from under the bar. Picking one up, he showed it to her. "Give me your wrist."

Her eyes flashed up and widened at the golden leather cuff in his hand. Even white teeth closed on her lower lip showing how her fears warred with her desires. Her fingers trembled as she laid her wrist in his open palm.

The first tentative gift of trust. "Good girl," he said softly.

He smiled at the solid feel of her arm. How long had it been since he'd had a woman who he didn't fear hurting with his size? The firm muscle overlaid a tender pulse hammering away. *Very nice.*

He buckled the first cuff on. When her whiskey-colored eyes met his, the unexpectedly vulnerable expression brought his protective Dom instincts roaring to the fore. Did all that crusty posturing of hers hide a little marshmallow inside?

The wash of satisfaction at putting her in cuffs surprised him, and he forced himself back to business. "Gold cuffs indicate a trainee," he said. "We'll put colored ribbons on your cuffs so everyone knows your limits. Red would indicate you enjoy serious pain such as a hard whipping. Yellow is for mild."

Still holding her wrist in one hand, he tugged on her hair, pleased with her startled jump. "As you read in the club rules, any submissive, trainee or not, who messes up can be spanked or paddled. The yellow ribbon simply indicates we can be more creative."

She said, "Oh, great," under her breath, and he barely managed to keep from laughing.

"Blue is for bondage. Green for sex. A trainee wearing a green ribbon might be given to any Dom here, for either reward...or punishment." The tiny pulse under his thumb increased, her bottom lip quivered, and her breathing hitched. Definitely intrigued at the idea.

As was he. What would her expression show when he chained her arms over her head with her legs opened and restrained, baring her to his sight and touch. Would her body quiver? Her eyes dilate? Her pussy turn hot and slick?

Her eyes were wide and vulnerable now as he pinned her gaze with his.

"But for now, you will wear no ribbons at all," he said softly and watched her muscles relax. "You'll spend tonight serving the club members drinks and getting accustomed to how the Shadowlands works. Do you understand, Andrea?"

She nodded, then added a hasty, "Yes, Sir."

"Very good. If at any time you wish to leave, you just let me know. Would you like a drink before you start?"

Her nerves yammering as if she'd fallen into a gang war, Andrea sipped her Seven and Seven. "Stay there, Andrea," Master Cullen had said after handing her the drink, and then he'd walked away.

His leaving had been such a relief. *Dios mío*, she hadn't expected Antonio's friend to completely overwhelm her. She shivered, remembering the feel of his hand in her hair, how he'd held her in place. That...control...had sent thrills through her like a downed power line. Totally what she wanted—talk about *instant domination*—so why did it terrify her at the same time?

Because he was too much. She'd expected the trainer to be...well, more commanding than the Doms in the club. Someone who'd give her a quiver inside—not one who turned her willpower to goo.

She snorted. Antonio would probably call this "The Story of Rambolita and the Three Doms." The Dom at the club didn't have enough, this Dom here had too much—*way too much*—so maybe the next one would be just right? Well, the ritzy Shadowlands gave her the best chance at meeting *Dom Just Right*, so no matter how intimidating Master Cullen got and how much he wanted her to leave, she'd be the greatest trainee he'd ever had. Her shoulders straightened.

She took another sip, and the leather cuffs he'd put on her caught her eye. They felt soft inside, yet snug, like a man's hands firmly wrapped around her wrists. A scary—exciting—feeling.

She was here. Doing what she'd dreamed about. *Dios help me.*

Pulling her gaze away from the cuffs, she took the time Master Cullen had given her and looked around. As intimidating inside as it appeared outside. She shook her head, remembering her first sight of the place. The massive three-story stone building with heavy oak doors and black wrought-iron trim had looked like a medieval castle dropped into the swampy Florida countryside.

Inside, the clubroom took up the entire bottom floor. The oblong bar of dark wood where she sat held ownership of the center of the room. A long table of munchies occupied one back corner and a small dance floor, the other. The light from wrought-iron sconces flickered over the equipment near the walls: St. Andrew's crosses, spanking benches, sawhorses, and stockades. Each within a more brightly lit, roped-off area. Rich leather couches and chairs created sitting areas where people could watch the scenes or just talk.

Everything in the place shouted rich, rich, rich and made her feel like she might get dirt on something.

The thud of footsteps sounded in the silent bar, and Master Cullen appeared on the stairs in the far corner. As he crossed the room toward her, she studied him, and her fingers tightened on her glass. Some men moved like cats, some like soldiers, some like they'd never mastered walking, but she'd never seen his style before. Not in a man...

Last year when hiking in Colorado, she'd witnessed a mountain avalanche. Carrying everything away in its path, the avalanche hadn't been graceful, but all that power had been stunningly beautiful.

She took a hefty swallow of her drink as he drew closer. In faded leathers and boots, he sure wasn't a clotheshorse like Antonio, and he was sure a lot bigger. The brown leather pants clung to long legs, and his vest opened over a thickly muscled chest. His neck was corded, his arms solid. A gold band circled one darkly tanned biceps. His face... She frowned. All rough lines and craggy bones, he looked like a hard-edged Boromir from *Lord of the Rings*.

His mouth was set in a firm line. And didn't that just figure she'd end up with Boromir? At least Aragorn had a sense of humor.

He stopped in front of her, and she looked up and even farther up, feeling like a tiny hobbit seeing a troll for the first time. No man had ever towered over her like this or made her feel so unsettled. Did short women feel like this? She started to stand—*never let them see you vulnerable*—and he set his hand on her shoulder, keeping her in place. Easily.

She swallowed against the heat that swept through her.

His eyes crinkled slightly as if he could see the effect he'd had on her. "Your papers said you'd been in a couple of the Tampa clubs before—and we'll discuss your experiences at a later time—but I was curious. Did any of the subs mistake you for a Domme?"

Oh, did they ever. In one place, a man in a chain harness had dropped to his knees, saying "*This one begs the honor of*—" Andrea grimaced. Just because she stood a good five feet ten and had some—*okay, lots*—of muscle didn't mean she was a femdom. It just meant she owned a cleaning agency and spent her days working hard. "They did. Um, yes, Sir."

"I'm not surprised."

"But—"

He held a finger up for silence, and a bit surprised at herself, she obeyed. Without asking, he unzipped her biker jacket and gave her a hard look when she squirmed. She wore only a bra beneath it.

"Little subs should never wear more clothing than Doms," he said absently. His knuckles grazed the bare skin below her bra, and she jerked, earning another stern look.

He moved closer, gripping her nape, holding her still. His other hand removed the clips keeping her hair on top of her head. He tossed them on the bar. "You look and dress and act like the stereotype of a Domme."

Her hair fell down, the uncontrollably curly strands brushing against her neck and shoulders. He finger-combed it out, leaving it messy. Tousled. "A trainee here must look like the very epitome of a submissive. You're an example to the other subs in your attire and demeanor. In your obedience."

Oh, great. She usually had trouble obeying—well, maybe not with this Dom, but with others—but she'd do it. "Yes, Sir."

"Better. That sounds like a sub. Now let's make you look like one." He dropped some fabric into her hands. "Master Z keeps an assortment of play clothes in the private rooms upstairs. You'll wear this tonight."

Grasping her upper arms, he lifted her off the bar stool. "Change. And leave those kick-ass boots off." Apparently he could smile after all, at least a bit. Sure didn't help much.

She glanced around, spotted the restroom sign, and started in that direction.

"No, Andrea. Right here."

In front of him? "Oh, Dios mío," she whispered. Embarrassment swept through her, heating her face and neck. Glancing over, she realized he half expected her to

refuse, and he wouldn't particularly care if she did. Antonio
had warned her the trainee boss had sworn up a blue streak
at taking her on.

She shut her eyes and pulled in a breath. *I knew I'd be
asked to do stuff like this, so why is it so difficult?* Difficult
and yet...exciting.

She didn't look at him as she struggled to get the jacket
sleeves over her cuffs. Her biker jacket dropped to the floor,
and she picked up what she hoped was a shirt. No such luck.
He'd given her a black latex minidress, low cut with thin
shoulder straps. Her pants wouldn't work, and her bra would
have to go too.

He leaned against the bar, his sea green eyes
disconcertingly light in his tanned face, and crossed his arms
over his chest. Waiting to see what she'd do, no doubt.

Would he kick her out if she turned her back to him?
She couldn't risk it. She bent and unzipped her boots, toed
them off, then wiggled and peeled out of the latex pants,
smelling the baby powder she'd used to get them on. As she
draped them over a chair, sweat trickled down the hollow of
her spine.

"The thong can stay," he said.

She gritted her teeth and removed her bra. *Chingalo*, but
she needed that bra. Her cantaloupe-sized breasts needed
support.

Almost naked. Standing in the middle of a bar. And he
sure was no gentleman since he hadn't looked away. Why
did this make her feel so terrified?

But she knew... The air moving over her naked skin felt far too much like...then. She could almost hear her shirt rip, feel the chain link fence cold against her back. Her schoolbooks had lain in the mud until the high school boys had kicked them out of the way. Carlos had grabbed her bared breast, and she'd punched his bony chin, crying as her fingers broke. Even as they backed off, the *culeros* had stared at her naked breasts, jeering, calling her a big, ugly *puta*. *Puta*.

Her spine stiffened. "You enjoying this?" she asked Carlos and his friends. "You want me to turn in a circle for you?"

"Excuse me?"

She blinked, and the stubbled grass of the empty lot melted into a hardwood floor. *The club*. She'd said that stuff to Master Cullen... When she looked at him, saw his mouth tight, his face cold, she closed her eyes in horror. What had she done? Would a hasty apology—

"You're new, Andrea. Normally we wouldn't accept a trainee without more experience, but as you know, Antonio didn't give me a choice." His voice echoed in the bar, deep and cold, like a cave lake. "I'm going to give you three choices and your first taste of Shadowlands discipline. One: you may serve the members tonight wearing just what you have on now. Two: you may select a paddle from the wall, bend over a bar stool, and receive five swats. Three: you may leave."

He didn't move. His expression didn't change as he waited for her answer.

And she hated him with every cell in her body. Maybe even more because she'd brought this on herself.

Pretty crummy choices. Walk around naked all night? Dios, no. The skimpy dress would be bad enough.

Leave? Give up and go home? That's what he wanted. *No.*

Be paddled? Papa had never spanked her, but this couldn't hurt worse than the bruises he'd given her, trying to *toughen* her up. She wet her lips, tried to speak despite her dry mouth. "I'll take the swats."

"Then bring me a paddle."

Forcing her shoulders back, she marched across the huge room, feeling his eyes on her. Humiliation vied with the disconcerting warmth of being naked in front of a man...this man. She'd wondered about instant domination. Well, now she knew. He had it in spades.

She reached the wall and stopped. Various "toys" hung between the scene areas. Iron bars to pull legs apart, leather straps, cuffs, rope. And whips and floggers and paddles. She moved closer to a selection of paddles. Giant-sized down to small and rectangular. One had holes in it. How did a person choose? She rubbed her clammy hands together. When Papa taught her karate, he'd said a woman's punch hurt more because the force impacted a smaller area. So, in this case, bigger might serve her better. She grabbed the largest paddle.

Walking back across the room, she felt her full breasts bounce and realized her nipples blatantly poked out...as if she were turned-on. The air-conditioning wasn't on yet, so she couldn't say the room's temperature caused her reaction.

Yes, admit it, Andrea—this intimidating, mean Dom turns you on.

His gaze ran across her, lingered on her breasts, and a crease appeared in his cheek. Her nipples tightened until they ached.

When she handed him the monster-sized paddle, he actually smiled. "Good choice." He pointed to the back of a nearby couch, amusement obvious in his voice. "Assume the position."

Biting her lip, she moved to the couch and bent, resting her stomach on the high back.

"Farther. Balance yourself on your hands."

Damn him, wasn't this horrible enough? She squirmed until her mound pressed against the cool leather. Her feet dangled in the air, and she braced her forearms against the cushions.

He ran a warm hand down her back. "You have a beautiful body, Andrea. As a trainee, you will be expected to strip on command, quickly and without the attitude. Is that clear?"

"Yes, S-Señor."

"Señor?" He chuckled low and deep. "Well, that's a nice alternative to 'Sir.' You may use that if you wish." He stroked down her bottom and her thighs. His touch might have actually comforted her…if she had more clothing on, and if he hadn't threatened her with a paddle.

"Why are you being punished?"

Her first answer included a nasty name for him, and she bit it back. *Look, Master Cullen, I* can *be taught.* "Because I was rude."

"Very good." He patted her bottom. "Count for me now. Since I don't encourage subs to lie, I won't expect a *thank you* afterward." A second later, the paddle slapped against her bottom.

"One." It stung but not too badly.

Smack. "Two."

Smack. "Three."

The stinging turned to hard burning. *Dios, it hurt.*

Smack. "Four."

Smack. "Five." With the last one, her bottom felt like he'd poured gasoline on it and set her skin on fire. She felt tears pool in her eyes and blinked furiously, hating him with all her heart. *Madre de Dios*, could she really do this? Was this what being a trainee would be like?

His hands gripped her waist, and he helped her to her feet. Breathing fast and hard, she dropped her gaze so he wouldn't see the anger.

He chuckled. "You're a stubborn little thing, aren't you?" Before she could back up, he pulled her into his arms.

"Hey!" She tried to shove him away.

He snapped, "Be still."

She stopped, standing stiff within his embrace.

Huffing a laugh, he set his back to the couch, pulling her against him. She realized her nose came only to the top of his shoulder. Another shock.

"Relax, little sub," he murmured. "Here's another lesson that apparently no one taught you—after discipline, you get cuddled."

Despite her nakedness, he didn't take advantage but simply held her. His warm hand stroked slowly up and down her back.

As her muscles eased, she started to tremble. Undoubtedly he could feel it, but he didn't say anything. He just pressed her head into the hollow of his shoulder. One arm kept her against him, firmly enough she couldn't get away but not enough to disquiet her. The smooth vest under her cheek felt soft but couldn't mask the rock-hard muscles beneath. He wore no cloying aftershave, and his scent of leather, soap, and man smelled just right.

His chest rose and fell slowly, and he seemed capable of standing with her in his arms all evening.

Her anger faded along with the shaking. She had definitely disrespected him, after all. She knew the rules. And he hadn't punished her cruelly. Just five swats, and with all his muscles, he could have hurt her badly. He hadn't. She sighed and leaned fully against him, somewhat bewildered at the unfamiliar sensation of someone bigger and stronger offering her comfort.

"There we go," he murmured. "All better."

Just as she started to enjoy being held, the door at the end of the room creaked open and footsteps thudded on the wooden floor.

"Back to business," Master Cullen said and released her.

Dios, someone had come in. Her hands flew up to cover her breasts.

With a snort of laughter, Master Cullen gripped her fingers, his knuckles brushing her breasts in the process. "Trainee, this is my body to bare or cover." His hard lips curved. "But you may put on your dress now if you want."

Oh, yes, she wanted. She darted over to the bar, snatched the garment up, and turned her back to the door, which left her facing Master Cullen, but at least he'd already seen everything.

His flashing grin startled her, but then he ruined it by saying, "That modesty is something we'll work on also."

Oh, *mierda*. She hurriedly stepped into the dress. Glancing down, she realized the hem stopped barely below her butt and the bust pushed her breasts up to an immodest level. Rather sexy. But the rest... Two lace-up panels the width of a hand ran all the way down the dress with only a too-small vinyl panel in the middle to cover her crotch. Hopefully. If she didn't move too much.

Having taken a seat on a bar stool, Master Cullen took her hand and pulled her between his outstretched legs. "I'll lace you up."

With a disquieting competence, he tightened the laces on each side until the dress fit more snugly than even her skin. Finished, he turned her from side-to-side like a doll to admire his work. Apparently she looked all right, for he grinned. As the lines beside his eyes crinkled and his cheek creased, her whole body felt like it had risen onto tiptoes, although she hadn't moved at all.

She took a step back and concentrated on regaining her breath. Madre de Dios, the man had an unholy effect on her.

His eyes narrowed, but whoever had come in walked up to the bar, breaking Master Cullen's focus on her.

The new person looked innocuous enough in a black silk shirt with the sleeves rolled up and black tailored slacks, but she hadn't survived the slums without the ability able to recognize a man who could be lethal.

She edged back a little and eyed the two men. Master Cullen looked just as deadly, in fact, but the smooth one would probably kill silently, whereas the trainer wouldn't probably enjoy making a mess.

"Master Cullen," the man said as his dark gray eyes assessed Andrea. "Is this our new trainee?"

"This is Andrea," Master Cullen said. "Andrea, Master Z owns the club."

The man's black hair gleamed silver at the temples, so he was perhaps a few years older than Cullen. A faint smile touched his lips as he held out his hand.

She gave him hers.

Rather than shaking her hand, he curled his warm fingers around her cold ones. He regarded her a minute without speaking, then glanced at Cullen. "An interesting challenge for you, I'd say." The gray eyes switched back to her, the impact like a punch to her chest. "Andrea, I'll speak with you tomorrow if you return." His lips quirked. "Good luck to you."

Good luck?

Chapter Three

Cullen rolled his shoulders. Almost midnight. At least Fridays were slower than Saturdays, probably because Z had only recently added Friday to the Shadowlands' BDSM schedule. Weariness pulled at him and slowed his movements, making him irritable. And unobservant. That new trainee had something going on with her, more than appeared on the surface, and he hadn't pursued it.

Part of him still wanted her to quit, but she'd taken everything he'd done and had worked hard tonight without complaint. And so, he had a Dom's duty to her.

The crowd around the bar had decreased, leaving only three Shadowlands Masters discussing the various scenes and a few others unwinding from their play. Wearing a black motorcycle outfit, Cat stalked up, trailed by her curvy sub. Cullen slid a Guinness down to the Domme and followed it with bottled water for her sub, whose red hair was matted with sweat. Cat nodded her thanks and waited until her sub drank before sipping her own beer.

Cullen glanced around and checked that he'd tended to everyone. Good enough. He needed to give some time to his other duty now. Pulling up Andrea's limit list in his memory, he considered his choices. A couple of the milder ones might do.

After lining up the remainder of Andrea's order on the bartop, he interrupted the Masters. "Raoul, your turn at the bar. I have a new trainee to harass."

The swarthy Dom grinned. "The Amazon? She's a beauty."

"She is, isn't she?" Cullen glanced across the room where Andrea handed out the first half of her drink order to a group of younger Doms and their subs. Finished playing, they'd kicked back to enjoy their second drink of the evening...and the scenery.

Definitely worth enjoying, Cullen thought. The dress he'd chosen fit her gorgeous body like a second skin. Of course, if her brain worked in the same way as his sisters, she probably considered herself overweight and hated every jiggle. But it happened that a soft, jiggling ass turned him on, and those lush breasts looked just the right size to fill his big hands.

She was definitely a large woman, another point in her favor. With her, he wouldn't have to bend like a pretzel to find her lips. He smiled. In an embrace, his cock would press against the softest part of her stomach. Nice.

But his personal plans didn't include getting involved. Nor was it appropriate for a trainer. The trainees came here to experience the various aspects of BDSM and submission but also to meet potential Doms. He wouldn't do them any favors by letting them attach to him. So although some intimacy went with being master over them, he set firm limits on the amount.

He watched as one of the Doms ran a hand down Andrea's thigh. She stiffened, frowned, and then pulled her lips into a smile. Cullen grinned. That looked like a good place to start. Under the bar, he located a couple of pieces of chain, one short, one long.

When he reached the Doms, he nodded and turned his attention to Andrea.

She smiled at him, then looked uncertain. "Master Cullen? Did I—" She obviously smothered the rest: "...*do something wrong?*"

Taking the tray from her, he set it on the coffee table and answered what she hadn't asked. "I've been watching you tonight, Andrea. You're doing a wonderful job."

Her eyes lit. He rubbed his knuckles over her soft cheek. A sub's need to please; how could a Dom resist? "Now I'm going to make your job harder and give the club members some enjoyment."

"Oh, Dios," she said under her breath, probably not realizing he had excellent hearing. Her hands rubbed against her thighs, and she edged away.

He chuckled. A sub *should* look slightly wary in a BDSM club. "Hold up your hands."

After wrapping the long chain snugly around her waist, he clipped the short piece between the chain-belt and her cuffs to ensure she couldn't raise her hands much past her waist. Definitely not to her breasts.

He stepped back and let her experiment with the restrictions on her movement. She tried to pick up a glass and realized she had to bend over to get it. He got a nice flash of curvy buttocks. When she turned, she smiled at him, obviously pleased that she could work around the limits and still serve drinks.

Didn't fluster easily, did she? Yet. Stepping closer, Cullen used a finger to nudge the thin dress straps off her shoulders.

Although the dress still covered her breasts for the moment, she obviously realized the slinky material wouldn't stay up long. She tried to lift her hands and discovered the chains prevented her from stopping the inevitable. Her smile vanished, and sparks lit her amber eyes as she glared at him.

"I don't like that expression," he said softly. She swallowed. When her scowl disappeared, she looked appealingly vulnerable. He cupped her cheek and felt the tiny tremble under his fingers. "Pretty little sub," he murmured.

She stared up at him like a mouse trapped between the paws of a cat.

He forced down the urge to push past her defenses and see what else she would yield. Instead, he stepped away. "I left drinks on the bar for the rest of the Doms and subs here. You can bring them over by hand rather than using a tray. Of course, that might require more trips." All of which would give the dress more time to fall down.

And she realized it too. The submissiveness disappeared, and her struggle not to glower was obvious. After a moment, she said, "Yes, Señor." And set off.

"Pretty new to the scene, isn't she?" Quentin asked. A sub knelt at his feet, and the Dom stroked the young man's hair absently.

"Yes. We need to go easy on her for a while." After chatting for a minute, Cullen walked over to sit by a roped-off area. He glanced at the scene and winced. One of the older Dommes had lashed her sub to the cobweb and slowly brushed a feather over the man's sensitive—and ticklish—areas. *Damn.* Cullen shook his head. He'd rather get whipped than tickled. After a minute, he turned to face the other way.

Andrea had made it back with two drinks without losing her top, but only her blatantly erect nipples kept the fabric up. Cullen grinned. She might feel embarrassed, but she was also aroused. Her face flushed when Quentin teased her, but she smiled at him as she handed out the drinks.

By the next trip, her bodice had fallen down, and she had a white-knuckled grip on the glasses. The last Dom, Wade, took his drink with a smile. He said something, probably about her breasts from the way her face turned red. He didn't touch, though. Although any Dom might command a trainee for basic service like barmaiding and cleaning, and might touch nonprivate areas, only the Shadowlands Masters could go further.

Cullen hadn't bothered to tell Andrea that; some anticipation never hurt a sub.

He relaxed and watched her trot back and forth with drinks for the submissives. In the flickering light, she looked like a golden statue come to life—one of the Greek ones where the women weren't stick figures. From her muttered curses and her skin coloring, he'd have thought her Hispanic, but her height and that whiskey-colored curly hair came from somewhere else. He thought about her application.

Andrea...*Eriksson*. Nordic and Hispanic? Odd combination. *Beautiful combination.*

"You look tired, Cullen." In his usual black leathers, Dan dropped onto the facing couch. "Problems?"

"Just work. I swear spring brings out the arsonists with the daffodils. There are days it feels like all of Tampa is burning. Where's your pretty sub?"

"Jessica grabbed her. Some party thing or such." The cop nodded toward Andrea. "How'd we get a trainee I've never seen before?"

Good question. Fuck Antonio anyway. Andrea's soft laugh floated across the room and erased Cullen's irritation. "Special case. Let me introduce you."

He waited until she finished serving, then called her name. When she saw him, red rolled into her cheeks. More than when she'd served the group of Doms. Interesting.

As she walked over, her breasts swayed nicely, and the brownish pink nipples tightened into hard peaks. Also interesting. He smiled at her as he and Dan rose. "Pet, this is Master Dan."

When she looked up at Dan's hard face, she appeared intimidated for a second before her chin lifted. "How do you do," she said, her frozen demeanor one of a queen. Or a Domme.

Dan blinked, and then his eyes narrowed. "I think I'd like you on your knees when you speak to me." He pointed at the floor.

Cullen smothered a smile. *Welcome to the Shadowlands, little sub.*

Her lips tightened, and she took a step back.

Cullen could almost feel wills collide as Dan held her gaze. And then she dropped to her knees with a hard thud and bowed her head.

"Very good. Stay there until I return," Dan growled. He walked with Cullen a short distance away. "What the hell kind of trainee is that?"

"I'll explain another time." Cullen shook his head. "Although I just met her tonight, I can already see she'll be an interesting addition to the group."

"If she challenged me, what'll she do to the novice Doms?"

"Looks like she needs a fast education in submission. But for now, we'll keep her limited to the Masters." He slapped Dan's shoulder. "Send her over when you've finished introducing yourself."

Cullen took a seat on a leather chair in an empty area and leaned back to watch.

Dan walked slowly around Andrea. Once. Twice. Not saying a word. A quiver went through her, making her breasts wobble. Dan bent, grasped her chin, and raised her face. Whatever he said made her cheeks streak red. Stepping back, he pointed to Cullen.

The flushed sub who scrambled to her feet and hurried over bore no resemblance to the haughty one of five minutes ago.

Cullen patted his knees. "Come and sit here." She hesitated, and he could almost hear her ordering herself to comply.

She turned to turn to sit sideways, and he shook his head. "Straddle my knees."

Andrea's hands fisted.

He raised an eyebrow. "That's an order, trainee." The softness of his voice didn't disguise the steel.

The demand sent heat sizzling through her, yet something—that damned fear of being vulnerable—made her try to resist. But when she met the controlled power in his eyes, nothing could keep her from moving forward. She lowered herself onto his legs. With her thighs open like this, the short dress didn't cover...anything.

And his gaze dropped there. Then he smiled and slid her forward until she could see the black flecks in his deep green eyes. His jaw had roughened with a day's growth of dark beard, and deep lines were carved around his mouth and eyes. He looked hard. Cold.

Her body tightened, prepared to fight.

His gaze grew more intent. "Easy, pet." He ran his hard hands up and down her thighs, the gentleness disconcerting. "Am I the only one who scares you, little sub? Or all men?"

The perceptive question took her off guard, and she hesitated. But she couldn't deny the trainer. "I...I have...when men"— *especially big men*—"get too close, too fast, I tense up." *A lot.*

"And strike out?"

She winced. "Uh...I grew up in a hard neighborhood. A girl either fought back or got...hurt." *The sound of fabric tearing, the feel of hands closing...*

"I see," he said softly. "And you, Andrea? Did you get hurt?"

Her breath caught. "Not...completely. I managed to get away both times before..."

His eyes had turned a cold, cold green, but his warm hands wrapped gently around her clammy fingers. "Poor baby. You had it rough, didn't you?"

"You're angry."

"Not at you, Andrea. I would enjoy meeting the men who attacked you, though." He didn't finish, but his craggy face and icy eyes looked as dangerous as anything she'd ever seen on the streets.

She shivered.

He squeezed her fingers, and his gaze softened. "That past is something we'll discuss later. For now, tell me about your snooty response to Master Dan."

Dios, talking about secrets sounded good in books, but in reality? Not that easy. She tried to move but couldn't. She looked down at the callused hands gripping hers so firmly. Restrained. Controlled. She shivered. She wanted to pull back and couldn't.

"I want your eyes on *me*, Andrea."

She raised her eyes to meet his. Penetrating. Focused. First he'd ordered her to strip physically, now he wanted her to strip emotionally? She'd felt less exposed when she'd removed her clothing, but she sucked in a breath and tried to comply. "If I'm scared, I act tough. And it's worse here because I'm not dressed, and being a trainee is scary. Kind of."

His fingers massaged her hands. "Have you ever fully submitted to anyone?"

The deep timbre of his voice made everything in her go weak. This was what she wanted and what terrified her at the same time. "I-I'm not sure."

"Then you haven't." He studied her until she squirmed. "When you were in the clubs, did you hook up with a Dom and do some scenes?"

She nodded.

"Did you do as he ordered?"

She stiffened. If she admitted what an inadequate submissive she was, then he'd toss her out.

"Answer me, pet."

Pet. Wrists leashed. Restrained by his hands. Commanded. Everything in her body melted, not with heat but with something far deeper, and the building seemed to drop away, leaving her without any security. *Falling.* "I did. At first. But they were... I didn't have to obey them, so I didn't."

"I see." His fingertips stroked her cheek gently, and she couldn't keep from tipping her face into his palm.

"What about me and Master Dan?"

God, with them she'd rolled over like a dog, especially with Master Cullen. She stiffened.

"Uh, uh, pet. Pulling an ice-queen act won't work." His eyes held her in place as thoroughly as his big hand on her face. "Did you want to obey us?"

The confusion that swept through her surfaced as a hard tremor. "You know I did," she whispered. "Mostly."

"Your honesty pleases me." His thumb under her chin tilted her face up just an inch higher, increasing her feeling of helplessness. Of exposure. "Andrea, do you trust me?"

"No." But part of her did. She'd never let anyone do this to her before. Hold her in place. Order her. Not even the boyfriend who'd tried bondage with her. "Some."

The harsh lines bracketing mouth lips disappeared as a laugh rumbled through him. "*Some* will do. Trust takes time."

When he rubbed his rough thumb over her lips, his muscular forearm grazed the tips of her breasts, sending sparks sizzling across every nerve. A startling wave of heat ran through her.

His eyes crinkled. "Well, now. Maybe this next part of the discussion won't be as hard as I thought."

"What do you mean?" No, that was a cop-out. She knew what he'd implied, although the fact he'd watched her closely enough to see her sudden arousal unsettled her. She closed her eyes for a second, and then nodded at him. "Go on."

"Brave girl."

Why did two words of praise please her so much?

"You got a taste of what is involved in being a trainee tonight. Bear in mind, you might be dressed one night, and aside from your cuffs, completely nude the next."

She bit her lip, then nodded. "I understand." *If I could handle tonight, I can handle the rest. Especially since the looks from the men here don't make me feel dirty, just nervous.*

"In a way, trainees belong to all the Doms. So the regular Doms are allowed to ask you for waitresslike service. They can also touch you, within limits...as you discovered this evening."

"That's no problem." Mostly. Unless they moved too fast.

"You handled yourself well, Andrea. However, the Shadowlands *Masters* have full authority over the trainees, and the Masters have no limits."

"Isn't every master here a Shadowlands Master?"

"No, pet. There's only a few of us with that title."

But *a few* was more than one. She swallowed, her mouth suddenly dry. "What...what can they ask me for?"

"Whatever they want, pet, depending on your cuff ribbons."

"If I don't wear the green, how far can you...they...go?"

"In the Shadowlands, not having a green ribbon puts cocks and pussies off-limits. Otherwise a trainee's body is available to any Master." His hand cupped her breast, his palm hot against her chilling skin. "We will touch you anywhere but there. Possibly put on breast clamps." He pinched her nipple gently, and she gasped at the hot zing of pleasure.

"Although you won't be asked for blowjobs or handjobs, a Master might display you bent over or spread-eagled, your pussy exposed for all to see but not touch. You'll be kissed, have your breasts sucked."

Her gaze fell to his mouth, and the thought of his lips on her breast made her tighten inside.

His thumb rubbed over her nipple as if to illustrate, and she could feel the aching tightness. Then he leaned back...and yet, his hands moved up her thighs until his thumbs rested in the crease between her hips and her crotch. So close to her wet pussy that she felt the warmth of his skin as he showed her exactly what he meant.

A shiver ran through her at the controlled heat in his eyes. She tried to ignore how the proximity of his hard hands made her pussy grow more and more sensitive.

Her hands jerked within her chains, and she looked away from his perceptive gaze.

Over in the nearby scene area, a Dom used a thin cane on his sub, flicking it over her breasts until the woman rose on tiptoes with pain...and arousal. Face flushed, voicing high whines, the submissive gripped the eyebolts on the top of the cross. Unrestrained physically, yet totally under control.

Is this what I want? Andrea wondered. She'd left her virginity behind years ago and had lovers off and on. She'd messed around some at the downtown clubs. So strangers touching her shouldn't bother her that much.

And she really wanted Master Cullen to touch her. Touch her more, and yet... How could a man both attract her and terrify her at the same time? Dios, she was swimming so far past her depth she might drown.

"Is this what you want, Andrea?" Señor echoed her own question. His intent gaze never left her face. "To have someone else make the decisions, to be pushed past your inhibitions, to be enjoyed by someone without asking your permission?"

When he pulled her more forward, the friction of his jeans against her sensitive, swollen folds almost made her moan. *Oh, yes, yes, yes.*

"Remember if something becomes unbearable, either emotionally or physically, you use the club safe word, 'red.' Everything will stop. To slow down, you may use 'yellow,' and we'll talk."

Although she nodded, her father's rules ran through her mind. *Never admit to a weakness.* She'd lived by that so long—could she even use a safe word if she needed to?

Cullen tilted his head, his eyes watchful. "I may push you to that point just to make sure you know when to use a safe word."

"Great," she said under her breath. His answering laugh was open and full and so contagious she had to grin.

"That's better," he said. "Now come here, sweetie, and let me hold you for a while before you head home."

He called her sweetie. The pleasure of that made her feel warm inside. As he snuggled her against his broad chest, she let herself sink into him, feeling safer than she had since a child, oblivious to the horrors of the world. The scent of leather and soap drifted up. "Don't you want to know my answer?" she murmured. Her fingers grazed his soft vest and touched the crisp brown hair covering his chest.

"I know your answer, little sub." His hand ran down her hair. "In fact, after a couple more nights, we'll discuss adding a green ribbon."

Chapter Four

The next morning, Cullen trudged down the sidewalk toward the riverside restaurant, breathing in the cool breeze off the Hillsborough and watching for Antonio. His eyes felt like he'd rubbed them in sand as he squinted against the bright morning sunlight.

Damn, but his ass was dragging. Last night, one nightmare had led to another and another, until he'd abandoned sleep to walk the beach until morning. Bad nights were just an occupational hazard for an arson investigator, but he couldn't handle dreaming of Siobhan or his mother.

He shrugged his shoulders, trying to loosen the tightness. He'd adored two women in his life, and both had left him.

His fiancée's death by fire had sent him into arson investigation.

His mother's death from cancer had left him scarred and bitter. She shouldn't have died, dammit. But not wanting to bother anyone, she hadn't sought treatment early enough. And as she wasted away to a fragile husk, so had his father in undeserved guilt and grief.

He spotted Antonio waiting on the riverbank outside the restaurant. The slender man leaned against a tree, watching the dark water flowing by.

Antonio glanced up. "You didn't have to intimidate her, you bastard," he said without much heat.

Cullen snorted. "I'm a Dom. It's what I do." He scowled at the reporter. "You might have mentioned that submitting is a bit of a problem for her."

"Ah, yeah, I wasn't sure if you'd agree if you knew." The slender man's expression eased. He pulled out a cigarette and rolled it between his fingers. "But you must not have been too much of an asshole; she said she's going back tonight." A smile grew on his face. "Apparently you didn't terrify her too badly. Not that you could."

"Care for her, do you?"

Antonio nodded. "We've been friends since grade school."

Doubtful that a pretty face could prejudice the gay reporter. Not just anyone inspired loyalty like this, so two more points for the little sub. Cullen turned his mind back to business. "You got anything on the fires in Seminole Heights?"

"I asked my sources to check into them. If I find any dirt, I'll give you a heads-up."

"Appreciate it. God knows you have better sources than me, however you do it." Cullen shook his head. "You must have every hooker and lowlife in the city trolling for news."

"I pay them better, and I talk their language. I came out of the gutter, you know."

"You must not have been in the gutter long enough to get a history."

"You ran me?"

"One of the perks of the job. I like knowing who I'm dealing with."

"You're a paranoid bastard, but I'll have breakfast with you anyway," Antonio said mildly. He hesitated. "You'll be good to Andrea, right?"

"The subs taken as trainees at the Shadowlands are experienced in the lifestyle and have spent a lot of time in the club. They know what they're signing on for. Your little innocent doesn't." Cullen remembered the smack of the paddle against her pretty ass and almost smiled. "But she survived her first night."

Antonio raised his eyebrows. "I can tell you're not pissed off anymore; she got to you, didn't she?"

A lot more than he found comfortable. Beautiful. Challenging.

Submissive.

He remembered the last woman outside of the lifestyle that he'd dated. When he'd asked her about bondage, she'd acted like he had turned into Hannibal Lector. Maybe he should have told her how much he liked to cook...

Nonetheless, the trainer, tempted or not, didn't get involved with the submissives. It wouldn't be fair to any of them.

* * *

Right on time. Surely that indicated the start of a wonderful evening. Holding the padlock and paper with the lock combination the guard had given her, Andrea pushed open the door to a very luxurious changing room. A marble tile floor. Glass-doored shower stalls on the right. To the left, a mirrored wall with sinks and counters. Clean with a faint scent of citrus.

The professional in her noticed a spot of mold on a shower door, a cobweb on a window. Her people would have done better.

The far corner held built-in wood lockers for trainees. Four women clustered over there, and Andrea halted as they all turned to look at her. *Time to run the gauntlet.*

"Hey, come on in," one pretty brunette said. "We don't bite." Her head tilted as she pulled half of her hair into a pigtail. "I saw you yesterday, but there was no time to talk."

"Hi," Andrea said. "I'm the new trainee." Hopefully, they wouldn't mind adding a complete stranger to their group rather than a regular club member.

"You're a *trainee?*" The question came from a woman with beautifully cut dark hair in a classic bob, impeccable makeup, and chilly blue eyes. Her turquoise leather bustier and skirt showed off her lineless tan and pretty much screamed "rich." *She* could obviously afford the fees here.

"Yes, I am," Andrea said firmly. "I started yesterday."

"I've never seen you in the club before this." The woman's lips thinned.

That's because I butted my way in.

"My name is Heather," a woman with big brown eyes and long hair said quickly. She gave Andrea a sweet smile. "We're glad you joined us. We've been short ever since Cody found a Dom."

"I'm Andrea."

"Well, that's Vanessa." Heather pointed at the bitch, then motioned to a woman with spiked blonde hair and heavy makeup. "That's Dara." She nodded at the pretty brunette who'd first greeted Andrea. "Sally has been here the longest. She can't seem to find anyone to keep her in line."

Sally laughed. "I was holding out for Master Dan, but Kari beat me to him."

"Aren't they sweet together? I just loved their wedding." Heather gave a happy sigh as she opened her locker. "But you could check out the new Dom, Master Marcus. When he said, '*Strip*,' with that southern drawl, I almost died."

"You could always try for Master Cullen." Dara pulled a silver skull earring from her locker.

"Oh, sure," Vanessa jeered as she leaned closer to the mirror to touch up her dark red lipstick. "Master Cullen isn't about to get involved with anyone, especially a trainee. He belongs to all of us."

After setting the padlock and paper on the bench, Andrea opened a locker. Empty with only the faint fragrance of wood. Much nicer than a gym locker. She shrugged off her jacket. "Uh, is there a rule about him getting involved?"

Vanessa gave her a snotty look as if she couldn't believe she'd spoken.

Andrea ignored her.

"No, no rule," Heather said hastily and shot Vanessa a reproving frown. "Master Cullen just isn't the type to tie himself down. Besides, if he played favorites, there'd be problems."

"I got him twice." Sally smirked. "Both him and Nolan at one time back before Nolan hooked up with Beth."

"Maybe the first time was so blah that he didn't remember." Vanessa fastened a cuff around her wrist. "I know he won't forget his scene with me."

Sally's smirk disappeared, and she turned away to wiggle into a short plaid skirt.

"Anyway," Heather finished, "he'll use us for demos and stuff like that, but he only plays…uh, *fucks*…once. And only in the main clubroom."

Andrea smothered a sigh. Well, there went any forlorn hope that Master Cullen had been interested in *her. Oh, well.* She stored her purse, shoes, and jacket inside the locker and, glancing at the combination on the slip of paper, opened the padlock. She put it on the locker and *snicked* it shut. There. She had an official place. Feeling pleased, she turned around to four sets of startled eyes. "What?"

"You're going to wear those?" Sally asked, staring at Andrea's latex pants.

"Sure." *Obviously.* At least Master Cullen couldn't complain about her attire tonight. She'd left her hair loose and her shoes off. Instead of a biker jacket, she wore a dark brown, leather bustier she'd bought earlier. *And look, Master Trainer, there's no shoulder straps for you to mess with this time.*

"Oh, well, good luck to you." Sally's voice contained all the optimism that Frodo's had when he first saw Mordor and realized he was going to die. A trickle of anxiety raised goose bumps on Andrea's arms as she followed the others out to the entry.

She tripped over someone a couple of feet in front of the door. Dara. On her knees.

"Get in line," the spiky-haired blonde muttered.

Line? They'd all knelt in a row with a young man holding down the end. *Oops.* Andrea hurried to the left end and dropped to her knees. She looked up and stiffened.

Resting a hip on the big guard's desk, Master Cullen crossed his arms on his chest, obviously waiting for Andrea to get in place. When his gaze skimmed over her, amusement lit his eyes.

Amusement?

Like a drill sergeant, he strolled down the line of trainees, passing Andrea first. She caught a hint of his scent—leather and soap and man—and it brought back the memory of his arms around her. His hard hands on her legs. His voice rumbling in his chest.

He stopped in front of the slender man at the far end. "Austin. Very nice."

The young man with curly brown hair acted like a dog told to stay, shaking with his eagerness to get started.

"You have the theme rooms tonight," Master Cullen said. "Lawson requested you for a demonstration on genital torture if you agree." Andrea barely suppressed a flinch, or perhaps she hadn't, since Cullen's eyes flickered over her.

Austin bounced to his feet. "Oh, yes, Sir!"

"Then you're good to go."

The sub took a few steps before Master Cullen called, "Austin."

He turned.

"You have a safe word. If I think you're past your limit and not using it, we'll be having a talk." A definite threat threaded through Master Cullen's deep voice.

The sub paled. "Yes, Sir. I'll remember."

Master Cullen nodded, dismissing him. When he looked at Sally, his laugh filled the entire room. "I like the outfit, sweetie."

Sally wore a prim English schoolgirl uniform with a very short plaid skirt, knee-highs, a white shirt tied just below her breasts, and her hair in pigtails. She grinned at him.

"You start late today, and then you and Vanessa will cover the buffet-side." He tugged at one pigtail. "Before that, find Master Sam if he's around and give him a treat by playing the bratty schoolgirl."

Grinning, Sally rose to her feet with appalling grace. After sticking her tongue out at Cullen, she skipped away, braids bouncing.

Cullen continued down the line, inspecting and giving Heather, Dara, and Vanessa their assignments. The room emptied except for the guard at his desk, reading a NASCAR magazine, Andrea, and the trainer. Hands behind his back, Master Cullen circled her, and her muscles tightened as a disconcerting heat ran through her. His thick hair, the color of rich, dark walnut, was disheveled, and her fingers curled, wanting to touch it, feel it against her skin.

"Stand."

She scrambled to her feet, totally graceless, feeling as gawky as she had in high school.

"I like the bustier," he rumbled, coming to stand in front of her.

With his gaze on her face, he ran a finger along the bodice, brushing her pushed-up breasts. "Very sexy. But the pants have to go."

Her mouth snapped shut before her annoyed response escaped. She smoothed her expression.

His dark green eyes crinkled. "Nice restraint, love." He picked up something from the desk and set it into her hands. "You'll wear this tonight."

This amounted to a bright pink vinyl skirt, or maybe *tiny tube* would be a better description. She held it up. "That's way too small."

His mouth flattened into a line. "Excuse me?"

The look in his eyes made her legs go weak, and she couldn't tell if it was due to arousal or sheer intimidation. Imitating the subs she'd seen in the clubs, she said hurriedly, "I'm sorry, Sir. Please forgive me, Señor."

He huffed a laugh. "You're not sorry." He paused as voices sounded from outside the front door, and his cheek creased as he smiled down at her. "You may change here— right where you are. No underwear, please. Store those pants in your locker and find me at the bar. Be there within five minutes."

And he turned on his heel and walked away, leaving her standing in the reception area, holding a skimpy skirt. A matching top lay on the desk. He'd obviously brought clothing out here just in case. She scowled.

Ben gave her a sympathetic look before turning to greet the couple who had just walked in. More arrived behind them.

Damn Master Cullen anyway. She'd like to beat the *cabrón* over the head with her biggest, wettest mop. She hauled in a breath and tried to pretend she stood in the women's locker room as she stripped out of her extremely tight pants. Getting them off took some serious sweaty work and created quite a show. Removing her thong felt harder, mentally at least, since none of her audience had left the entry, and more kept crowding in. From the heat in her face, she'd turned red. Very red.

"Don't we have a dressing room to change in?" one woman asked.

"New trainee. I daresay she annoyed Cullen," a man answered, laughter in his voice.

Andrea kept her eyes lowered and pulled on the skirt, squirming like a worm to get it past her full hips and bottom. *Finally.* But... She stared down in disbelief. The damned thing looked even smaller *on* her than it had before. Stretching like Saran Wrap over her butt, it covered her from the top of her hipbones to only a quarter inch below the cheeks of her bottom. *He has got to be kidding.*

A ripple of laughter snagged her attention, and she realized she'd spoken aloud.

"Nice ass," a Dom with silvery gray hair said.

She stiffened and glared at him before stalking into the locker room to put her pants away.

* * *

Cullen shook his head as Sam finished his story.

"It was a cute glare," the other Dom said, "but nonetheless…"

"Nonetheless," Cullen agreed with a laugh. "We'll be working on that little problem."

He shoved a Coors to Sam and watched the new trainee stalk up to the bar. He could almost see smoke coming out of her still red-tinged ears. She'd have to turn damn red for a blush to show against her dusky golden skin. He also noticed how her tanned legs went on forever, or at least up to the tiny excuse for a skirt. The hot pink glowed in the dim light of the room, and he felt certain he wasn't only one who enjoyed the way it stretched over her round ass.

After checking that the members crowding the bar had drinks, Cullen stepped out from the bar, deliberately infringing on Andrea's personal space. Damn, he liked her height. The top of her head came to just under his chin, and if he wrapped his arms around her, he could rub his face against her curly hair.

Right now, she'd probably deck me. So he tucked a finger under her chin and tilted her head up. "You look as if you'd like to say something. Go ahead."

"That wasn't fair," she spit out. "You could have let me change in the restroom instead of in front of all those people. It felt like you were punishing me."

"I was."

"But...why? I got this." She patted her bustier. "I'm wearing less."

Ah, now we get to the heart of the issue. "What did I give you to wear last time? And why?"

"A dress, because you said a sub shouldn't wear as many clothes as a Dom."

"Did I put you in a long dress so you could cover your legs?"

"No."

"So, from where I'm standing, you did as little as possible, and did so only to meet my rules, rather than trying to please me." He ran a finger down her cheek, smiling slightly at the bewildered look in her big eyes. When she truly submitted to someone, she'd understand his point.

He rather envied the Dom who would compel this sub's complete surrender. "We'll talk about it later."

"Yes, Sir."

He held his hand out. "Give me a wrist."

Master Cullen buckled the golden-tan leather cuffs on Andrea's wrists, and the feeling of his strong hands sent chills through her.

The cuffs fit snugly, and he checked to make sure they didn't impair her circulation before smiling at her. "You look lovely in cuffs, Andrea." His thumb stroked over the palm of her hand. "And you like having them on."

She opened her mouth to deny such a wussy trait and realized she did. She enjoyed the feel. She nodded.

"Very good." He gave her hand a warning squeeze. "Don't ever lie, pet. Preferably not to anyone, but never to a Dom."

Well, at least that was easy enough. "I don't lie, Señor."

"Good. The punishment is rather unique and not very pleasant." He pulled a yellow ribbon from his pocket and threaded it through tiny rings on her cuff, then added a blue one. *Mild pain. Bondage.* She swallowed hard.

"You had a night to get used to the place, to wearing less"—his grin flashed as he glanced at her skirt—"and to taking orders, wearing cuffs, and having your movement restricted. Tonight you'll get to try real bondage."

Oh, Dios. Anxiety warred with exhilaration in the pit of her stomach.

"How does that make you feel, love? Knowing someone will restrain you, maybe on a cross, maybe on a bench?" His intent eyes were the color of high mountain forests.

She swallowed again. The gentleness of his hand on her hair made it possible to answer. "Scared. Excited. Both."

"Good." His cheek creased. "Nothing too drastic at first. Not tonight." He ran a finger over her lips, and his look intensified. "Someday, however, I will restrain your hands, maybe with chains so I can enjoy the clinking sounds you'll make as you get close to coming."

Her mouth dropped, and his finger slid inside, returning to brush the wetness over her lower lip.

"When I tie your legs apart, you won't be able to move. You'll be open and exposed for my pleasure." His hand on her upper arm tightened, and she could feel the sudden dampness between her legs. "I look forward to touching and tasting and taking every part of your body, little sub."

She shivered, and his smile increased.

He tangled his hand in her hair and tilted her head back. The lips that came down on hers felt as firm as the body that pinned her against the bar. He held her in place as he deepened the kiss, as his tongue took possession, then coaxed her to respond.

A rigid erection pressed against her lower abdomen, and heat pooled in her pelvis. When her legs wobbled, she curled her arms around his neck. The sheer size of him made her feel so soft and feminine...and controlled. He took what he wanted, and oh, but she wanted him to take more.

He pulled back and murmured in her ear, "But for tonight, you only get bondage. Say, 'Yes, Sir.'"

"Yes, Sir." Her husky voice sounded as if she'd just gotten out of bed, and the thought of bed—and him—turned her legs to jelly.

His laugh boomed out, making her lips curl up. Dios, she liked his laugh.

"Off you go. You're with Heather on the dance-side. Find her and tell her she has the first two hours off." He smiled. "Your shift as barmaid ends at eleven, and that's when Raoul takes over the bar. Come to me then."

As she watched him walk back to the bar, her shoulders felt cold and empty where his hands had rested. The way he affected her was just scary...and wonderful. This was so what she wanted, someone who could make her feel like this.

But she needed to remember the other trainees' warning: he didn't get involved.

Back behind his bar, Master Cullen laughed at something a Domme said, then glanced at Andrea and lifted an eyebrow.

She realized she hadn't moved. Flushing, she headed for the dance-floor half of the bar. Hopefully she didn't look too much like a cowed mouse scurrying away.

As she wound her way between the small sitting areas, she nodded and smiled at the members. Some even remembered her and called out a hello. How totally cool. Halfway across the room, she spotted Heather serving a group of Dommes and the male and female submissives at their feet.

Andrea walked over. "Hey, Master Cullen says you're off for two hours."

"All right." Heather glanced at her and laughed. "Nice skirt, Andrea. You know, I didn't think those pants would last long. Masters like to touch skin."

"Wish I known before," Andrea said with a rueful smile. "He made me change out there in front of Ben and everybody else who came in."

"That was nasty of Sir what with you being so new." Heather frowned in the direction of the bar, then shrugged. "But you might as well get used to it. We get a lot of strip orders."

"Oh, great."

Heather grinned. "Hey, when the order comes from a Dom you're interested in—well, it can be really hot, you know?" She glanced over her shoulder at a Dom with dark brown hair sitting nearby. Legs extended, arms resting on the back of the couch, he was listening to another Dom talk, but his eyes rested on the brown-haired sub. Openly watching and obviously enjoying her. When his gaze met Heather's, the look sizzled.

Andrea suppressed a stab of envy. "No, I don't know. Someday maybe I will." But if she found someone she liked and wanted to date outside of this fancy place, could he overlook her background?

"You will. And in the meantime, you'll learn a lot. All the Masters give us some of their time."

As Heather sped toward the bar to return her tray, Andrea frowned. Just how many Masters were there? And how did a person identify them?

Later that night, as Andrea stood between two bar stools, waiting for Master Cullen to take her drink orders, she couldn't stop smiling. She owed Antonio big-time for getting her in as a trainee. If she were here just as a member, she'd sit on a bar stool, hoping someone would approach her, yet terrified they would, and she'd have to come up with something to say. Instead she had things to do, stuff to keep her hands busy, and everyone seeing her trainee cuffs treated her like she belonged here.

As the death metal of Agonize pounded out from the dance floor, her hips swayed in time with the hard bass beat. The Dom paddling a sub tied to a nearby spanking bench kept the same cadence...as did the sub's groans a belated second later.

At the adjacent station, an older Domme in a tailored business suit and wicked stiletto heels used a thin cane, but not with any rhythm Andrea could detect. *Whack.* A pause. *Whack.* A longer pause. Then the Domme walked to the sub's other side, waited, and struck again. The gray-haired sub on the cross had bowed his head and locked his jaws. His muscles tightened over and over as he waited for each blow.

Andrea tilted her head. Apparently suspense proved as effective as an actual blow. The Domme paused to run her hand across the thin parallel lines the cane had caused. As the man groaned, she bent to stroke his cheek and whisper in his ear, her affection obvious.

"They've been married just over twenty years." Cullen's deep voice sounded behind Andrea. "He presented her with that cane as an anniversary present."

"Awww, that's sweet. Nothing says 'I love you' like a well-made implement of pain."

His roar of laughter made satisfaction well inside her, and she grinned and turned.

He leaned an arm on the bar—his damn forearm was bigger than her biceps—and looked down at her. "How are you doing, love?"

"I'm good, Señor." Every cell in her body seemed to yearn toward him. *Touch me again, again, again.* She took a step back and pushed him the tiny piece of paper she used for the drink orders. Lacking an apron, she had dropped the pencil stub into her cleavage and tucked a pad of paper under the overly tight skirt band. Since the membership fee included drinks, she didn't have to worry about carrying money.

"You look good. I've been admiring your skirt."

The one he'd made her wear, the cabrón. She grinned, unable to stay mad in the face of his good humor. Hard to imagine that she'd actually wondered if he ever smiled. The man was a natural bartender; people made trips to the bar just to talk to him. He joked with the men and teased the women. He also flirted with the other trainees, and Andrea tried not to let that bother her. Besides, all the trainees probably fell for him, like with Stockholm syndrome or something.

Or maybe like a woman and her gynecologist. As his comment about tying her legs open ran through her mind, heat surged into her face, and she looked away.

Unexpectedly his big hand cupped her cheek, tilting her face until she stared right into his penetrating eyes. "Now, what was that thought?"

How did he shut that easygoing nature off and turn into this...Dom? She tried to pull away, but the man sitting beside her set his foot on the bar stool to her left and penned her against the bar. Unable to escape, she scowled at the stranger.

"Subs answer questions put to them." The man's low voice had almost the same punch of power as Master Cullen's...as Señor's.

Trapped. She looked at Master Cullen, felt the hardness of his hand against her face, and her insides went liquid. "I was thinking I...well, that I like you and I blamed Stockholm syndrome."

Amusement flickered across his face, but he didn't release her. "Considering how red you are, I think there's something else."

A girl could get to hate Doms. "And about how women fall for their gynecologists."

"That's a leap," the man next to her muttered, putting his leg back down.

"Oh, not really," Señor murmured, his gaze still holding hers, and she could see he knew exactly how she'd made that leap. "But since you're so fond of gynecologists, I may adapt my plans."

He pulled back, and when his hand left her face, she had to grip the bar, as if he'd taken her strength with him.

His eyes glinted with laughter. "I don't think I showed you the theme rooms where Austin is working?"

She shook her head. He knew full well he hadn't.

"One of the rooms is a medical setup complete with an exam table. With stirrups."

Jesús, María, y José. The thought of lying naked on a table...of Señor setting her bare feet into the cold metal stirrups. Of looking at her down there. Heat sizzled through her so hard and fast that she almost fell.

The man beside her gripped her arm. "Steady, chiquita," he murmured.

"Thank you," she whispered.

When she looked at Señor, his eyes were intent on her face, and the crease in his cheek deepened as he said, "Definitely a plan."

He picked up her drink ticket and strolled down the bar. Such a big man. The tight leathers showed off his hard leg muscles. All muscle with not a speck of fat on him anywhere.

And a man beside her still held her arm as she drooled over Master Cullen. Oops. She turned. "Um. Thank you, sir."

About six feet tall. His chest and arms bulged with muscles like a powerlifter. Dark brown eyes, black hair, and he had her coloring. "I'm Raoul. And you are Andrea, our new trainee?"

Our. "Are—" Was she allowed to ask anything? She smothered the question, then stood there looking stupid. "Yes. I am."

His brows drew together, and he didn't release her arm. "What did you want to ask?"

Another overly perceptive Dom. At the downtown clubs, the men didn't always comprehend her meaning even when spelled out; here she didn't even have to talk. Why did that seem a bit scary?

She took a breath and answered, "Señor said I needed to obey the Shadowlands Masters, but I haven't met them. How can I tell who is who?"

"Very good question," he said and let her arm go. He didn't appear offended in the least, and she relaxed. "And you're not the first trainee who ran into problems with not knowing. In fact, last fall, we had one presumptuous Dom who dubbed himself a Shadowlands Master. Now we often politely refer to someone as *Master Whatever*, and a Dom can order his own sub to call master, king, sire, or anything else he wants. But technically, in the Shadowlands, *Master* is an honorary title and has to be earned and voted upon."

"I see. Thank you, Master."

He blinked, and then laughed. "No, *gatita*. If you call me 'Master' without my name, it sounds as if you belong to me. Use Master Raoul or Sir."

"Oh. Um, thank you, Sir."

"No problem." His dark eyes turned serious. "I look forward to the day you call someone your 'Master.'"

The thought sent a thrill—an uneasy thrill—through her. *Master.*

Change the subject. "So what happened to the Dom who called himself a Master?"

"Oh, he had his membership revoked. But Z didn't like having the subs confused, so he makes us wear these." He slapped an elastic armband of gold rings that circled his biceps. "Dungeon monitors wear gold-trimmed leather vests, trainees wear gold-colored leather cuffs, and now Masters wear gold armbands. Do you see a trend here?"

She laughed at his rueful question. "I, for one, appreciate it. Thank you for the information." And she'd keep a wary eye out for golden bands.

Chapter Five

Later in the evening, Cullen walked over to Nolan. "Can you tend the bar for a bit? Raoul's late—he had to drive a panicky sub home—and I need to release the second-shift trainees and oversee a scene with the new trainee."

His friend scowled at a mouthy Dom who sat at the end of the bar. "Don't know if I can take the noise."

"Hell, if you walk down there, he'll shut up." Although Nolan had mellowed after taking Beth as a sub, the scarred-up master still looked like he'd rather gut a member than serve them.

"Well…" Nolan frowned down at his slender redhead, obviously wondering what to do with her. He rarely left her unaccompanied.

"She can help if you want or just hang out behind the bar." Cullen shook his head. "Considering how many women you used to share, you're damned territorial now."

"Some women you don't want to share." Nolan slid a hand into Beth's loosened corset to cup a small breast. The sub's fair skin reddened.

"Ah-huh." *Sure made for boring parties.* His friends had turned into little old women, all right. Hell, Dan had already married his sub and forced Cullen to be best man. Looked like Z and Nolan would soon follow. How many times would he have to rent a fucking tux? "She's ruined you, buddy."

"I don't think so," Nolan said softly, kissing the top of Beth's head. "But, all right; I'll babysit your fucking bar."

Once Nolan had taken over, Cullen did a quick walk through the room to check on his trainees. Earlier he'd seen Heather accompany Jake upstairs, but she'd returned with a pretty glow in her cheeks. If things continued like that, he'd lose another trainee. Still, he understood why Z liked matchmaking; seeing two people well-paired, one's needs and wants met by the other, felt oddly satisfying.

In the dungeon, Austin handed a drink to a Domme seated on the Queen's throne with a sub worshipping her gleaming red boots.

"Cullen." A Dom in his thirties paused in wiping down a sling and nodded toward Austin. "May I have him again if he's willing?"

"His serving time is over, so it's up to him now. Be aware he can be so eager to please that he won't use his safe word appropriately."

Lawson's brows drew together. "That's not good. Want me to work on that?"

"Please." Back in the long hallway, Cullen checked on Dara. A satisfied look on her face, the pretty Goth had stripes across her thighs, probably from a session in the office room. Good enough.

Vanessa had left early. He found Sally entertaining two Doms with schoolgirl pranks.

What about his new trainee? He spotted her watching a violet wand scene, her eyes wide. Cullen grinned. New subs; you had to love them. Now to find Marcus... Cullen looked around. *There.*

Marcus sat off to one side, studying Andrea even more closely than the wand play.

An odd itch tickled Cullen's neck as if he'd brushed against a cobweb; he'd have preferred to be the one introducing Andrea to bondage. But as the master in charge of the trainees, he walked a tightrope between creating enough attachment that the subs wanted—needed—to please him, yet keeping enough distance that they would bond with the right Dom when he came along. Andrea seemed especially vulnerable; she could easily become too close to him.

And she was too intriguing for his own peace of mind. Unlike his chums, he had no intention of getting tied down to one woman. Or at least not for a long, long time. Hell, the members of the O'Keefe clan traditionally found their loved ones late, after they reached their thirties.

Cullen frowned. He'd hit the midthirties. *Well, I'll just bring up the rear.*

After catching Marcus's gaze and nodding, Cullen dropped into a chair by the chain station. Had he read the little sub correctly?

Marcus walked up to Andrea, stopped close enough that she took a hasty step away, then set a hand on her shoulder.

She knocked it off, and her hands fisted.

Marcus snapped something, and she blanched and dropped to her knees, her hands still fisted.

Perfect. Cullen strolled over to the two. "Problems, Master Marcus?" he asked and grinned as Andrea's shoulders tightened at the Master title. He could almost hear her telling herself she was in deep shit now.

Oh, I am so screwed. Andrea stared down, seeing only her bare thighs, her knees, the hardwood floor, a man's dress shoes. Not boots. The man—Master Marcus—wore a suit. *Madre de Dios, I almost punched him.*

The men talked, their voices too low for her to hear the conversation. Would Señor kick her out? Would he order her punished?

Was he disappointed in her? That thought made her chest ache like a foot rested on her ribs.

"Andrea." Master Cullen's voice.

She looked up.

His hard jaw was stern, his eyes the color of emeralds and just as cold. She'd let him down, made him mad. Her eyes filled, and her gaze dropped. "I'm sorry, Master," she whispered.

He exhaled hard, almost as if she'd hit him. Then he sighed. He closed hard hands over her upper arms and lifted her to her feet. His face still looked angry, but his eyes no longer held the cold expression that terrified her. "Andrea, we have a problem. You instinctively strike at any man who gets too close. Pet, that's not a bad habit, especially in bad areas, although even there, you might pause to make sure you're not wiping out some poor blind guy who stumbled."

Her face flamed. It could easily happen.

"As you mentioned, part of the reason you're jumpy is the atmosphere. Sex and violence. But here in the club—or anywhere in the lifestyle—hitting someone who touches you just won't cut it."

"I know." He was going to kick her out. She couldn't control her—

"So we'll work on that instinct in two different ways. First, if you make an aggressive move toward a Dom, you'll forfeit clothing." He tapped her bustier. "Take it off."

He's not throwing me out. Thank you, thank you, thank you. She didn't even give a thought to the increasing number of people watching as she fumbled the hooks open on the bustier. After tossing it on a nearby couch, she looked up at him. *Was that okay?*

His approving smile sent relief rushing through her. "Very nice, sweetie," he said softly. "You ready for the harder part?"

Harder part. Her breath hitched, and then she nodded.

"Since you see a strange man as an enemy first, a possible friend second, we'll increase your friends and decrease the strangers."

That didn't sound so bad.

"Master Marcus." Cullen turned to the tall, lean man.

Master Marcus's hair was a shade darker than hers, his tan lighter, and his sharp blue eyes held a daunting expression. He wore a Master's armband, but the suit fabric concealed it—which seemed a lot like cheating, didn't it? Then again, she shouldn't punch any Doms at all, master or not.

Master Cullen grasped her hand. "This is Andrea. Please take her to the St. Andrew's cross and get better acquainted." He set her wrist in the other Dom's hand.

Cross? Acquainted? But—Andrea's mouth dropped open. *But, but, but...*

"Thank you, sir, it will be my pleasure," Master Marcus said.

Señor smiled and walked away. *Walked away.* She took a step after him and got a surprise when the Dom's fingers squeezed her wrist. She turned to stare at him.

He stood silently, giving her time to regain her composure.

After a minute, she managed to at least close her mouth, though her breathing was...really fast. She probably owed this man an apology too; after all, she'd almost hit him. "I'm sorry, Master Marcus," she said, her voice barely audible.

She glanced at Master Cullen's back one last time, then looked up at the Dom and met a keen gaze. Not dark, more of a true blue.

"You are most certainly forgiven, darlin'," he said, his voice slow and rich. He held her eyes as he stepped forward until only an inch separated them. His free hand cupped her cheek, his thumb rubbing over her lips.

When she tried to step back, his grip on her wrist tightened in warning, and she froze.

He smiled, easing the lethal expression on his face. "Being as you're new, we'll take this slow. Say, 'yes, Sir.'"

"Yes, Sir." Her heart started to hammer. Master Cullen had a massive, overwhelming power; in this one, it was sharpened to a bladelike edge.

"What is your safe word?"

"Red. Sir."

"I mean for you to use it if something becomes too much for you, either physically or mentally." His hand stroked from her cheek down her neck to her bare shoulders. "You ever been bound, sugar? Restrained?"

She nodded. "A couple of times. In bed." She'd always bailed before that point in the clubs.

"Well now, that's fine." His hand moved down her upper arm, his eyes never leaving hers. The sensation of being touched—and not able to touch back—unsettled her, and she raised her arm, wanting to—

"Don't move, sugar," he said, very softly, and her hand dropped. "Did being restrained frighten or excite you?"

She tried to look away. Talking to Master Cullen about her intimate experiences had embarrassed her badly enough, but this person—she didn't even know him.

"Answer me."

"Excite." That's why she'd come here. "Mostly. He didn't... When I realized he didn't like it..."

"He didn't like tying you down, so it wasn't fun for you after that?"

She nodded, embarrassed as all hell.

"You're a good girl to be so honest." His smile rewarded her. "Do you have any physical problems, joint problems, arthritis, or tendonitis?"

"No, Sir."

"That's fine, then." Never releasing his grip, he led her through the crowded room, murmuring, "Excuse us, please," until they reached the St. Andrew's cross near the front. A small reserved sign hung on the rope. Master Marcus chuckled and removed it. "Z mentioned your trainer is always prepared."

Master Cullen planned this? Andrea frowned, an unsettled feeling creeping into the pit of her stomach.

Master Marcus backed her up to the cross. The wood on the giant X-shape felt satiny smooth but cold against her bare skin.

The Dom knelt, grasped her leg, and buckled her ankle to the bottom of the X. After moving to the other side, he did her right leg so she stood with her legs spread widely. With no underwear and her skirt way too short, her pussy seemed awfully vulnerable. The knowledge sent heat through her.

And yet...would he remember she didn't have a green ribbon on her cuffs?

She wanted this, though, to do this kind of thing, right? And the man was a master. Experienced and everything. Only, once again, her body had turned off, just like in the other clubs. *Why couldn't it have been Master Cullen instead?*

The Dom checked the leather ankle cuffs, running a finger under each, then simply remained kneeling. His warm hand glided up her calf, then down. He stroked a finger over her ankle. "You have very smooth skin, sugar," he said, his hand running up her leg again, higher this time, stopping on the ticklish area just above the knee.

He rose to his feet and clipped each wrist cuff to the upper arms of the X. She tugged on them and found no give. Her legs wouldn't move either.

Anxiety surged into her like a tidal wave, filling her completely between one breath and the next. She yanked on the arm restraints harder. "I—"

A firm hand tipped her face up. He moved in front of her, hiding her from the room, his gaze on hers. "Take yourself a breath, darlin'. I'm here, and you're safe. Do you remember my name?"

She sucked air, and the panic drained away as if he'd pulled a plug. "Master Marcus." *Embrace the fear, then step past it.* "I-I don't know why I reacted like that."

His hand against her face gentled her nerves, and he stood close enough she could feel his warm breath on her temple. "It's a normal fear. You're new, and you don't know me." He toyed with her hair, pulling a curl out and letting it spring back. "I do like your hair."

"Um. Thank you."

Her answer made his eyes glint with laughter. Then he abandoned her curls to circle one finger around her ear, lightly teasing. His touch brushed down her neck and dipped into the hollow of her collarbone.

"What are"—she swallowed, her mouth having gone dry—"what are you doing?"

The brilliant blue eyes met hers, hotter, brighter, searing her. "I am pleasing myself with a little sub's body."

"But—"

"Andrea, be silent."

She wanted to talk, to question, to stop the increasing heat in her body, and the way his hands wakened her skin, leaving each area aroused and sensitive. He skirted her breasts to encircle her waist with his hands, to tease the dip in the hollow of her spine. His hand slid under her skirt and one finger grazed the crack between her buttocks. She stiffened. *He wasn't supposed to—*

He smiled into her eyes and moved his attention forward. His hands ran up and down the front of her thighs, each time stopping just short of her pussy, and his avoidance caused more throbbing than if he'd actually touched her. Her hips tilted out involuntarily.

He didn't take the hint. Instead, his long fingers squeezed her waist. "Now, sweet darlin'," he murmured. "Apparently these pretty breasts don't count as being on the green ribbon list."

He cupped one breast, drawing a gasp from her that made his lips curve.

"You know"—he braced one arm on the frame beside her restrained wrist—"some women have sensitive nipples." His finger circled her nipple, around and around, barely touching, until just the drag of his fingertip over the increasingly puckered areola made her toes curl. He switched to the other one, and within a minute, both breasts ached.

"I do believe you're one of those women," he murmured.

The room had heated past bearing, but he didn't seem to notice as he leisurely played with her breasts, teasing one, then the other, until they swelled to the point of pain, and her nipples spiked hard with need.

His body still only inches from hers, he slid his hand down to the inside of her thigh, tracing more circles...and each stopped just short of her pussy. The seething tension left her strung like a taut wire.

And then his firm mouth closed over hers, taking possession so swiftly her head spun. His tongue plunged within even as his hand squeezed high on her thigh, barely brushing her pussy hair. A tremor of need shook her body, then another.

He abandoned her lips to bend down and capture one nipple in his mouth. He pulled, sucking strongly, sending an excruciating jolt of pleasure through her. Her body arched on the cross.

She tried to move, to touch him, but her arms stayed fastened to the cross. No control; she had no control over what was happening at all. The knowledge filled her with heat until each breath seemed to sear her lungs.

Even as he moved to her other breast, his hands slid up under her skirt to knead her bottom, spreading and closing her cheeks. Her pussy clenched as pressure built to a clawing need.

When he returned to her mouth, she could almost feel how his lips would touch her down below. His hand fondled her breast, gently, but hard enough that she knew a man, a powerful man, touched her. A moan broke from her.

Surely he hadn't heard. But she couldn't exactly hide her arousal. She'd grown increasingly wet and realized, with her legs open, everyone would be able to see. She tried to close her legs, but the restraints held her in place and exposed, and she couldn't do anything about it. Her insides seemed to melt.

As if he'd heard her thoughts, he knelt and ran his hands up her thighs, then pressed outward, telling her without speaking how he would open her for himself.

His teeth closed on the tender inner skin of her leg, biting just hard enough to draw a gasp from her as arousal sizzled like a hot wire straight to her pussy. His mouth, hot and wet, moved higher.

When his tongue flicked over her skin, tracing circles on her thigh, her clit throbbed, begging him to go higher yet. Her legs trembled.

He straightened, his face inches from her mound, and his breath riffled the hair there. She stifled the whimper rising in her throat. Then his hands squeezed her legs, his thumbs grazing the crease between her legs and hips, so very, very close to her aching folds. "Ah can smell your arousal," he said, pressing her thighs as far apart as her restraints would allow. "You're wet, sugar."

Oh, she knew that. Could feel the dampness and how swollen she was down there. Dios, she wanted him to touch her.

He rose to look into her eyes again even as his fingers grazed the very top of her mound, where the hair started. "If you were my submissive, I'd want your li'l pussy shaved, slick and bare," he said softly. "I'd probably do it myself the first time, just to enjoy the scrape of the razor on your sensitive skin."

She quivered, drawing his gaze to her breasts. "And I'd put jewelry on these pretty nipples." His hand pressed against an aching breast, and then he grasped the hard peak, pressing into a steady pinch that arched her back. "I'd tighten them, like this, so when I played with your pussy, when you trembled at what I was doing, the clamps would pull on your breasts."

Heat shimmied in the air around her; his blue eyes pierced through the waves.

He closed his hands on her forearms and leaned his weight against the frame, adding to her feeling of being restrained. "I'd set your legs on my shoulders, opening you completely, and I'd take that wet pussy over and over until..." He bit her earlobe, the sharp pain wringing a whimper from her. "Until that sound was all that would come from your lips."

He kissed her then, deeply, thoroughly. When he pulled back, Andrea blinked the haze from her eyes and stared at him, every part of her aching with need. He smiled down at her and stepped away, no longer blocking her.

People stood outside the roped-off area, and Dios help her, Master Cullen sat in a chair nearby. She felt blood rush into her face like a hot wave.

"I believe Andrea and I have become bettah acquainted." Master Marcus set a hand on her shoulder. "Are there others she should meet now?"

"No, you can release her."

Master Marcus undid the restraints and put a hard arm around her waist when her legs buckled. "Easy there," he murmured. He raised her chin with his free hand. "I do like seeing you in chains, darlin'. I enjoyed becoming *acquainted.*"

She smiled at him, unsure whether to thank him for a lesson or punch him for leaving her so very, very aroused.

He obviously saw both expressions on her face, and he chuckled. "If you take a lick at me, I'll string you up again and make it much worse."

Madre de Dios, just the thought made her ache even more.

He drew a finger over her swollen lips. "Say, 'Thank you for the lesson, Sir.'"

"Thank you for the lesson, Sir," she repeated, then added sincerely, "Really."

"You are very welcome, sugar." He walked her over to Cullen and released her.

Cullen patted the couch so Andrea dropped down beside him. His arm came around her, muscular and strong, sending a shiver through her. After a second, she leaned against his hard side, snuggling into his embrace, a sense of safety enveloping her.

"Nice job," she heard him say to Marcus.

"It was my pleasure, sir. Thank you for entrusting her to me."

As Marcus walked away, Cullen turned his attention to the little sub quivering against his side. Watching Marcus rouse her had definitely been enjoyable. Her face had flushed, her full breasts swelled, and her focus had shifted inward until the room and observers had obviously disappeared from her consciousness. Marcus had played her perfectly.

At the same time, seeing Marcus touch her had created a hard knot in his gut, one that only started to ease as she nestled against him. Fuck, but he wanted to keep her to himself. *Mine.*

What the hell was wrong with him? He didn't get involved with trainees. He preferred not to get involved with anyone at all.

And he didn't have time to examine this idiocy now. *Trainee, Cullen, she's a trainee. Get back on track here.* "So, little sub, did you enjoy the cross?"

She sat up, her still-swollen breasts swaying, begging for his touch. "You know, Master Cullen, aside from my father, you're the only person who ever called me little."

Trying to evade the question, was she? But he'd go along for the moment. "You are little. See?" When he lifted her hand and set his forearm next to hers, his thick muscles made her toned arm look like a toothpick.

She snorted a laugh. "Compared to you, I'm a midget."

"Now answer my question. Did you enjoy being restrained?"

That earned him a glare for his persistence. Then she hastily wiped the attitude off her face.

He snorted. Apparently she'd mastered one lesson, at least. A pity. He wouldn't have minded smacking her round ass a few times right now. "Answer me. Now."

"Uh. Yes. I... It scared me at first, but then, yes."

"That's a good girl." Honest little submissive. He'd already known the answer. Her excitement had increased each time she'd attempted to move and couldn't.

And he hadn't been immune. Seeing her in chains had given him a hell of a hard-on. "All right. More bondage. Do you think you'll punch Master Marcus next time he approaches?"

She scowled, and then laughed. Her voice, still husky with arousal, made his cock tighten to the point of pain. "I think he's safe. That was a weird punishment," she added. "I thought you'd probably beat me."

"Beating you for being wary of men wouldn't be practical."

"Good point." She settled back against him with a sigh, and he pulled her closer.

Her cheek rested on his chest, and her hair spilled loose, the colors ranging from pale whiskey colors to a dark rum in the flickering lights. He poked a finger into one curl, then lifted until the weight dragged the silky strands off. Cullen shook his head. *We're discussing discipline. Right.* "You should realize that punishment depends on the transgression. It won't always be this pleasant, sweetie."

"I know." Her lips curved in a wry smile. "My butt hurt this morning. And wiggling out of tight pants in a roomful of people really sucked."

He laughed, enjoying the way her eyes lit at the sound. A sub with a sense of humor and an attitude. *I could be in trouble here.* When he cupped her face and she rubbed her cheek against his palm, the trusting gesture derailed his thoughts.

Brushing his thumb over her velvety lips, he brought his mind back to business. "You realize, pet, being a trainee isn't like a real Dom-sub relationship. What you experience here is just a taste of what you'll feel when you settle into a relationship and learn to truly submit to your Dom."

Oddly, her face stilled at that comment. Why?

"Cullen," Nolan yelled from the bar.

Hell. Cullen straightened. "Looks like Raoul's not back yet, and Master Nolan has reached his limit of socializing. I need to let him off the hook."

She smiled up at him, her eyes the same golden brown as her cuffs. Lion eyes. "Thank you for the snuggle."

He kissed the top of her head, inhaling the vanilla-citrus scent. She even *smelled* edible, damn it. "You're off now, so you can observe or arrange to play. However, you may play only with a Shadowlands Master for now. No one else."

He waited for her nod.

"And shave that pretty pussy before you return next week."

He grinned at her gasp of outrage and walked away. Thank God he'd have a week to get his fucking head back in the right place.

Chapter Six

Soon after Sunday mass, Andrea drove through Tampa into the Drew Park area where rundown apartment buildings rubbed shoulders with small houses. Water from last night's rain puddled in dips in the narrow streets, and she veered the van to avoid the deepest. After slowing to let a palm tree frond blow across the road, she pulled up to the curb. Bag in hand, she walked down the cracked sidewalk to her aunt's small, white house.

Every Sunday since she'd moved out at eighteen, she returned to have dinner with her family. Today, the routine seemed immensely comforting after the strangeness of the weekend. Church and family—so maybe the dark side hadn't taken her over completely. Although she hadn't quite decided what...exactly...she should include in her confession next week.

Grinning, she trotted into the house and called a greeting.

Aunt Rosa poked her head out of the kitchen in the back, her silver-streaked hair falling out of the once-tidy bun. "I won't be starting on dinner for another hour. Mama is still in her room. She fell yesterday, so she's not moving too fast now."

"Madre de Dios."

Rosa held up a hand. "No, no. She's fine. Just a bruise on her hip and stiffness."

Anxiety twisted Andrea's stomach anyway, and she paused only long enough to say, "I'll visit for a bit, then be out to help."

She walked down the hallway where the scent of paint still lingered. Last week, Julio's children, Miguel and Graciela, had helped her paint the walls a pretty blue in hopes that, having missed a whole day of play, the kids would confine their artwork to paper. Then again, they'd all had so much fun, the children probably hadn't learned a thing.

Would she ever be blessed with children? A husband? Andrea touched the paint and sighed, before moving down the hall.

"*Abuelita?*" Her "little grandmother" had shrunk so much over the past few years that the affectionate term really applied. Andrea tapped lightly on the bedroom door.

"*Mija*, come in," called an old voice, still strong and clear.

The sight of her grandmother, up in her rocking chair, her brown eyes twinkling squeezed Andrea's heart. "So what are you thinking, falling down and bumping things?" she scolded and bent over the frail body for a hug.

"Tsk. Such a fuss *por nada.*"

After a discussion about falling and using her cane and how the good Lord should have made old people sturdier, Andrea dug into her bag. "I brought you some new nightgowns." Last week, she'd heard Rosa's teasing comments that she could see her hand through the thin fabric. Abuelita didn't like waste; given the chance, she'd mend her clothing until it turned to tatters.

"Oh, they're lovely, mija." Her grandmother beamed, and her aged hands stroked the soft cotton.

Dry hands. Andrea frowned and made a mental note to bring lotion next time. Since Rosa wouldn't accept money, Andrea brought gifts instead. Trivial things to make her grandmother's life easier and indirectly ease Rosa's burden.

"I brought some goodies too." She'd celebrated her acceptance at the Shadowlands by making chocolate chip cookies. Abuelita could share with all the cousins, except maybe Estelle who was usually so methed-out she wouldn't eat anything. But around here, to lose only one child to drugs seemed a miracle. "Some cookies."

"That's a good girl."

Cullen had said that to her in a voice so deep and rough it had resonated to her bones. Andrea shook her head. No thinking about the Shadowlands here. *Keep the dark side where it belongs.* She smiled at her grandmother. "Are you hurting or anything? Maybe we should take you to the doctor?"

Ropy, blue veins showed like scrollwork on the thin hand that patted Andrea's knee. "My Rosa took me yesterday. She's as bossy as you."

"Well, good. You're so stubborn, somebody needs to be bossy." Andrea pulled her chair closer. "What are you working on now?"

"This will be a sweater for Estelle. That girl is too thin, no fat to keep her warm."

"That's a good idea." Andrea reached under her chair and pulled out her sewing basket. "So, how is Miguel doing in school?"

A while later after getting all the current news, Andrea tucked away the soft pink blanket she'd started for her cousin's soon-to-be-born baby. The knitting kept her hands busy and pleased her grandmother who had taught her. It certainly wouldn't have pleased everyone. She grinned as she slid the basket under the chair. "You know, Papa would have been horrified to see me knitting."

Abuelita's wrinkled lips turned down. "Your father should have brought you home to Tampa when my Maria died, not kept you with him."

True, but Papa wouldn't accept help from others, and he couldn't have managed on his own. Alone and half-crippled, missing one hand and his leg. Andrea winced from the memory of her father sprawled on the kitchen floor, bleeding, broken glass around him, and the stench of alcohol filling the room. She'd been nine and terrified at the sound of his drunken sobbing. Up until then, she'd thought grownups, especially her father, could handle anything. She'd slid down into a corner and cried too.

She'd never been so lost again. *Maybe Papa never learned to cope, but I did.*

Andrea shrugged. "He tried, you know, and he made me strong and independent." Cooking, shopping, cleaning. She had it down by the time she'd reached twelve. And she'd liked the lessons in fighting...on the days he stayed sober.

She forced her lips to smile. "I could beat up anybody in Miami before I was fifteen."

"A girl needs her family." Abuelita's knitting needles clicked angrily as she rocked back and forth.

Andrea smiled and didn't reply. She had a record because of that "family." Thank Dios the judge had sealed it, and the rich people at the Shadowlands didn't know. Maybe some wouldn't care that much, but others, like bitchy Vanessa, would take full advantage.

Her grandmother sniffed. "Julio and Tomás should never have left you for the police. Your cousins were the older ones, were men. You shouldn't have protected them."

"Hey, I protect everybody." First Papa and Antonio, then her Mama's family here in Miami. Andrea pushed to her feet and bent to kiss her grandmother's cheek, the firmness long gone but soft with the sweet fragrance of gardenias. "Let's get out there and help Rosa. I can't stay too long after dinner. I have a walk-in clinic to clean."

Afterward maybe she'd do some shopping for next Friday. She could get something sexy. And, oh, Dios, how did a person go about shaving private parts?

That master of the trainees was awfully demanding. Her lips curved. And she loved it. The way his voice would drop when he... Her gaze caught on the knitting basket under the chair. If Papa would have hated the girly hobby, what would he think about the Shadowlands?

Her skin seemed to chill. He'd had taught her to stand up for herself, to knock down anyone who tried to push her around. And here she was, almost begging someone to dominate her. Papa would hate her for this.

She lifted her chin. He'd taken enough from her life. He wouldn't take this too.

* * *

Andrea managed to get one step into the room when the noise of the Shadowlands burst over her like a vat of hot oil, scalding in its intensity. Screams, cries of climax, shouted commands. Deep, throbbing music mingled with slapping sounds and moans. Just past the crowded dance floor, a female Domme used an oversize paddle on a man chained to a St. Andrew's cross.

The muscles in Andrea's butt tightened as she remembered how Master Cullen had walloped her with one. Why did people say that it felt erotic? It had *hurt*.

Well, first things first. She needed to check in with the boss. Maybe he wouldn't punish her for her lateness. She eyed the paddle-wielder. Surely Master Cullen wouldn't do that again. Considering the news had reported the massive pile-up on the Parkway, and anyone coming from the Tampa area would arrive late, he'd probably cut her a break.

Inhaling a breath for courage, she noticed how the scent of sweat and leather, pain and sex overwhelmed the fainter fragrances of cologne and perfumes. Shaking her head—*Antonio was right; I should have picked an easier kink*—she headed for the huge circular bar in the center of the room.

The roped-off scene areas were busy already: a tall, thin woman spanking a hefty man tied to a sawhorse, a man in a stockade being caned, a Dom holding a candle over his sub's naked body.

Andrea winced at the last one even as she stopped to watch. She'd never had hot wax dripped on her girlie bits. Was that a good thing or a bad thing? From the sweat beading on the sub's face and her rapid breathing, she'd climax soon—apparently, for her, hot wax was good. *Maybe I'll get a chance to find out.*

But would she trust someone that far?

The crowd had all migrated away from the bar, leaving only a few people chatting, some drinking alone. Andrea smiled at the sight of a white-haired man in a black suit feeding pineapple slices to an elderly woman in a shiny blue collar. The couple must be at least seventy years old.

Master Cullen's deep laugh rang out, and Andrea felt her spirits lift. People around him always had a good time. Why couldn't she be so relaxed and gregarious?

She waited at the part of the bar the servers used and watched him talk with a Domme, giving her advice on discipline. *Ay caray*, he was big, but so perfectly proportioned and muscled, a person wouldn't notice until Señor stood next to someone else. His darkly tanned arms were only a few shades lighter than his brown leather vest. His incredibly broad shoulders made his butt look small. Of course the way the leather pants fit over—

He turned then, and although she looked up quickly, he'd obviously seen the direction of her gaze. He smiled, and the impact of his penetrating stare pushed her back a step.

"About time." He ducked out from behind the bar. After resting a hip on a bar stool, he checked out her attire, then made a circling motion with his finger for her to spin in place.

The rest of the people at the bar turned to watch, and her cheeks flared with heat. She might have models' height, but she sure didn't have their slenderness. And she'd tried hard to wear something Señor would like which meant skimpy clothing. She'd chosen a black latex top like a running bra, and matching shorts that rode low on her hips and stopped just past her butt cheeks. If she bent over, well, he could see that—

"Bend over," he said.

"What?" She took a step back.

The smile disappeared. "Wrong answer, sub. I'd thought to be nice, but... No matter. I'll enjoy this more, as will everyone else." He paused long enough for all the blood to rush out of her head. "Drop the shorts. I want to see if you obeyed my instructions from last week."

Mierda. No friendliness showed in his face now, just a Dom's utter self-confidence and authority.

She didn't hesitate even though her fingers trembled as she unzipped the shorts. She wiggled them down. And exposed her newly shaven pussy.

He didn't say anything for a very, very long minute, letting the people at the bar look their fill. "Good job," he said. "Zip on up."

Her breath released in a relieved sigh, and she hastened to pull her shorts up. A minute ago, they'd felt way too skimpy; now they seemed wonderfully covering.

He waited until she'd finished, then said, "You'll be handling the buffet-side area with Heather, and will have the end of the night free again. Before you start though, Master

Z wants to speak to you." Cullen pointed. "He's over by the stockade."

Master Z? She bit her lip and rubbed her suddenly clammy hands on her thighs. He planned to kick her out, didn't he? But she didn't want to leave. She'd learned so much about herself and the thought of never coming here again...never seeing her Señor... "Did I do something wrong, Master Cullen? Is he... Do I have to quit?"

His dark green eyes softened. He rose and set his big hands on her shoulders, squeezing gently. "No, sweetie, he's not going to ask you to quit. This is just a talk. Master Z checks in with all the members off and on, especially the trainees. He considers you under his care and protection."

The rush of relief made her head spin. *But Master Z!* "Not *your* care? Señor?"

Cullen's eyes crinkled, and he bent his head until his lips paused only a breath away from hers. "Mine too, Andrea," he whispered, and then kissed her, long and slow and deep. Her knees sagged, and he had to pull her against him to hold her up. Everything about him was massive and hard, from his iron arms around her waist to the erection pressing against her stomach.

When he released her, she could only stare at him. Christos, but no one had ever kissed her like that before. The floor rocked like she was a small boat swamped by a killer wave.

He tapped her cheek with a finger. "Master Z, little sub. Go talk."

As he walked away, she tried to push the buzzing out of her brain and think clearly, but arousal still fizzed through her veins. Want more kisses, her body said. She hauled in a breath, then another. *Master Z. By the stockade.* She walked that direction, relieved she was barefoot. The way her legs wobbled, high heels would have killed her.

The Shadowlands owner occupied a couch as he watched the nearby scene where a woman had her head and hands locked down in the stockade. Her gray-haired Domme tossed the woman's skirt up and lifted a thin stick with something flattened at the end. What an interesting-looking cane.

Master Z must have noticed her frown. "It's called a crop." He rose to his feet, a sleek and smoothly groomed man, the direct opposite of Master Cullen who always had the disheveled appearance of someone who'd recently beat the stuffing out of someone. And yet, as with Señor, power radiated from Master Z like a furnace on a cold day.

"Please have a seat." He joined her on the couch, totally at ease. One arm rested across the back cushion as he turned toward her, and his face in the shadowy light looked lean and dangerous. He didn't scare her, but he really, really made her nervous.

"Relax," he murmured. "I've already had my quota of pretty subs for breakfast." His smile lightened his dark eyes and made him...almost...human. "You had two days of being a trainee, then a week to think. You returned." He paused.

She nodded.

"So, little one, did you enjoy being disciplined? Tied to the St. Andrew's cross? Your body made available to someone you'd just met?"

She licked her lips, feeling her face redden. "I..." Her chin came up. If she wanted to do it, then she should acknowledge that. "Yes, Sir. I did."

"Brave girl." He studied her. "And when Master Marcus roused you, did you want more?"

Dios, she could still remember the way she'd felt, how her whole body had craved his touch. His hands on her had seemed wrong somehow, and yet, if he'd continued much longer, he'd have had her begging. "Yes, Sir."

"Well, then." He picked up her wrist, one finger rubbing her cuff. "Are you ready for a green ribbon?"

The question blindsided her. Although now that she examined the conversation, she saw he'd planned to arrive at this question all along. To this. Basically, did she want sex included as part of her training? "It could be anyone in the club? I don't have any say over it?"

"You always have a safe word, kitten." His eyes were gray, she remembered. Dark gray, not black. "But any Master here can take you. Anyone else has to ask Master Cullen for permission. Only Master Cullen or I can give you to someone who isn't a Master."

Any Master could have sex with me. She hadn't even met them all yet. But the ones she'd met were truly dominant. Unlike the Doms at the downtown clubs, she hadn't considered arguing with either Master Marcus or Master Dan. And she wanted that domination.

But to go further? Put on a green ribbon?

Then Master Cullen could take me. The shudder of excitement hit her like a small earthquake. Master Z had a faint smile as he waited. He probably knew just by looking at her what she'd decided. "I'm ready for the green," she said firmly.

He tilted her head up, his hand warm. He studied her for a long moment, and then nodded. "Yes, you are." He pulled a green ribbon from his pocket and added it to the ones threaded on her gold cuffs. "Very nice. All ready for St. Patrick's Day in a couple of weeks."

She stared down at the new ribbon, and suddenly the air disappeared from her lungs. The music receded until the sound of her heart thudding inside her rib cage filled her world. What had she given permission for? What if they grabbed her and …

"Andrea." Master Z lifted her chin again and forced her to look at him. "This isn't a brothel. Most of the Masters have their own subs, and even the ones who don't never lack for partners. Although we enjoy having trainees here, we could easily do without." His thumb stroked over her cheek in a slow, comforting touch. "What you will do in the Shadowlands, sex or bondage or discipline or whatever, is for you, little one. And we will do our best to give you what you need." After holding her gaze for a moment longer, he rose to his feet, pulling her up with him.

Well, that went well. Yes, give me a green ribbon, she'd said, then panicked like a baby. She looked up at him. "Thank you, Master Z."

His cheek creased. "You are welcome. Go ahead and get on with your duties."

She nodded and headed for the other side of the room, acutely conscious of her cuffs. Although she knew the green ribbon hadn't turned fluorescent, shining out for everyone to notice, it sure seemed that way.

But the evening went well. Several Doms eyed her cuffs and tried to engage her in conversation. She talked with them but couldn't muster up any enthusiasm. Dammit, she didn't want any of them. But she mustn't get fixated on the Shadowlands trainer. Both Antonio and the subs had made it clear that Master Cullen didn't get involved with any sub, especially a trainee.

All right. She firmed her mouth. Time to get acquainted with the other Doms.

* * *

Elbow on the bar, Cullen watched Andrea chat with one of the younger Doms. Good. She was meeting people and making herself at home. Exactly what he wanted for her. He barely suppressed a growl when the Dom ran his hand down her arm.

"Hey, Cullen." With his arm around his sub, Dan turned to follow his gaze. "Pretty trainee, even if she does have an attitude problem."

More than one problem. Knowing she'd been attacked and almost raped when younger infuriated Cullen. Why the hell hadn't he been there? "She'll learn," he answered.

After lifting his short sub onto the bar stool, Dan took a seat beside her.

Kari pushed her long brown hair back and smiled at Cullen, showing the sweetness that had captivated his friend. "She looks like a good size for you."

"She is that." After handing Dan a glass of ice water, Cullen mixed a rum and Diet Coke for Kari. "You little subs make me nervous. Being around you is too much like walking into a room filled with tiny kittens and trying not to step on one."

Dan snorted. "So true. They're constantly underfoot."

Kari poked him in the side. "That's rude."

She squeaked when Dan fisted her hair. "Did you jab your Dom with a finger?" he growled.

Kari's eyes went wide. "No. Yes. I'm sor—"

Catching on, Cullen grabbed their drinks just before Dan hefted Kari facedown across the bartop.

"Hey!" Her bare legs kicked frantically as Dan shoved her tight skirt up and delivered three sharp swats to her round ass. "Ow!"

"Want more?" Dan stroked a hand over the pinkening cheeks.

"No, Sir. Master. No."

"Open for me."

With a high whine of embarrassment, Kari moved her legs apart. Dan's fingers slid across her pussy and came back nicely wet. "Well." He grinned at Cullen. "I think this little sub and I will go play on the spanking bench."

The tremor that ran through Kari obviously had nothing to do with fear, and then Dan plucked her off the bar and onto his shoulder. He carried the small, curvy woman away as if she didn't weigh more than a lady's purse.

Cullen shook his head. He enjoyed that size—hell, he enjoyed every size—but he'd take bigger any day. Holding

Andrea had been incredibly satisfying. Rather than her head barely reaching his chest, her cheek fit against his shoulder. And unlike Deborah, another big sub he'd played with, Andrea snuggled like a kitten, taking obvious pleasure in the comfort he offered.

He sighed, dumped the two untasted drinks, and wiped down the bartop. Across the room, Dan finished fastening Kari to a sawhorse-type spanking bench. Despite her arousal, she'd apparently objected pretty noisily, for Dan now gagged her, something he rarely did to the little schoolteacher.

Cullen grinned, envying his friend. Kari's lush ass was made for spanking.

How long since he'd spanked anyone? Cullen rubbed his chin. Last week with Andrea? But a discipline spanking differed from an erotic one. He checked the diminishing crowd. In another hour, he'd kick free of the bar and find her.

He really should teach her the difference between the two types.

Chapter Seven

Andrea winced at the crack of a whip—a single-tail someone had called it. Looked nasty to her, and it sure left long red marks. The Domme handled the whip well, placed each mark carefully, and never hit her sub's dangling balls. As a kid, Andrea had envied the guys their equipment. They could pee in long arcs and didn't have to squat. But those guy-bits seemed awfully vulnerable. The whip edged up the man's thighs, and the sub's muscles tightened. No, the trade-off wouldn't be worth it.

As Andrea turned from the scene, a huge guy grabbed her arm. With a grunt of shock, she knocked the hand away and threw a punch, unable to stop when she realized—

He caught her fist in a rock-hard hand as easily as if she'd tossed him a tennis ball. She tried to pull back, but he didn't let go.

"Master Cullen's doing a lousy job of training these days." His voice sounded like a garbage disposal with a spoon caught in it, only this guy could probably chew up the spoon himself. He wore black leathers, a black T-shirt over a muscular chest, and Madre de Dios, he had the gold armband of a Master.

Oh, mierda, she'd done it again. "I'm sorry," she rushed out. "Sir, I'm very, very sor—"

"Silence." Mean black eyes narrowed.

She choked back the rest of her apologies.

He released her hand. "I believe the penalty was clothing. Strip."

Dios, was she going to end up naked every night? With a sense of resignation, she yanked off her newly bought shorts and top and stood before him. One unclothed body, and now, she'd added a shaved—naked—pussy. She kept her legs tightly together

"Has Cullen taught you any positions?"

Positions? "No, Sir," she said, with extreme politeness.

He grunted and turned his head. "Beth. Show her *present.*"

A slender redhead in a gorgeous rippling latex skirt and a golden bustier walked closer. She gave Andrea a sympathetic smile, then stood at military-like attention and put her hands behind her neck with her elbows pointing outward.

"Do it," the Master said to Andrea.

She eyed Beth and duplicated the pose.

"Almost acceptable." He stood in front of her, much like Master Cullen during inspection, only right now she hadn't a stitch on. She didn't even know his name. She barely managed to keep from jumping when he put a big foot between hers and shoved her legs further apart. He moved behind her. "Lace your fingers together."

She adjusted her hands, then tensed as he pulled her elbows farther back, making her breasts raise and tighten. Dios, how humiliating.

He circled her again. "Better." Glancing at the other sub, he nodded. "That's perfect, sugar. Thank you."

When he held his arm out, the redhead snuggled into his side without any hesitation. Andrea blinked at her bravery. The guy looked like he ate rocks for snackies.

The black eyes examined Andrea again. "Come with me."

Oh, no. She had green ribbons on her cuffs. Surely he didn't want to... He had a sub already.

He picked up his toy bag and walked into an unused scene area. From his bag, he pulled out rope, still in its package.

Rope? Andrea took a step back, then froze, hoping he hadn't noticed.

He had. A glint of humor appeared in his eyes before he pointed to a spot in the center of the scene area. "Stand there, take the position you just learned, and don't move."

As he ripped open the plastic, Andrea heard whispers from the gathering audience. "Nolan...Shibari...trainee..."

The redhead smiled at Andrea and knelt gracefully off to one side. The Dom glanced at Beth then grabbed a bottle of water from the bag and joined her. "Drink this, sugar." He stroked her hair, and the tenderness in his face changed it completely. "You panted so much in the dungeon that you're probably dehydrated."

Beth gave him a disgruntled look. "And whose fault was that, you evil-minded bastard?"

Rather than striking her dead, he chuckled. When he returned Andrea, he said, "I'm Master Nolan. What's your safe word?"

Her arms felt as if someone had attached lead weights to her wrists. "Red, Sir."

"Very good. Master Cullen said you have no medical problems." He fixed her with a black stare. "Is that true?"

"Yes, Sir."

"Good." He looped the rope behind her neck with the lengths dangling down between her bare breasts. "This is called Shibari, and it's not only bondage, but it can be erotic and beautiful. We'll try for all three." As he spoke, his hands worked, tying the rope into intricate shapes. Over, between, and below her breasts, pressing them out. Snugly around her waist, creating a sensation like a corset. Then across her buttocks and around her thighs, squeezing them like tight shorts.

He studied her for a second before drawing the rope from the back up between her legs. After glancing at her pussy, he added a knot and tied the end to the rope circling her waist. When he tightened it, the knot pressed right into her clit.

Dios! The pressure on the most sensitive spot on her body sent shockwaves through her.

"Now the Japanese style tends to immobilize, but I think bondage is even more erotic when it's in motion." He laced her arms behind her back, not uncomfortably, but tightly enough that her breasts pressed forward. And securely enough she couldn't touch any of his ropes.

"That'll do." He folded his arms over his black T-shirt and looked down at her. "Find Master Cullen and explain why you're naked. Remain in the ropes for at least a half hour." A faint smile crossed his face. "Of course, if Master Cullen is annoyed, you'll be in them all night."

And then he slapped her on the butt as if moving a horse along.

She took two steps and stopped, completely horrified. Each movement scraped the rope between her labia and dragged the knot across her clit. With her hands behind her back, she couldn't adjust it or move it away. She glanced over her shoulder at Master Nolan. No smile showed on the hard face, but laughter glinted in his eyes.

Maybe I'll just stand here for the half hour and pretend to be a statue.

"You were given an order, sub," he said softly.

Or not. She tried walking slowly, tried not moving her hips, tried not breathing. Nothing helped. Each step moved the knot, and yet the stimulation never intensified enough to get her off. By the time she approached the bar, her rapidly swelling clit burned with need. She halted to try to regain her composure. Like that would happen.

"Pissed off Master Nolan, did you?" Master Cullen's deep, rough voice.

She looked over and saw him and Marcus sitting on bar stools.

Master Marcus glanced at Cullen. "That's beautiful work. Why do you think he's angry?"

"He adds the crotch rope only for discipline," Master Cullen said.

Andrea flushed as Marcus's gaze dropped to her groin. "I do see how that might become a tad uncomfortable," he said.

Cullen's laugh didn't amuse her at all.

Cullen tucked a finger under the crotch rope, making the knot press harder on her clit. She barely kept back a moan.

When he pulled her between his outstretched legs and rested his hands on her shoulders, she wanted him to hold her so badly she quivered with it.

"What happened, sweetie?"

"He startled me." She looked down. "I swung at him."

"Wrong guy to take a swing at."

Understatement of the year. "Yes." She considered not mentioning the remainder of Master Nolan's instructions; then again, good Catholic girls shouldn't commit suicide. "He said he wanted me in the ropes for at least half an hour." Maybe Señor would think that excessive?

He smashed her tiny hope flat. "A half hour it is." He glanced at Marcus, "Nolan prefers the Japanese style that uses almost no knots. See how the ropes twine without being knotted?" Master Cullen's fingers ran over the ropes, brushing her skin lightly. He traced the rope running around her swollen left breast, and the nipple tightened so hard that it ached.

"You look lovely in ropes, Andrea," he said. "And I see he tied your arms so you can't take a swing at anyone else...no matter what they do." He looked her straight in the eyes and ran his knuckles over the tight peak of her nipple.

A whimper escaped her, and her arms jerked helplessly behind her back.

Master Cullen's eyes crinkled. Rather than stopping, he played with her swollen breasts, rubbing his thumbs over the hard points and making heat streak through her in waves.

When he finally stopped, her legs shook like jelly. "For the next half an hour, you will walk laps around the bar. Stop in front of me with each lap," he said.

Carajo. She looked at him.

He raised his eyebrows.

"Yes, Señor." She moved away. Carefully. Slowly. *Cabrón. Hijo de puta.*

Whistling with the music, her Señor returned to his bar.

One lap. Two. With every lap and stop, he came back out. And each time, he teased her, playing with the ropes, fondling her breasts. Once he moved the crotch rope, not away from her clit, but just a fraction of an inch sideways so it pressed on a new place. She grew even more swollen and tender.

Almost twenty minutes later, as she started another lap, she realized her head felt light. Oh, Dios, no. Sometimes, especially if she missed meals or didn't drink enough fluids, she'd get dizzy. She'd only fainted a couple of times, since she usually had the brains to stop and sit until it passed, and then fix whatever caused it. But she couldn't sit, not this time. "*Never show weakness.*"

She gritted her teeth, trying to force away the blackness wavering at the edges of her vision. Her mouth tasted as if she'd chewed on tinfoil, and her face felt hot, then cold. *I can do this, dammit.* She staggered into a table, shook her head, and kept on walking.

A hand grasped her chin, and she blinked, trying to see through the haze. "Don't. I don't need help."

"Hell you don't."

Her head spun so fast that her stomach twisted, and then she realized Master Cullen was carrying her. He laid her on a couch.

With her feet up, the dizziness receded, and shame ran through her. She'd failed. Couldn't even cut walking around a bar a few times.

"Heather, bring me a water," Señor called. When it came, he held the bottle to her mouth. She tried to take it, but he hadn't released her arms from behind her back.

"Drink."

"I—"

"Drink, sub. We'll talk in a minute."

The water poured into her, removing the taste of tin. Every time she swallowed, she got more until most of the bottle was gone.

Then Master Cullen took a pair of scissors from his pocket and cut the ropes off her, dropping them in a pile on the floor. As blood rushed into every compressed area, her skin tingled and burned. When he pulled her arms forward, she groaned.

"Poor baby." Chuckling, he slid her down so her head rested on the arm of the couch, then massaged her sore muscles with strong hands. Her neck, her shoulders, her upper arms, squeezing to the point of pain.

The knots in her shoulders relaxed, and she sighed. But having him tend to her felt wrong. That was her job. She tried to sit up.

He pushed her flat, holding her there with a firm hand between her breasts. "Don't move, sub."

She eyed his stern face. He looked so angry. Now he'd yell at her for screwing up. She couldn't even walk around the room without wussing out. "I'm sorry, Señor," she whispered.

His eyes narrowed. "What exactly are you sorry for?"

His hand still pressed her to the cushions, leaving her no retreat. "I didn't do what you said, didn't finish walking my half hour. I—"*I'm a failure, a weakling.*

"I see." His knuckles brushed along her jawline. But he'd stopped holding her down, so she started to—

"Lie still," he snapped.

She dropped back on the cushions, although she couldn't relax.

"Andrea, did you realize you were dizzy?"

"Yes." Oops. "Yes, *Señor.*"

"Why did you keep walking?"

What kind of a question was that? "Because you told me too."

He snorted. "And if you'd continued another minute, you'd have been passed out on the floor."

She flushed and dropped her gaze. *Loser.*

"Hell." A finger under her chin raised her face. "Look at me." He regarded her for a long minute. "Sweetie, I expect a lot from my trainees, but you're only human. If you get dizzy, or if it's the wrong time of the month, or if you're feeling puny, I want to know. That's part of the honesty between a sub and Dom."

Like he would listen any more than her father?

His eyebrows drew together, and his mouth went taut as if he'd heard her. "And if for some reason, I'm not listening, I'd better hear the word 'red,' coming from those pretty lips, loud and clear."

Admit to a weakness? Quit? Not me.

The little sub's muscles had tightened up again. That sure wasn't looking like agreement to Cullen. And why the hell had she kept walking despite obviously heading for a faint. He hadn't seen determination like this since his wildland firefighting days, watching candidates take the three-mile pack test.

He'd known she had a never-back-down spirit, but did that include a problem with requesting help? Too many cops and firefighters often had that mindset, especially the macho idiots who figured asking for assistance made them pussies.

However, he'd never seen shit like this in a sub. "Why am I not hearing, 'Yes, Sir-Señor If I don't feel well, I'll ask you for help'?" When her hands clenched, he realized he'd growled the question. Nonetheless. "Answer me."

"I don't like asking for help." Her eyes met his. Serious. Stubborn. Ms. Macho all right. Time to remind her that—at least in the Shadowlands—subs didn't make decisions or say, "I don't want to." He pinned her left arm down with his hip, grasped her other wrist, and used his free hand to cup one breast.

The startled look in her eyes gratified him. She tried to lift her arms, realized she couldn't move, and her eyes dilated. *Little submissive.* He teased her breasts, circling the nipples with his thumb, pressing the fullness upward, enjoying himself as was a Master's right. Her breathing increased, and a pulse hammered in her neck. But the pleasure he got from seeing her response to being restrained had nothing to do with this conversation. "Why don't you like getting help if you need it?"

When his answer didn't come quickly, he pinched one tender peak.

She barely managed to muffle the squeak, but her back arched.

"Why?" He rolled the nipple between his fingers, keeping the pressure hard enough that her cheeks flushed. Sensitive breasts. Someday he'd have to see if she could come just from breast play.

"It doesn't do any good." Her eyes had a haunted flash.

Someone had let her down. Maybe several someones?

She added rapidly, "No. I mean—I mean, my father didn't like... He was military. You don't ask for help."

Her hips wiggled as her body wakened to his touch.

Cullen snorted, released her breast, and moved to the other. The low moan she gave delighted his ears, and his cock hardened. Bending her over the couch and taking her from behind would please both of them, but he needed to understand this problem of hers. "Wasn't he ever in a squad? Didn't he ever ask a buddy for help with his pack? Stripping a weapon? What kind of teamwork is that?" He pinched her again when she obviously tried to find the right words. "Don't think. Just answer me."

She whimpered and said, "He was a sniper. He didn't like teams."

Covert ops with no backup? That sucked and explained much. Those guys seriously believed the *depend-only-on-yourself* bullshit. Hell. "Sweetie, what he said about counting only on yourself won't work here. We need to know you'll use your safe word."

"I-I don't..."

Not the answer he wanted, but at least she hadn't lied to him. He gentled his touch and simply stroked her, from her graceful neck to just above her pussy. Pretty bare pussy where her swollen clit still poked out between the lips.

So should he dump her from the trainees? Her unwillingness to bail out created a safety issue. But little Miss Independence truly was submissive, and the Dom in him wanted to fix this. Especially since she might end up somewhere else where they wouldn't know her hang-ups or care for her properly.

As he continued petting her, she pressed her legs together with a tiny squirm. Her color mounted. He smiled, even as his cock turned rock hard. She needed to come, and badly.

"I'm going to go home now." Her voice started soft but ended up firm.

Probably dying to find some privacy and get herself off, especially since she wouldn't ask for help. One of these days he'd drive her right to that point...over and over. Another fun lesson to look forward to.

Apparently he'd made the decision to keep her, after all. She'd stay, and he'd work on the safe word issue with her. He traced the pink line left from the rope, down her stomach to her mound. "You're not going home yet."

Her eyes closed, and her hips tilted into his hand like a cat begging for more. He chuckled. Master Z called his sub a kitten. Andrea was no kitten but a tiger. Bigger, the claws faster and deadlier, but she liked to be petted just as much.

Let's see just how much... "You know, earlier this evening I realized I'd given you only one side of a lesson that first night."

The flush of arousal pinked her cheeks. His finger slid down a fraction into the crease between her outer labia, staying well above her clit. As aroused as she looked, any stimulation would send her over. Her brows drew together as she tried to think. "What lesson?"

"I spanked you, remember?"

"I'm not likely to forget someone slapping my butt with a big piece of wood."

He laughed. When her lips curved in response, he surrendered to the urge and took her mouth—hard. Deep. Satisfying, especially since she gave as good as she got, participating fully. When he pulled back, her lips were as swollen and wet as her pussy.

"I am going to spank you now." He gripped her arms, forestalling her instinctive attempt to retreat. "I gave you the first spanking for punishment; this one is for fun."

"Your fun, maybe. I didn't like it at all. No." She actually struggled, and he had to smother his laugh.

"Trainee," he said, sharply enough that she had to look at him. "I didn't ask your permission."

She stilled, her breathing rapid. Her lips moved—*No*—but no sound escaped.

He let his voice warm with approval. "Very good. Now give me your hand." They both knew he could overpower her, but that wasn't submission. Submission was the war in her eyes as her desire to refuse fought with his command.

Submission was her hand settling into his.

They crossed the room through the pools of darkness left by the dimmed flickering sconces. A deep Gregorian chant throbbed under the murmur of the members, and the sounds of pain indicating the Shadowlands had transitioned to late-night play.

As he led her to the specially designed spanking throne, Cullen knew he should have given the task to another master. But he wanted to show her this side of desire—and to bring her to orgasm in the Shadowlands for the first time.

He took a spreader bar off the wall. "Don't move."

After buckling a cuff on her left ankle, he pointed at the other end of the metal bar. "Put your foot over here."

When she paused to consider, he slapped her thigh briskly. Her legs moved apart.

He strapped the other cuff on. The metal bar prevented her from closing her legs and kept that pussy open and available. As he knelt on one knee, he could smell the heady scent of her arousal and see the glistening moisture between her thighs. Her abused pink clit, still too swollen to retreat behind its hood, waited for his touch.

He almost peeled her farther open to use his tongue, but if he did, then she wouldn't have this lesson. So he rose and took a seat on the chair, setting his feet on the metal footrests. The height of the pedestal chair put his knees even with her upper stomach. He grasped her wrist and drew her closer, smiling at her impaired steps. "Over my knees, pet."

Her look of disbelief made him laugh. He could explain the added intimacy of over-the-knee, bare-handed spanking, but she'd discover it soon enough. He simply held her gaze until her eyes dropped, and she laid herself over his lap. Barely. Her stomach rested on his thighs.

He grunted, amused. "I'm not planning to spank your shoulders, love." With a hand between her legs, he repositioned her, head down.

Even with her height, her fingertips barely brushed the floor. Her legs on the other side dangled without any leverage. Cullen grinned. Z had made the carpenter mount the chair extra high just to induce that helpless feeling.

Andrea gulped.

And that was just the right response. Cullen pressed his left hand to her shoulders, increasing her sense of helplessness. With his right, he massaged her bottom. Soft and round, with hard muscle underneath. Perfection.

"You have a gorgeous ass, Andrea." He ran his hand over her low back and down the tiny hollow of her low spine.

When his finger teased the crack between her cheeks, she tensed.

"Not this time, love, but I intend to give you a sample of anal sex one of these days." And he knew her anticipation and worry would only increase as time went on.

He patted her ass lightly to warm her skin and sensitize it. Then he slid his hand between her legs.

Since he had her shoulders pinned, she could only squirm helplessly as he ran a finger through her slick labia and over her clit. It was swollen and too tender to press directly—at least right now. He slid his finger up and down one side, very gently, feeling as always that his hands were too huge for such delicate work.

Finding, as always, that it didn't matter.

Slowly, as he teased her, the muscles of Andrea's back tightened into long hard lines. Her breathing increased.

There we go. Abandoning her pussy, he smacked her right ass cheek, then the left. Her legs tried to kick, but the spreader bar prevented much movement. He swatted her harder, taking her just to the edge of pain. Her golden skin took on a pink hue.

And then he slid his hand back between her legs.

Chapter Eight

Master Cullen pushed down on her shoulders as the fingers of his other hand touched her pussy, setting every nerve on fire. Dios, what was he doing to her? She squirmed, but his fingers never stopped. He traced every inch of tender flesh, over and over, until her clit engorged, and her whole pussy felt tight.

When he eased a finger into her, yet more nerves shocked awake. The feeling of fullness startled her, but then, she hadn't had a lover in a long time.

"Been a while for you, hasn't it?" he murmured, his finger sliding deep inside, then out and over her clit again, until she was drowning in burning pleasure.

She tried to move, and he pressed her shoulders down mercilessly, even as his finger entered her again. Held down, invaded. The helpless feeling sent heat roaring through her, increasing every sensation.

When he abandoned her pussy, she whimpered at the loss.

Slick fingers touched her buttocks. Then he slapped her bottom. Harder, much harder than before, and she yelped, then moaned as, somehow, the pain moved into her sensitive pussy, sending her even higher into need. "I want—"

"Little sub…" His open hand came down on her bottom with a smacking sound, and the stinging impact seared straight to her clit. "You will get only what I give you." Two more remorseless slaps; her bottom burned like fire.

His hand returned to her pussy.

Oh, yes. She tried to open her legs farther, and the bar stopped her, reminding her of her helplessness. Her clit throbbed, pulsing intensely. Just one touch, one more, and she'd get off. "Please—"

"If I hear you speak again, I'll gag you and strap you to the wall," Cullen said and drove two fingers into her.

"Oh oh oh." She tried to arch at the intense pleasure and couldn't move. *Dios.* He pulled his fingers back and thrust harder. Her nerves flared as her vagina stretched around him. The throbbing arousal moved deep inside her, trying to merge with her clit. Oh, Dios, almost. She heard whimpering. *Her.* She pressed her lips together.

Two more stinging swats drove her higher, each impact creating a sizzling wave straight down to her pussy. Her legs, held firmly apart by the bar, trembled.

His fingers slid into her again. In, out, circling her clit, in out. Everything inside her coiled tighter and tighter, and she tensed. Her fingernails scratched the floor. Nothing to hold. She grabbed his ankle, digging her fingernails in.

"Hang on, sweetie," he murmured. His fingers drove into her again, pressing deep, deeper. The hand on her shoulders disappeared, and then he slapped her bottom so hard that brilliant fire shot through her.

"Come for me, pet." A finger slid over her clit, right on top, rubbing, the exquisite sensations too...too...

The explosion ripped outward in searing waves of pleasure. She buried her face against her arm as cries escaped her. Her hips bucked under his hand.

Before the spasms inside her had ceased, his fingers plunged into her, and he slapped her butt, sharp, stinging strokes—and she came again, shaking hard. Her spasming vagina seemed to collide against the thick intrusion inside, sending more convulsions through her.

When her hips wiggled, he pinned her with a hard hand on her bottom, keeping her from moving, as his fingers thrust in and out. The unyielding control triggered another tremor through her.

His hand eased as her quivering lessened. When he removed his fingers from inside her, she couldn't suppress the whine as her whole body shuddered, toes to shoulders. Her heart pounded so hard she felt the impact against her ribs. *Dios mío.* She didn't try to move, just lay there like a ragdoll over his knees as he stroked her back.

"You come beautifully, love." His low voice made her insides quiver as if he'd entered her again. "Sit up now." He lifted her and sat her on his lap, his big hands settling her as easily as if she'd been that ragdoll.

Her skin, damp with sweat, started to cool, and she shivered. Mouth dry, she sat stiffly as he reached down and unbuckled the bar holding her legs apart. It dropped with a nasty thud on the hardwood floor, and she put her knees together, hiding her swollen parts.

What was she doing here on a stranger's lap? This felt wrong. In the center of a room full of people, she felt horribly alone. Her skin grew more sensitive, and the glances of the members around the scene area scraped against her like a hard-bristled brush. She stared down at her hands clenched in her lap. *I want to go home now.*

Why did she feel so upset? *I got what I wanted, and it had been great.* A mind-blowing orgasm. But shouldn't there be more? Her chest felt hollow, too empty even for the tears that prickled at her eyes. Dios, she would not—would not—break down and cry.

He started to pull her closer, and she resisted. He stilled. A big hand brushed over her tightly woven fingers, and then he lifted her chin.

She wrenched her face from his grip and looked away.

"No, love, look at me." His hand cupped her cheek, his thumb under her chin exerted steady pressure as his voice deepened. "Look at me."

Knowing her eyes must be watery, she met his narrowed gaze.

"Ah. Like that is it?" Ignoring her attempt to pull back, he leaned her against his chest, his hard arms enfolding her in his warmth. "Austin," he called. "A blanket, please."

A second later, his embrace loosened, and he wrapped a fuzzy, soft blanket around her. He rose, lifting her, his biceps bulging with the effort.

Her head spun, and she inhaled sharply. "What...?"

"Shhh, little sub." He walked across the room to one of the more secluded areas and chose a low chair, leaning back so she rested against his chest. He pressed her head down into the hollow of his shoulder. On this side of the club, the Gregorian music throbbed like a heartbeat; the voices and noise of the room dimmed to only a murmur.

"I'm leaving." Her voice came out slurred, as if she'd sucked down a bottle of gin.

"No. You need to let me hold you for a while until you recover." She could feel his chin rub over the top of her head, the press of his lips. "You've had a rough night, but I didn't expect you to drop like that." A low chuckle. "What are you going to do after a flogging or wax play?"

She was so...elsewhere...that the words didn't even bring up a good scare. She laid her cheek against his soft leather vest and breathed in his masculine scent. His arms tightened around her, gripping her so firmly she couldn't move, and his strength gave her comfort rather than fear. As his hand stroked her hair, as the empty spot inside her started to fill, she could feel her feet and her arms. Like she'd stepped back into her body again.

Footsteps. Austin whispered, "Master Z said to bring you this stuff. He said his kitten likes chocolate."

Something settled on the blankets in Andrea's lap. "Thank you, Austin," Señor's voice rumbled under her ear. "Return to Master Z and tell him, 'Thank you, Mommy.'"

"Sir," Austin sounded appalled. "I can't do that."

"Do just that." As Austin's footsteps receded, Master Cullen reached inside the blanket and pulled out Andrea's arm. He put a bottled water in her hand, curling her fingers around it, and guiding it to her mouth. She took a sip, and it stuck before finally going down.

"Again," he said, and she swallowed another. Suddenly her mouth felt horribly dry, the water like a rare treasure, and she sat up and started drinking greedily.

A rumbling laugh. "There we go."

When she'd finished most of the water, she stopped with a sigh. "Thank you."

He set the bottle on the end table beside the chair and picked up something from her lap. "Open up."

Feeling like a baby, and just the thought made tears prickle in her eyes again, she obeyed. Chocolate—Hershey's. The rich flavor swirled through her mouth, and she moaned, then looked up to see Señor studying her, a faint smile on his face.

Ignoring her hand, he fed her another square of chocolate. When she sighed in pleasure, his eyes crinkled. "I can see an easy way to reward you from now on."

She leaned her head against his chest, the hollowness inside her gone, replaced by warm contentment. "Chocolate's better than sex any day."

Oh, rude, she realized when amusement lit his eyes. His eyebrows rose, bringing back the memory of his fingers stroking her clit, then filling her.

She quivered, and her cheeks warmed. "Well, so I thought."

His laugh filled the area, and the way he snuggled her closer completely topped off her happiness meter.

* * *

What a pretty day. Andrea stepped out on Antonio's balcony and paused. As gorgeous puffy clouds floated across a deep blue sky, the palm trees dotted around the apartment complex swayed in the cool, salt-laden breeze. A row of sea gulls lined up on the next building's roof with military precision, in marked contrast to her best friend slouched down in a chair.

"Hard night?" She set a cup of coffee in front of him.

"I'm getting too old to party, and doesn't that suck?" Antonio muttered. With dark circles under his eyes, his color almost gray, and his breath nasty enough to kill a rhinoceros, he'd definitely overindulged. "Why are you so disgustingly cheerful? Weren't you at the Shadowlands last night?"

She rubbed his shoulder in sympathy and took a chair across the small, round café table. "I was. But the place has a two-drink limit; even if I wanted to get plowed, they wouldn't let me."

But a couple of strong drinks before leaving might have helped her forget Señor's merciless hands holding her, controlling her. The memories had kept her awake and aroused most of the night. She shifted in the chair, uncomfortably aware of her tender bits and bottom. Especially her bottom.

"Things going all right?" He sucked coffee down with the single-mindedness of a junkie needing a fix.

"Good enough." No, she owed Antonio more than a throwaway answer. She took a bite of the still-warm glazed donut. Sugar high, caffeine, a friend to talk with, a special man to see tonight—who could ask for better? "Really good, actually. Thanks for getting me in there, although I'm not sure how you did it. Are you and M—Cullen friends?"

"Casual friends. We have a couple of interests in common." Antonio set his empty cup down. "Did he get over being pissed off?"

"Oh, yes." The way his gaze had softened, how he'd held her, his kisses...everything in her just melted thinking about him

Antonio's eyes narrowed. "Andrea, you're not getting hung up on him, are you?"

"'Course not."

"Oh, hell," Antonio muttered under his breath. He leaned forward, taking her hand across the table. The worried look in his red-rimmed eyes was disheartening. "Listen, *chica*. Cullen's really well known in the BDSM community. He started the trainer program out there, has been doing it for years, and loves it. He never, ever gets involved with any of the subs. Yeah, he'll screw around in the club, but he never dates them. Hell, he doesn't even get involved for more than a few months with anyone. The guy's a hard-core player, and he's totally upfront about it."

The sweet pastry in her stomach turned into a hard lump, and she pushed the remains of the donut away. With an effort, she smothered the protests welling up inside her. *He really likes me, though. This is different. He'd change for me.* Dios, but she'd been a fool. *Dumb as a rock.*

She glanced up at the sky, but the sun hadn't disappeared...just the hope she hadn't realized she'd harbored. "I'm not hung up on him," she said firmly. *Not anymore.* "He's been very patient with me. And it's fun being around someone really bigger than me, you know?"

"Oh, yes, he's bigger." Antonio waggled his eyebrows and gave her an, "I'm gay and gorgeous, and you're lucky I don't go after your men" expression.

"Cabrón." She frowned at her feet, thinking of how she'd painted her toenails, wondering if Señor would notice. If he'd like the color. *Estúpida.* "But all the Masters I've met so far are big guys. Is that some Dom thing?"

"Nah. The percentage of big dudes there is probably skewed because the owner has a lot of ex-military and cop friends."

Cops? *Oh please, no.* She shivered at the horrible thought of a cop's hands on her, of one having control over her. That couldn't happen; just couldn't. She must have met the ex-military guys though; some of them—including Master Cullen when he wasn't smiling—definitely had that fuck-with-me-at-your-own-risk aura. "Well, makes it nice for me."

"Good." Antonio frowned, and she could see him worrying over her like a dog with a bone. "But, Rambolita, I'm serious about Cullen. You two wouldn't suit. *Comprendes?*"

Her cousin had people-reading down to a fine art, so he must know something about the trainer that she didn't. She tried a sip of coffee, and it tasted like mud. "*Comprendo.*"

Time to get out of here. Find someplace where she could kick something really hard. "I need to get going." She pushed to her feet and paused. "How'd last night go for you? Did you meet anyone nice?"

"A hunk named Steven. Reminded me of you, in a way. Thick, yellow hair and he has your coloring too, only lighter." His lips curved.

She snorted. "His Swedish father probably didn't marry a Hispanic woman." She walked around the table and pressed a kiss to his cheek. "Just be careful. It's not a safe world out there, and I can't afford to lose my best friend."

He didn't even try to stand up. "Don't worry. Besides, you don't need me anymore. You've got all those Masters to beat on you now, right?"

"Oh, that's right." Annoyed, she smacked him on the head and grinned when he yelped.

But tonight there would be one less Master beating on her. *No more Master Cullen daydreams for me.*

Chapter Nine

"Is there a problem?"

Cullen jerked his attention back to the bar and frowned at Z. When had he arrived? "No. No problem."

Z turned and looked over his shoulder and, canny bastard, spotted what or rather *who* Cullen had been watching.

The little Amazon. Over the past couple of weeks, she'd definitely gotten into the spirit of submissive clothing. "You give her some of the play clothes?" Cullen asked.

"Indeed. I doubt her budget extends to many new outfits, so I told her to borrow from the armoires upstairs and discover what style suits her." Z smiled. "She has good taste."

The creamy flowing skirt went to her ankles and was transparent enough to glimpse her darker legs, to tantalize a man with hints of her pussy. Her halter top of the same material showed brownish pink nipples pressing against the thin fabric. Seductive as hell. Scowling, Cullen poured Z a Glenlivet and set it in front of him.

Z took a sip. "How is she doing?"

"Fine."

Z raised an eyebrow at the terse answer, obviously expecting more of a discussion. Fuck that. Cullen glanced down the bar. Olivia needed a refill. So maybe she hadn't quite finished her drink. Be prepared, right?

As he walked away, he felt Z's gaze on his back and knew he'd made a wise choice staying at least a bar-length from the damned psychologist mind reader.

By the time Cullen had served everyone at the end of the bar, Z had left, and Raoul had arrived for his shift at the bar. "All yours," Cullen said.

"Got it, '*mano*. Go."

As Raoul stepped behind the bar, Cullen headed out.

He released Austin from the theme room, ran into Jonathon and helped him with a flogging technique, then told Vanessa her shift was over, and finally checked on Andrea.

Cullen stood for a minute, watching her laugh at Gerald's jokes. No wariness there, not with the old man and his wife. Andrea's golden brown skin gleamed in the flickering sconce lights, and Cullen's hands curled as he remembered the feel of that silky skin under his palms. How sweat had dampened the tiny hairs at the nape of her neck. The smell of her arousal on his fingers.

He jerked his head. *Trainee, buddy. She's a trainee.*

And she had made it very clear she harbored no interest in more. Not that he'd let himself get sucked into that trap. Dammit, he was *not* getting sucked in.

She glanced around, and her eyes widened when she noticed him. He saw the gulp of breath, and the control she imposed on herself before she turned away without smiling.

He frowned. When she'd said good night after her spanking, she'd been soft and flushed and obviously wanting more. More holding, more stroking—he could have taken her then and there, and she'd have welcomed him.

But ever since that evening, she'd looked like she might snap his cock off at the root if he touched her. And yet...

"Hey, Cullen." Wade walked over, his black leather pants not yet softened from use.

"How's it going?" Cullen leaned a hip against a table, keeping Andrea in his sight. "You connected with any subs yet?"

"Well, I did a scene yesterday, but it didn't go quite right. Z suggested I use a trainee and have you watch and give me pointers." He nodded to Andrea. "He said Andrea was new enough that she wouldn't be as...critical...as the others."

Cullen ran his hand through his hair. What the hell was Z thinking? The Ice Age starting in Florida had as much chance of happening as Andrea submitting to this insecure Dom. But a suggestion from the owner translated to an order, and Cullen would need a damn good reason to ignore it.

He didn't really have a reason—aside from the fact that he wanted to break this guy's neck for even thinking about touching her.

But that was his problem, not Andrea's. She had made it clear she didn't want any intimacy between them, and he had to respect her choices. Instead he'd direct his efforts into finding her a Dom of her own. "All right. Go collect your sub. Tell her I gave my permission. I'll follow."

Wade lit up. *God, was I ever that young?* The baby Dom started to hurry over to Andrea, then caught himself, and slowed to a dignified walk.

Cullen watched Andrea's face. The frown, the confusion. She looked at him, and he nodded. Her lips tightened before she bowed to Wade.

As the two headed for the nearby bondage table, Cullen wandered over to Gerald and Martha. The old man raised his eyebrows. "Hate to say it, Cullen, but you let that boy get in over his head. That's not a sub who will give it up for just any Dom."

"Agreed. But it was Z's suggestion."

"Odd. I wonder why." As Gerald stroked Martha's hair, the old woman rested her head against his shoulder. Quite the couple. When her knees had become arthritic, Gerald refused to let her kneel any longer. He said if she didn't know her place after more than twenty years, then kneeling wouldn't help.

Growing old with someone...strange how Cullen could actually see the appeal now. Maybe he was getting old. "With Z, who knows why?" Cullen smiled at Martha, nodded at Gerald. "I'd better get over there; I'm supposed to watch and give suggestions."

As he walked away, he heard Martha whisper, "It's long past time that man found himself a sub." She'd said it often.

Cullen expected to hear Gerald's usual response, that Cullen would in his own good time, and he almost stopped, when instead, the old man said, "Yep."

Wade seemed like a nice enough person, Andrea thought, as he buckled her arms over her head, then her legs open at the end of the table. But if he figured his actions and commands had made her submissive or aroused, he had another think coming. She could see him trying to be all dominant, but all she felt was annoyed.

Apparently dominance came in different sizes since she sure became submissive around some of the Doms here, especially the Masters. Scary guys. Especially Master Cullen, whose deceptively easygoing nature covered a well of enormous power.

Wade checked the tightness of her restraints—he was well taught—then undid her halter straps and exposed her breasts.

At least she'd gotten past being so embarrassed about nakedness. "*That modesty is something we'll work on also*," Master Cullen had said the first night. And why did he keep popping into her mind?

This Dom—she shouldn't think of him as the kid, they were probably about the same age—tried hard. Really he did, messing with her breasts, then her pussy. Very pleasant and very boring.

Finally the kid stood up and said to someone outside of the ropes, "What am I doing wrong?"

"First of all, this is a stubborn sub." It was Señor's deep, rough voice. Her heart actually skipped a beat before it started hammering inside her chest.

"Few people get through to her. Keep that in mind," Señor said. "After that, Wade, it's not what you're doing wrong; it's what you're not doing."

Master Cullen walked into sight, and her whole body seemed to jump awake like an internal alarm had gone off. *No, no, no, bad body.* She would not get involved with this...player...Antonio had called him. So maybe her breathing increased, but it wasn't her fault if the giant Dom used up all the air in the area, leaving none for her.

"Not doing? Like...?" Wade prompted.

A big hand touched her pussy—Master Cullen's hand— and her hips squirmed uncontrollably.

"She's dry. This tells you something right there: that you haven't captured her mind. Dominance isn't about the physical, and neither is sex."

Señor pressed Wade's hand against her pussy, then moved up the table to stand beside her. His hard fingers captured her chin. "Look at me, Andrea."

The command in his authoritative voice sent a thrill through her, and when her gaze lifted, his eyes focused on her so intently that she had to look away.

"I want your eyes on me, sub."

Again that melting feeling. No. She didn't want that feeling. Didn't want him. She tried to pull her chin out of his grip, to move anything, but unfortunately the kid had done a good job on the restraints. Nothing moved.

"You can't move, little sub." His thumb caressed her lips. "Your body is bound, and every part is open and available for my use."

Just the thought of Señor *using* her, taking her, touching her, sent a tremor through her.

"Hell, she's wet." Wade sounded shocked. "I work on her forever and get nowhere. You *look* at her, and she creams."

Master Cullen's focused gaze stayed on her as she flushed. Then his cheek creased. But it wasn't a real smile, not a Master Cullen smile, and the loss set something aching in her.

He undid the arm restraints, his hands sure and efficient, and sat her up like a doll with her legs still bound. "And that's the lesson Z wanted you to have, Wade. Domination starts in the head."

Just the feel of Señor's touch made her needy, like her skin had been sandpapered all over and every contact with his fingers grew more acute than the next.

Wade released the ankle restraints, and all too conscious of her wetness, she started to put her legs together.

"Did I give you permission to move?" Master Cullen asked, the chill in his voice freezing her in place.

"No, Señor."

He turned back to his conversation with the kid. "Think about why you're doing this. What you get from it and how you feel when a woman willingly submits to you. Hold that in your mind and find one of the younger subs—one who won't look you in the eyes for more than a second. Take her to a scene area and dominate her. Have her kneel, ask her questions, and don't let her evade you. Dig deep. Make her look at you and watch her eyes. Read her body language. No sex, Wade. Just enjoy the feeling of dominating someone."

Wade nodded and headed off, leaving Andrea alone with Master Cullen. This was so what she didn't want. If she stayed away, far away from him, she could cope. If he didn't touch her or—

He moved closer, and she stared down at her hands.

"You going to tell me what's going on with you?" he asked, his tone deceptively mild.

Don't lie. "No, Señor. I'd rather…" Stall. "I just need some time to think." *Time to get myself back under control. My control, not yours.*

His hands engulfed her own, warm against her cold skin. He chafed her fingers gently. "All right, Andrea. You do your thinking. We will discuss all these thoughts next week." He paused. "Is that clear?"

"Yes, Señor."

"You're off duty. Let me know if you find someone you want to play with." He gave her hands a squeeze and walked away.

I want to play with you. You, you, you.

* * *

"Look, I finished before the baby came this time." Andrea shook out the tiny blanket, and the sun glinted off the pink and white yarn.

"Very pretty." Andrea's grandmother fingered the fringed edge. "And very soft. You did a fine job, mija."

"I'm getting better." Nice and even, no lopsided corners, no gaping holes. With a contented sigh, she leaned back in the patio chair and glanced over Aunt Rosa's tiny backyard. Not much had changed since when she'd lived here for her last two years of high school. The straggly line of bushes dividing it from the neighbor's yards had grown only a foot taller. A lemon tree had replaced one of the orange trees marking the corners. Off to one side sat the massive truck hubcap that Julio had turned into a barbeque. On the other side, grass still refused to grow under the aged swing set.

And Andrea still came to Aunt Rosa's house every Sunday to immerse herself in belonging.

At least now that her cleaning business had edged into the black, she could give something back. Earlier, Andrea had made an excuse of using the bathroom and had unpacked her bag of all the items she'd bought. New sheets went on the bed, lotion to the bedside table, treats and some high-calorie shakes into the tiny cupboard in the corner. When she finished, only the box of cookies remained in the bag. Her grandmother wouldn't see the new things until Andrea had left; it was part of the game they played. Pride ran strong on both sides of the family.

After pulling out the box, Andrea folded the quilt and put it into her bag to wrap later. "Here, Abuelita, I made some cookies."

As they munched and enjoyed the unseasonably warm weather, Andrea heard all the gossip about the area. Who got pregnant, who had a divorce, whose marriage failed, which husband beat on his wife. Whose children landed in jail or went to college or found a new lover.

"But we haven't talked about you, mija." Aged eyes studied Andrea. "You look different. Softer."

Over the past few weeks, she'd discovered she liked looking feminine. Now she left her hair loose, wore tighter shorts and a tank top that showed off her shape.

"Have you found a man?"

"Abuelita!" Andrea's jaw dropped.

"I may be old, but I'm not blind. You look like a woman in love."

"I wish." The wanting to be with Master Cullen got worse every time she saw him. "I met someone, but he's not interested in getting involved."

Her grandmother nibbled a corner of the cookie like a mouse. "But you want him?"

Just the thought made her heart scramble. "Oh, yes. But he wouldn't get involved with someone like me."

"Like you? You're pretty, smart."

"The place where I met him is all rich people." Although a bartender probably didn't earn all that much, right? "Eventually he'd discover that I come from here." She waved her hand at the surrounding neighborhood of older housing, rundown apartments. Two streets over, prostitutes stood on corners, drug deals went down in the alleys, and knifings occurred every weekend.

"Is he so shallow to judge a woman by her background?"

"People do." Rosa's husband had been a notorious drug dealer; her cousins had spent time in juvie. Job opportunities dissipated once potential employers checked Andrea's background. Banks wouldn't loan her money after discovering where she came from. Boyfriends disappeared after their parents found out about her family. She'd learned the irrelevance of a person's character compared to her background.

Abuelita's eyes narrowed. "Is he a good man?"

Andrea's lips curved as she thought about Señor's sense of humor, his insistence on honesty. How he watched over the trainees so carefully and how everyone, from the club members to the Masters, turned to him for help and advice...how he'd wrapped her in his arms and fed her chocolate. "Oh, yes."

"Then go after him. Your past may matter, mija, or it may not. You won't find out if you don't give him a chance." Abuelita clasped her arthritic fingers together. "People—especially men—don't always know what they want. You try, and if it doesn't work, then you may quit."

With a broken heart.

As if she'd read her mind, Abuelita frowned and scolded, "Hearts mend, but lost chances are gone forever.

"But—"

"My granddaughter is not a coward."

Chapter Ten

Cullen walked into the Shadowlands a good two hours late and in a crappy mood. The only thing worse than getting a nasty burn and a visit to the emergency room was filling out incident report forms. *Damned rules and regs.*

To hide the bulky gauze dressing, he'd worn an old shirt from college days when he'd belonged to a SCA group. The medieval look with full sleeves didn't go too bad with his leather jeans, and the green color worked just fine for St. Pat's Day.

Cullen nodded to Ben at the guard desk, received a token salute, and stepped into the clubroom. Z had apparently decided upon a romantic Celtic theme for the evening, and the lilting music of Clannad drifted through the room rather than the harsh beat of aggrotech. Not bad. In fact, the atmosphere felt almost like his grandfather's Irish pub...aside from the sounds of whips and chains, screams and groans.

Cullen ducked under the bar and saw Dan filling drink orders.

"'Bout time you got here," Dan said, throwing a token punch.

Cullen stepped out of range and winced when the hasty movement pulled on the bandages.

Dan stilled. "What happened?"

"Just a burn. Not bad." Hell, here only five minutes and he was outed.

"Go sit. I'll play bartender this evening."

"I've got it." Cullen moved his arm and sighed. Who was he fooling? It would hurt like hell if he did a complete night. "For a couple hours or so."

Dan studied him, then nodded. "I'll set the rest of us up to rotate through after that until Raoul comes on."

"Thanks. I owe you." Cullen stepped around him and set a beer on the bartop for Adrian. "How are my trainees?"

"Pretty as all get-out. They coordinated their outfits, even Austin." Dan pointed across the room.

"Well, now," he murmured at the sight of Andrea serving drinks to a group of Dommes. As cute as a button, his gramps would say. The rich brown vinyl skirt was good, but the green ribbons knotted like macramé to cover her breasts were excellent. She'd pulled her hair back and more green ribbons mingled with her streaky curls. The tiny bows tied around her ankles showcased her tanned legs. "Very nice."

She'd had her week of thinking. Tonight she'd tell him what the hell had happened in that pretty head of hers. Why had she chilled out like that? Snuggling in his lap one night and avoiding him the next. And why the hell did he care?

Another sub, Cullen, she's just another sub in a long line of subs. And she doesn't want her trainer. He glanced at the next person waiting and snapped, "What do you need?"

The young brunette sub paled and took a step back.

Fuck, now he was scaring the little ones. "Sorry, love," he said gently. "What can I get you?"

Giving him a wary look, she edged closer and started reciting her order.

After her, Cullen worked his way around the bar, concentrating on the music and his friends, and slowly his mood lightened. Bartending at the Shadowlands balanced the intensity of his arson work. He liked meeting people's needs, either for drinks or talk or advice.

As Cullen set a White Russian in front of a new redheaded sub, Marcus stepped behind the bar, saying, "Dan sent me over to assist you and learn how to tend the bar."

Doms could be pain-in-the-ass mother hens. Cullen had the same trait, but that didn't mean he had to like landing on the receiving end. He heaved a sigh and gave in. "The beer is kept in this refrigerator..."

Once they'd dealt with the current batch of drinks, Cullen leaned on the bar, Marcus beside him.

Over at the chain station, Nolan indulged in flogging his pretty redhead—very lightly, as usual. Then he stopped. From the annoyed look on his face, Beth had sassed him. He tossed the flogger aside and stepped over to her, burying his fist in her hair. When he stared down at her, the increase in sexual tension was obvious from across the room.

"She's a spirited little thing," Marcus commented. "But I do tend to prefer the quieter ones."

"I usually do too." At least until recently, until a little Amazon started giving him trouble. "You have someone here in mind?"

Marcus shook his head. "I am still making the acquaintance of the members."

New prosecuting lawyer, Cullen recalled. The cops who'd seen him work a jury said he was damn good. "You're here from Virginia, right?"

"I wanted some distance from my divorce."

Now see, that right there demonstrated why a man shouldn't get involved. "Makes sense. You enjoying the Shadowlands?" Cullen turned back to the scene at the chain station.

When Nolan picked up a cane, Beth's eyes widened. Trust came hard to that sub, and Nolan kept pushing her limits. Now he started with mild flicks up her body, warming her up, waiting until she relaxed. The first light snap across her breasts raised her up on tiptoes.

Cullen grinned.

"I do like this club," Marcus murmured with an identical grin. "You've got an interesting group of trainees too, although one seems to be rather attached."

Cullen felt his gut tighten and kept his muscles loose. "Andrea?"

"Yes, sir, that would be the one." Marcus gave him a level look. "I did enjoy the time you graciously shared with her. But if she has come to be important to you…"

"The master in charge of the trainees has to keep distant from the subs," Cullen said. Which was why he didn't plant his fist in Marcus's face right now. He rubbed his chin. Dammit, his possessiveness kept increasing.

"So I've heard," Marcus said. "But even that master might be tempted."

Yeah, and that master was in deep shit.

Andrea's energy had faded like pink panties laundered with Clorox. She'd spent much of last night cleaning two new businesses and then couldn't get to sleep afterward. Too excited over tonight. Here she'd been all primed to put her grandmother's advice into action, but Master Dan had manned the bar instead of Master Cullen. Talk about a letdown. Despite the cheerful crowd and the fun Celtic music, the fizzle had vanished from the evening like a Pepsi left out in the sun.

Heaving a sigh, Andrea wrote more drink orders and went back to the bar. She set her tray on the bartop.

"Pretty outfit." The deep voice took her breath away.

"Master Cullen, you're here!" Dios, look at him. He actually had a shirt on rather than a vest and the full-sleeved medieval style made him appear even bigger, his shoulders even wider. The rolled-up sleeves revealed his muscular, tanned forearms and wrists.

"Very observant of you, love." He didn't come around the bar as he'd done in the beginning, didn't lean over the bar. Her attempting to stay away from him had worked too well.

"*Go after him,*" her grandmother had said. *All right, Abuelita, just watch me work.* If he wouldn't move closer, then she must. She rested her forearms on the bar in an imitation of his usual posture. Only she had breasts and knew full well that her arms squeezed them together, making serious cleavage.

He definitely noticed.

"You look really nice too," she said. And everything in her wanted him. "The green in your shirt matches your eyes."

Those green eyes narrowed.

She could feel his gaze as she rummaged for the scrap of paper she'd tucked into her token bra. Considering the open spaces outnumbered what the ribbon covered, she was lucky it held paper at all.

"Want some help?"

She looked up, knowing his perceptive gaze would catch how much she wanted him. Not that she wanted to hide it anymore.

"Well now," he murmured. He leaned across the bar and tucked a finger into her knotwork bra, securing her while he pulled the paper out...and took the time to rub his knuckles over her rapidly peaking nipples. She'd tried arranging the ribbons to hide her nipples, but her breasts had soon jiggled them out.

Then again, if things sticking out interested him, she'd wear macramé every night.

She closed her eyes as her nipples tightened into sensitive nubs, and she could feel herself dampen. When she opened her eyes, she realized he wasn't looking at her breasts. Instead he was studying her face as he touched her. Somehow that just made the heat worse.

He smiled and ran a finger across her lips. "Once you're off duty, we're going to have a talk, little tiger."

"Yes, Señor."

He straightened and stepped back, wincing as if his shoulders hurt. She frowned. He was moving funny too. Stiff, like—

"Master Cullen, you made it!" Vanessa nudged Andrea to one side without even a glance. "You promised me you'd use the flogger on me tonight. I've been waiting and waiting."

"I did promise that, didn't I?" Cullen looked at Andrea's orders. "Let me get these drinks, and then we'll talk." At the mixing station, he reached for a bottle, winced, and moved closer to the counter before picking it up.

"I saw the way you looked at him," Vanessa whispered, her eyes slitted like a feral cat. "Don't get any ideas. I also saw the van you drive, and I can tell you, he wouldn't be interested in a maid."

Vanessa's scorn filled the air like a foul stench, and Andrea took a step away. There was no answer she could make.

"You don't belong here," the other sub muttered before her mouth curved into a sugary smile as Master Cullen approached.

He set the drinks in front of Andrea. "There you go, sweetie."

Dammit, he still didn't look right. The laugh lines beside his eyes and mouth had tightened, and his easy humor disappeared.

"Vanessa, give me an hour to finish up here and I will—"

"No," Andrea interrupted.

His brows came together as he turned to look at her. Oh, carajo, she was so screwed. But that didn't matter. She turned to Vanessa. "I don't know what he did, but his shoulder or arm isn't moving right. It hurts him. He's not going to use a flogger tonight."

Andrea winced at the look he gave her and added, half under her breath, "I bet that's why he's wearing a shirt."

Vanessa glared at Andrea, then turned to Master Cullen. "I wouldn't want you to be hurt, Master Cullen," she said so sweetly that Andrea rolled her eyes. "How about next week instead, Sir?"

Master Cullen smiled at the brunette. "Thank you, Vanessa. Next week would be good."

As he spoke, Andrea grabbed the drinks and headed back to her area. Maybe after some time had passed, he'd forget how she'd actually butted into his conversation and said "No" to him.

She could feel his eyes on her back, and a chill crept through her. Did she really think that the bartender who never forgot anyone's drink would forget that a sub tried to boss him around?

* * *

"What happened to your shoulder?"

Still watching his little Amazon, Cullen jerked his gaze away and realized Z had taken a seat at the bar earlier. "Got under a ceiling that fell in. Burned a patch of skin."

"She watches you closely, doesn't she?"

No use pretending he didn't know who Z meant. "Apparently so." He grinned. "Brave little thing, isn't she? Laid the law right down."

Odd to have a sub dare his displeasure because of her concern for him. He'd had subs sass him to get punished, subs who defied him because they couldn't quite submit, subs who just didn't want to obey, but Andrea—he caught a glimpse of her across the room, moving with that graceful, strong stride—she was something different.

"What are your plans for her tonight?" Z asked.

Cullen poured him a drink and pushed it over, then picked up a beer for himself. "I didn't push her last week, so she's due. Since she has a green ribbon, she should do a scene with one of the uncommitted Masters. Maybe Marcus."

The thought of Marcus taking Andrea didn't sit well. Or Sam or... The can in Cullen's hand crumpled, spilling beer over the sides. Hell. *Not mine. Trainee. Here to be taught.* "Marcus should work fine."

Z had a slight smile on his face, one that didn't seem to go with the conversation. "Indeed." He rose and paused long enough to say, "Daniel will be along as soon as I find him. He and the others will handle the bar tonight."

The flat tone said argument would be futile. The Masters weren't paid by the Shadowlands, but the owner still laid down the law. "Yes, boss."

* * *

The night had started sucky, revived for all of five minutes, and gone straight downhill from there. First she'd annoyed Master Cullen with her unsubmissive behavior—had she really told him what he could do? Madre de Dios, she'd gone mad. Then before she could go back and apologize, Master Z had given her to this...this incredibly boring Dom.

Totally naked, with her hands chained over her head, she looked down at the sandy-haired, young Dom using a vibrator on her. Surely that should get her off. *You'd think.* She stifled a sigh.

Gary pushed the vibrator into her harder and said, "Come now!"

Did he really imagine he could order her to get off?

Then again, if she did, she'd be finished with him, right? Enough was enough. Andrea closed her eyes and moaned, giving some nice hip jerks for emphasis.

Gary rose to his feet, a pleased smile on his face. Good. Maybe now he'd release her. "Well," he said. "I think—"

"If we might intrude on your scene, Gary?" Master Z walked into the roped-off area. "I believe Master Cullen needs to have a word with his trainee. And I'd like to speak to you for a minute."

"Oh. Okay."

Master Z looked at her with no expression on his face, then escorted the Dom from the area, leaving her still chained. Well, he certainly appeared awfully cross.

She didn't care, not with Master Cullen right here in front of her. She looked at him...and froze. His jaw was tight, his mouth straight, all humor gone from his eyes as he unclipped her restraints.

"Señor?"

He pointed to the floor, and heart hammering, she dropped to her knees and lowered her head. Her hands felt cold as she set them carefully on her thighs in the position she'd learned last week. She could see his boots in front of her. Not moving. He just stood there, and the weight of his gaze bowed her shoulders.

"Do you know why I am displeased, trainee?" Even his deep voice had chilled.

Dios, she'd really made him mad. Amazing that he hadn't yelled at her earlier. "Because I told Vanessa she couldn't be flogged."

"No. Try again."

But what could she have done to make him so angry? She waited on tables well enough. Hadn't tried to hit anyone. Behaved properly submissive when the Dom chained her. Even faked a... Her breath stopped. Surely no one realized she'd faked it. She'd certainly fooled the Dom.

She hadn't fooled Master Z or Cullen. Madre de Dios. "I...I'm sorry."

"Tell me what you're sorry for."

"I pretended to have an orgasm," she whispered to her hands.

"Look at me." A finger under her chin tilted her face up, but she didn't want to see those icy, green eyes.

"Look. At. Me."

She flinched and raised her eyes, and he held her gaze as he said, "The relationship between a Dom and a sub is based on honesty. If you can't be truthful about something as basic as your own pleasure, you don't belong here."

His words thudded into her chest harder than any blow. "No. Oh, no." She grabbed his wrist, holding him so he had to listen. "I didn't think. I just wanted…" To make the Dom quit. To manipulate him with a lie. She had lied with her body, if not her words. Her eyes burned as the enormity of her error hit. She closed her eyes against the lack of emotion in his.

But he didn't move. Didn't walk away. Did she still have a chance? "I won't mess up again. Now that I know." She couldn't say the word that kept reverberating through her head. *Please, please, please.*

His gaze softened slightly. "Sweetie, you—you especially —won't enjoy the punishment we use for something like this."

"I'll do it. Beat me, whip me, whatever." *Don't make me leave you. Not yet when I haven't even tried to see if you like me.*

He sighed and lifted her to her feet. "*Whatever* is the word for it all right." His hand closed over her nape, pushing her to the back of the main room and down the hallway past the themed rooms, and into the dimness of the dungeon.

Not polished wood and glowing bronze like the rest of the Shadowlands, the dungeon decor came from an earlier era. A brutal one. The manacles embedded into the rock walls held submissives, male and female. On the right, a skinny sub rocked in a sling, her master pounding into her; the left had an empty bondage table. A woman hung suspended in the center of the room, her eyes half-closed, deeply into subspace as her Dom placed a row of clothespins down her back.

Andrea had started to shake by the time they reached the far corner and stopped. A carved statue of a brown horse rested on a tall stand. A leather saddle adorned the narrow back. Against the wall behind it stood a small table with various dildos. An uneasy sensation crawled into Andrea's stomach. This didn't look like a whipping station.

Master Cullen pointed to the floor. "Kneel."

She dropped down and lowered her eyes. Her fingers trembled so hard that she clasped them between her thighs. Her legs hurt from the rough slate floor, and as she stared at her knees, she listened. What was he doing? A whip cracked across the room. Low commands came from a Domme elsewhere. A man's groan. The crinkling sound of a condom wrapper very close. Low murmurs and whispers, increasing and getting closer. To here. Oh, Dios, her punishment had turned into a spectator sport.

What exactly was that horse thing?

As if he'd heard her, Master Cullen said, "This wooden horse is a relative of the Sybian, and you're going for a ride, trainee." He grasped her upper arms, lifted her to her feet, and pushed her over to the statue.

She looked at it and jerked back a pace. A long plastic piece ran down the fake saddle with a condom-covered dildo poking up in the center. Master Cullen squirted a package of lube on the dildo, then shoved a wooden step closer to the device. "Mount up, sub."

She shook her head, her stomach knotting. This... She couldn't do this. She took another step back.

Face expressionless, he crossed his arms over his chest and waited.

She had only two choices. Take her punishment—ride this thing—or walk out of the Shadowlands and never come back.

Her eyes filled with tears. *I don't want this.* And then she stepped up on the wooden box and swung a leg across the saddle, trying to get over the dildo. It bumped against the inside of her thigh.

"Up you go, little tiger." He grasped her waist and lifted her up above it, then lowered her, letting her position herself. The dildo slid into her, startling her. It was smaller than a man, but she hadn't had anything there in so long...except his fingers. Teeth gritted, she let it enter her completely, and discovered that the plastic in front of the dildo curved upward, pressing the pebbled surface against her clit.

Master Cullen ran his hands up and down her arms, his nearness and touch so warm and comforting that a tear spilled over. She lowered her head and closed her eyes. Bad enough that she'd been a liar, now a crybaby? What he must think of her.

"Oh, sweetheart." His fingers brushed the wetness on her cheek, and then he cupped her face. "Look at me, Andrea." The coldness had disappeared from his voice.

She looked up, the unshed tears rendering his face a blur. "I'm sorry, Señor," she whispered.

"I know, honey." His voice wrapped around her, rumbling like thunder in the distance. He leaned against the saddle just in front of her leg, making her far too aware of the thing up inside her. Why couldn't it have been him inside her?

"Now what happens is you're going to ride until I am satisfied you know the difference between a lie and truth, and a fake orgasm and a real one. What is the safe word here?"

"Red, Señor."

"Use it if you need to."

Never. He'd see she could bear anything.

His eyes narrowed. Then he sighed. After fitting her bare feet into the stirrups, he adjusted the length until she could push herself up off the saddle slightly, but not far enough to escape the dildo.

She pulled in a shuddering breath and worked on regaining her composure. Just sit on this thing, not that difficult. But if he thought she'd bounce up and down on it for the entertainment of the people watching, he had another think coming. Not gonna happen. Orgasms—her orgasms—weren't for public viewing.

That one time she'd gotten off with Master Cullen, he'd swamped her so hard and fast that she hadn't noticed anything except him. But now? Now she could see every single person standing near the edges of the space. Expectantly. *Ugh.* She wrapped her arms around herself and sat still.

Master Cullen picked something up from the table. A control box? Suddenly the whole saddle hummed, and then the dildo started to move, rotating inside her vagina, slowly going around and around. Oh, dear God, what was this thing? *Around and around.* She stiffened, trying not to respond even as heat washed through her.

A minute later, the nubby area pressing against her clit started vibrating. She leaned away from it, but that made the dildo stroke harder on a sensitive place inside her. She couldn't slide back either.

If she pushed up in the stirrups, she escaped the vibrations at least. Her teeth clamped tighter. He wanted her to come here, in front of everyone. This wasn't like making love or anything even close. It just felt wrong.

She could use the safe word... *Never.* No, she'd ride the thing, but damned if she'd come for his or anyone else's entertainment. Not today. She put her hands on the horse's neck for balance, lifted up, and kept herself as far from the nubby vibrator as she could.

A snort of amusement sounded behind her. Then his hand slapped her bottom, and she yelped.

"Are you trying to do what I want, sub? To please me?"

His questions dug into her soul, burning worse than the blow. She knew the answer. She was doing as she wanted. Defying him. Her head bowed, and she dropped down into the saddle. *A crybaby and a wuss.*

The vibrations hit her clit, but it no longer mattered. She didn't feel at all excited, even less than when the Dom had used a vibrator.

"Such a stubborn little sub," Cullen murmured.

Relief filled her at the lack of anger in his voice.

"I think I'll give you some assistance." Suddenly the saddle creaked as he swung himself up behind her. He reached around her and set one hand just above her mound. His other hand flattened over her right breast.

Arousal streaked through her so fast and hard that she gasped.

His muscular chest warmed her back. When his groin pushed against her bottom and shoved her up against the nubby pad, vibrations thudded into her clit, waking it instantly. She felt it swell, tighten. His fingers circled her nipple, then rolled the tip, sending more sizzling fire straight to her pussy.

Her breathing sped up as the vibrations against her clit and the dildo circling inside her kept increasing her excitement. She grew close, closer, an orgasm inevitable. There was nothing she could do about it. Her legs tightened around the saddle, her hands clenched the horse's neck.

Suddenly the vibrations stopped, and the dildo rotated slower. She didn't move for a second, shocked at the sudden halt to everything, and her lips closed over a low whine of frustration. Her whole pussy throbbed, inside and out.

After a few seconds, she pulled in a long shaky breath. *Good. This is good.* She didn't want to come out here in front of everyone.

"I was surprised you didn't get off earlier, considering the Dom had a vibrator." Master Cullen's fingers rubbed gently against the top of her mound. The small caress moved her sensitive nub, and her breath hitched. "But you weren't even close, were you?"

"No."

His hand massaged her breast, eased out to tease her nipple. His warm breath brushed her ear and sent a quiver through her. "Why, sweetie? Why didn't you feel anything with him?"

She shrugged. She didn't want to think about the other Dom, not now. Her head tilted back against the hard shoulder behind her, and his scent drifted to her: clean soap, leather, his own masculine scent. Had anyone ever smelled more like a man?

"All right, then." His hand moved away from her mound, and the vibrations kicked on again.

Her whole body went rigid as she shot straight into arousal. This time, he used his hips to rock her against the vibrating pad, and the rhythmic movements combined, growing bigger and—

The vibrations stopped, and she moaned. Being cut off like that hurt, dammit.

Then he slapped her thigh with his big hand, the blow as shocking as the sting that bit through her. "Andrea, why did you have to fake it? Why didn't you get off with him?"

She shook her head, her body trembling, her lower half aching. The dildo still circled inside her, but ever so slowly, just enough to keep her excitement from dying.

He slapped her leg again. She tried to rise, but the unyielding arm around her waist kept her in place. The vibrations surged back on, harder, much harder, and the dildo circled faster.

"Oh, oh, oh." Her hands tightened on the horse, and she leaned into the clit piece. Just a bit more.

The vibrations stopped, and his hand struck her again, higher on her thigh. It hurt. Another stinging slap sent her thoughts splintering into fragments, and she trembled as the arousal and pain mingled inside her, confusing her. What did he want from her?

"Why didn't you come with him?" He waited, then slapped her thigh again, and tears filled her eyes.

Vibrations started, sending her soaring upward. Almost...

Stopping. Even as she whimpered, he smacked her leg one more time. "Why?"

She couldn't think, couldn't come, everything burned and throbbed as need churned inside her. He wouldn't let her move. He held her...he hurt her...he kept her safe...

"Why, Andrea?"

"He isn't you." The words burst from within her. "I trust you." Her head bowed as she whispered, "I only want you."

Chapter Eleven

Her whispered words blew through him like ignited phosphorus. *She wanted him.*

Fuck, he hadn't planned for this to happen. His arm tightened around her, pulling her soft body back against his chest. She hadn't gotten off for someone else because she wanted *him*. Specific. Not just any Dom or Master, but him. The knowledge made him want to roar as if he'd scored a touchdown or flattened an opponent. *His.* She was his; she said so.

She couldn't be his. *What the hell am I going to do about this?* He knew the appropriate response, but damned if he wanted to pull back.

When she trembled, he set his thoughts aside. Right now, he had a little sub to reward, although she probably didn't even realize what she'd said. He turned the vibrator dial, and her body reacted as if he'd used an electrical charge. With his half-erect cock pressed against her ass, he could feel the vibrations right through her body.

As he upped the rotation, her low whine of excitement rose over the hum of the machine. Her hands opened and closed on the horse's mane, and her body quivered. Very close. He wrapped his arms around her, held her tight, and then bit the vulnerable curve between her neck and shoulder. She jerked and arched as the tiny pain sent her right over the edge.

"Dios," she wailed, the husky cry of an out-of-control woman, one who trusted him to care for her. It hardened him into granite, even more than the vibrations and the rocking of her bottom against his cock.

The orgasm shook her, over and over, and when he finally flipped off the machine, she sagged in his arms. The satisfaction of holding her, flushed and hot and sated, filled him to overflowing.

He pressed a kiss to the tiny hollow under her ear, to the juncture of neck and shoulder, to the top of her shoulder. Each touch of his lips sent another tremor running through her soft body.

"Make her come one more time, Master Cullen." Z stood a short distance away beside Gary. "I'd like to show Gary exactly what to look for."

Cullen frowned. *Again?* Andrea leaned limply against him and tremors wracked her frame at intervals. At Z's order, she tried to sit up, and her tiny whimper broke his heart. He tightened his grip. "No. She's had enough."

"One more time," Z insisted. What the hell was wrong with the bastard?

Every protective instinct in Cullen surged to the front. Vulnerable little sub...*my* little sub.

"No, Z. She's done." Cullen swung down and lifted her off the horse. Argument over. If Z got pissed off, they could fight it out later.

He wrapped her in a subbie blanket from the table, took long enough to toss a NEEDS CLEANING sign over the horse's neck, then lifted her. He grunted as her weight pulled against the burn on his shoulder. Hurt like hell and he didn't give a damn. Not a tiny lightweight, his sub, but a solid armful of woman. *Just my size.*

She blinked up at him. "You're not supposed to say no to Master Z," she whispered, her words slightly slurred. "He's the owner."

Cullen growled. "And I'm your Master. He'll have to live with it." He glanced around, prepared to be as hard-assed as it would take, but Z and Gary had disappeared. What the fuck was that all about, anyway?

No matter. He pressed a kiss to her soft curls and headed for the quiet area of the main room. Her words still sang in his head like an unnoticed tune. "*I only want you.*"

In a back corner, he settled in his favorite chair and leaned her against him. The scent of her arousal and fragrance of her body drifted from under the blanket, pushing him past hard into serious pain. His balls felt as if they were being squeezed in a wrench. He frowned. Seemed like he hadn't taken a sub since Andrea had arrived. He'd not gone that long without sex in years; no wonder he hurt.

The woman had snuck up on him, hadn't she? He shifted her, and her eyes drifted up. Golden brown lion's eyes.

When her soft ass wiggled slightly, he tightened his arms, keeping her in place. Much more of that and he'd bend her over a chair and take his pleasure right then and there.

She frowned, undoubtedly noticing what her ass rested on. "You need…" Her brows drew together. "May I offer…?"

He could see her trying to come up with the appropriate words. "Um, if you want to... I'd be..."

So worried and generous. He chuckled and saw her shoulders relax. With one hand, he held her for his kiss.

Her lips softened, and her mouth opened to him, her entire body surrendering. He kissed her gently. Thoroughly. A woman could lie with her words, sometimes with her face, but rarely with a kiss. Not for long.

The submission that had given her so much trouble was offered now with her whole heart. Was he going to take it?

His cock ached like a sore tooth when he pulled back.

"You need me," she murmured.

"Sweetie, I fully intend to have you before the night is over. But I'll wait until your body recovers. Did you enjoy your horse ride?"

Her gaze held accusation, and she struggled to sit up. "How could you do that to me? In front of everyone?"

With a hand between her breasts, he pressed her back down. "In the Shadowlands, lying at all is a problem; lying about having an orgasm is a crash-and-burn offense."

"Well, fine."

"Now answer my question."

Her eyes snapped up. "I... Obviously I got off. But it was so impersonal." She hesitated, then added with a truthfulness that pleased him immensely, "Having you holding me helped."

"Good girl," he said softly and watched a happy smile lighten her face.

A little submissive with a giving heart. Damn, he couldn't hold out forever, not if he stayed around her.

But, hell, he didn't even really know her.

And then again, he did. BDSM cut past the polite rituals and into the naked core of a person. He knew the courage she showed when afraid. Her sense of humor might be quieter, but was as ingrained as his. He'd seen her pleasure in helping and serving, seen her modesty and her passion. If he didn't know her favorite color—though he doubted it was pink—did it really matter?

Andrea realized she'd drifted off when she woke to hear low voices.

"That is unacceptable." Master Z sounded furious.

Oh, Dios, would he fire Señor for telling him no? She jerked upright, still in Master Cullen's arms. "Don't be mad at Señor. He was only defending me," she said. "It's his job because he's the trainer. He shouldn't get in trouble for that."

Master Z looked confused; then a smile erased the hardness off his face. He glanced at Señor. "She defends you well. I'm pleased." His dark gray gaze dropped to her. "I'm not angry at Master Cullen, little one. We were discussing a problem at a downtown club."

Ooops. She'd broken right into a conversation between Doms—Masters, no less. And once again had given orders. "I'm sorry."

She crawled back into her blanket like a kid trying to pull the covers over her head and rested her head against

Señor's shoulder. A laugh rumbled through his chest, and she closed her eyes. Maybe she wasn't totally screwed.

As she inhaled his wonderfully masculine scent, the memory of him saying no to Z enveloped her with more warmth than a blanket could provide. No one had ever stood between her and harm.

"We're taking advantage of the heat wave and having the after-hours St. Patrick's Day celebration outside," Master Z said. "Bring your sub and come on out."

Your sub? Did he mean her? She lifted her head far enough to peer over the folds of the blanket.

Master Z's eyes glinted as he said to her, "Don't bother to dress."

Oh…Dios. As Master Z walked away, Señor set Andrea on her feet and stood. He tilted her chin up. "Will it be a problem for you to stay up late?"

"No. I spend a lot of time awake at night." She rubbed her eyes and realized the room had emptied. Her lack of sleep had obviously caught up with her, and she'd sacked right out on Master Cullen's lap. "Sorry about falling asleep."

"I enjoyed holding you, sweetheart." His eyes held something…different, something that made her want to snuggle back in his arms.

She'd better not push her luck. She retreated a step. "What kind of party is this?"

"Just remember you have a safe word, pet." At the words and his amused smile, worry and anticipation slid like an ice cube up her spine.

He pulled her blanket off and tossed it on the chair, leaving her completely naked as he led her across the empty barroom.

A door marked PRIVATE on the buffet-side opened to a hallway at the end of which another door let them out on the side of the house. The unseasonably warm night air surrounded her. A tiny rock path, damp against her bare feet, led around the corner to the back and a covered lanai. Dim lighting came from wrought-iron sconces that matched the larger ones in front. More light flickered from candle lanterns on the tables.

She heard laughter and talk, and her feet stopped without her orders. Dios, she didn't have any clothing on.

Cullen set a hand on her low back and nudged her forward. "You've met all the Masters already, love. I think you'll like their subs."

The lush plantings around the lanai edges and flowers cascading over the sides of hanging pots filled the area with a tropical fragrance. The center of the outdoor room held chairs and a wrought-iron and oak table on a rich Oriental carpet. The far end of the patio contained a massive barbeque. Near it, a naked woman pulled soft drinks from a tiny refrigerator.

Too many people... Andrea's feet stopped again.

A small distance away, Master Dan stood with his arms crossed and watched a short, curvy sub as she stripped off her dress. Master Nolan of the Shibari ropes had his arm around his slender redheaded sub who was also naked.

Andrea's muscles loosened slightly. Maybe she wouldn't feel so out of place as she'd thought. All the Doms wore clothing though. Didn't that just figure?

"Better?" Cullen murmured.

She glanced up, saw the crease in his cheek. He'd seen her discomfort and let her look. How could she not adore the man? "Yes. Thank you, Señor."

"Good." He raised his voice. "This is my sub, Andrea, and she's never been to a private party before, so go easy." He pulled Andrea closer and pointed to each woman in turn. "Master Nolan's sub, Beth. She runs a gardening service and does the gardens here. Master Dan's sub, Kari. She's a schoolteacher. Master Z's sub, Jessica. She's an accountant."

The subs all smiled but didn't speak, so Andrea decided to keep her mouth shut. She nodded instead.

A door closed softly overhead, and Andrea looked up. A flight of steps led to the third story. Master Z walked down with a tray in his hands.

"He lives on the third floor," Cullen said as Z strolled over.

"Andrea," Z said. "Welcome. We have a few rules you must observe during our parties. Follow the usual trainee rules. And subs speak only when spoken to or after obtaining permission. What is your safe word?"

Why did that question always make her shiver? "Red, Sir."

"Very good." He held out his hand, and his sub who had just walked up took it. How had he sensed Jessica's arrival? "Kitten, I don't think Andrea had any food tonight." His lips quirked. "And please have her drink a bottle of water before moving on to something more substantial. Master Cullen made her ride the Sybian earlier."

"Yes, Sir," his sub said.

Master Z kissed his sub's fingers, then left.

"Let Jessica feed you, love," Cullen murmured, his knuckles brushing her cheek. "I'll be right over there if you need me." He followed Z.

The feeling of abandonment made her hands clench. Dios, she didn't belong here with these rich people. The women worked, she told herself, but still, none had crawled out of the slums, had they? She—

"It's a bit overwhelming, isn't it?" Jessica interrupted her thoughts. "The Doms, the place, the party."

Andrea gave her a startled look.

"I haven't been in the lifestyle that long either." The short blonde pointed to a table by the barbeque. "Let me find you something to eat and drink before I get in trouble."

"What would he do?" Getting on Master Cullen's bad side scared her, but she trusted him at least. Making Master Z angry? Ay, diablo.

Jessica rolled her eyes. "He's way too inventive. The last time was when I—" She giggled so hard that Andrea's lips curved. "Well, I mailed him an invoice for my 'services.'"

"To Master Z? Are you insane?"

"Hey, I'm an accountant; it's what I do. You know, the bastard actually analyzed it line by line and told me I wasn't worth those prices?" As Andrea choked on a laugh, Jessica aimed a dirty look toward the Doms. "Anyway, I got a choice of wearing an anal plug to work or getting strung up and paddled down in the Shadowlands."

Well, getting paddled wasn't so bad. "What did you choose?"

"The plug." Jessica winced. "Major bad choice. Do you know how hard it is to sit on one of those? My co-workers probably thought I had fleas or something."

Andrea snorted. "I've never tried one. But…" She eyed Master Cullen warily. "He doesn't… Do you know if he…?"

"Good luck. That's all I'm going to say." Jessica's eyes danced. She pulled out a bottled water from the fridge.

"Oh great." Andrea took the water. She picked up a sugar cookie from a plate and bit in. Butter rich, creamy, soft. "This is wonderful. Like what my grandmother bakes."

"Kari likes to cook. Have you met her or Beth yet?" Jessica nodded to the other two subs standing near the group of men.

"No, but I did manage to smile at Beth before her Dom wrapped me in rope like a fancy Christmas present."

Jessica's snicker drew the men's eyes, and Señor grinned at Andrea before turning back to the Doms' oh-so-serious discussion. Probably the latest basketball scores or something.

Kari glanced over, then rubbed against Master Dan like a cat. He didn't seem to notice.

The sub's eyes narrowed and—Andrea's jaw dropped—she pinched his side. Andrea well remembered the scathing lecture Master Dan had given her just for looking snooty.

Although Master Dan frowned down at his sub, the crease in his cheek gave him away. After a second, he nodded, but she got a ringing swat on her bottom as she left him.

Kari rubbed her bottom as she walked up to Jessica and Andrea. "Guess I should have been smoother about my request, huh?"

"You have no class." Jessica grinned. "Watch Beth; she's a pro."

The three turned in time to see Beth kneel at her Dom's feet and rub her breasts against his legs. When he glanced down, she clasped her hands and looked up entreatingly at him, obviously begging.

A grin came and went on the lean, dark face. He pulled her up onto tiptoes for a hard kiss, before letting her trot across the patio to the others.

"You're so manipulative," Jessica said admiringly. "What did you call him this time?"

"My magnificent and generous liege." Beth grinned and wrinkled her nose at Kari. "I save that one for parties because it makes your master so envious. He keeps asking Nolan why he can't get you to beg."

Kari burst out laughing. "You're just plain evil."

"I know," Beth said with obvious satisfaction. She glanced at Andrea. "I heard Master Cullen tell you our occupations. What do you do for a living?"

"I own a cleaning service."

Jessica turned around from pouring a drink, her blonde hair swinging. "Really? Houses or businesses?"

"Houses and small businesses only. I don't like the big ones."

"Cool. Maybe we could talk sometime. Z isn't happy with who he hires now. The old owners sold out and…" She shrugged. "You know how that goes."

Take on the Shadowlands? Andrea studied the big building. *Doable.* She might even handle this one herself since she had a vested interest in keeping it very, very clean. "Once I get my clothes, I can give you a card."

"Great."

As Jessica turned to Kari and asked what she wanted to drink, Beth leaned a hip against the table and said in a quiet voice, "You know, part of my payment for maintaining the Shadowlands gardens is free membership."

Jesús, María, y José. Right when she'd decided serving as a trainee wouldn't work out any longer. "That would be…really good."

Beth nodded. "I figured. I saw you with that baby Dom earlier."

"Yeah. Major disaster." With her heart set on Cullen, being forced to submit to other Doms felt gut-wrenchingly wrong. But a trainee couldn't turn down men, not without a good reason. However, a member could. "Thanks, Beth."

Beth gave her a smile. "I've been wanting Master Cullen to find himself a sub. He's always taking care of everybody else, but there are times you can see he needs someone."

Andrea crossed her arms over her chest and nodded firmly. *That someone is me.*

Beth nodded back, no further words needed, and then turned to check the Doms.

Andrea's eyes widened at the sight of the white scarring on the redhead's back. Whip marks and more. Dios mío, what kind of a monster was her Dom? She scowled at Master Nolan.

A hand clasped her wrist. "It wasn't Nolan," Jessica said.

Beth glanced back over her shoulder, saw the direction of Andrea's glare, and laughed. "I got these before him. Nolan saved me." Her mouth twisted. "Only now he's trying to teach me self-defense. Nightmare time. He's awesomely good, but a lot of his moves don't work for me—he's never been smaller or weaker than his opponent."

Jessica patted her shoulder. "Oh, girlfriend, I know just what you mean. I have the same problem with Z."

"Ah, I've had training," Andrea offered.

Kari set her hands on her hips. "Might I point out that you're not exactly short?"

"True." Andrea grinned and threw a mock punch toward an imaginary giant. "But I started learning when I was ten or so. My papa taught me tricks for being smaller: shorter is faster; long legs are more vulnerable to crippling, stuff like that."

"In that case, sign me up," Beth said. Kari nodded.

"Me, too," Jessica said. "That sounds—"

"That sounds like we'd better get our subs back under control." Master Nolan's gravelly voice. He glanced at Master Cullen. "Your sub is a bad influence."

"Ooops," Andrea whispered, remembering her simulated punch.

"Gentlemen," Z said. "I propose a game of volleyball to cool off and remove some of this aggressive behavior. Doms versus subs. Any Dom who makes a point may decorate his sub. Whatever team wins collects favors from the other one. We'll go to seven points."

"Volleyball to cool off?" Andrea murmured.

"The net is in the pool," Jessica whispered.

The Doms gathered their subs, leaving Andrea unable to ask what *decorate* meant. Didn't sound good. Master Cullen took her hand, and they followed the others down a winding path to what no one in their right mind would call a swimming pool. Okay, maybe it was Olympic sized, but with rocks, bushes, and tropical flowers all around and a tiny stream splashing into one end, it looked like a forest pond.

Chapter Twelve

After stripping and pulling on swim trunks, Cullen jumped into the heated pool and held his arms up for his sub, ignoring the pain in his shoulder when he lifted her. Naked, warm woman, soft in all the appropriate places, a nice, heavy armful. Perhaps he should shove her against the side and take her right there.

"Put her down, Cullen," Dan said. "We're playing a game here. You have to wait."

He set her on her feet, pleased when she leaned into him, not in any hurry to get away. He removed her wrist cuffs and tossed them onto the path, put a kiss on her soft lips, and pushed her toward the shallower water of the sub's side of the net.

As Cullen joined the men, Z frowned at the large dressing, Dan scowled, and Nolan's brows drew together. Cullen shook his head at them. Overprotective Doms. "I'll just change the bandage when I get out."

"Play ball," Z called after giving Cullen another frown. He sent the ball sailing over the net.

Shrieks, giggles, laughter. Splashing. Breasts jiggled and gleamed in the garden lights hidden in the vegetation. Dan scored the first point and motioned Kari over. From the basket Z had set beside the pool, Dan pulled out a set of breast clamps and fastened them to his wife's nipples. She squeaked, and he frowned. "You kind of sensitive these days?"

"Must be," she gritted out. He snorted and loosened them.

Despite using only one arm, Cullen made the next point. Being tall had advantages. He crooked a finger at his sub.

Andrea waded over, her breasts bobbing just above the deeper water on the Dom's side.

"What's your favorite color?" Cullen asked. He'd wondered about it ever since it had crossed his mind earlier.

"Blue."

He riffled through the jewelry until he found a set with blue jewels. Putting a hand on her ass, he kept her still while he bent and took a nipple into his mouth. Velvety texture, cool from the water, rapidly bunching into a hard point. He sucked slowly, getting the peak nice and long. Watching her face closely, he applied the tweezers clamp and slid the ring upward until the tiny muscles around her mouth and eyes tightened. The little sub wasn't one to squeak, was she? He loosened the clamp slightly, going for just enough pain to keep her awareness on her breasts.

He did the other and stepped back to survey his work.

"Very pretty, pet. You have gorgeous breasts."

The compliment made her smile; his light tug on the jewelry made her eyes widen.

Madre de Dios, but this felt weird, Andrea thought as she crossed the pool back to the other subs. She'd never tried to move with stuff hanging on her nipples before. The jewelry swayed as she walked, sending hot zings through her, reminding her of the feeling of Master Cullen's mouth. Hot. Sucking. He'd put his hand on her butt to keep her from retreating, and why that seemed so erotic, she didn't know.

The game continued. Dammit, even raising her arms to get a ball made the clamps pull. More zings. She jumped up to get a high serve, came down hard, and barely managed to muffle her squeal. She grabbed her breasts. Carajo, that hurt.

"That looked painful," Jessica commented. "It's why they put us in the shallow—"

"Kitten," Master Z interrupted. "Did you have permission to speak?"

"No, Sir," the blonde said, adding, "Damn, damn, damn," under her breath.

"Come here."

Jessica waded to the other side. Z laid her over the edge of the pool where a rounded rock formed a high lip. He smacked her sharply three times on the bottom and ran his fingers between her legs until she squirmed.

Andrea bit her lip as she watched. The clamps on her breasts made her skin so sensitive that even the water lapping around her waist felt like a caress. And seeing how Master Z spanked and teased... Andrea swallowed, remembering Master Cullen's big hands between her legs, his finger... Unable to help herself, she looked at him.

Arms crossed, he leaned against the side of the pool, and rather than watching Jessica and Master Z, he was studying her, his lean face shadowed in the dim light. A wave of heat went through her. Dios, she wanted him; wanted his hands on her.

When his lips curved, she shivered.

Jessica returned to the sub side, her face dark with embarrassment.

The game continued. Andrea realized the cabrónes deliberately passed the ball to each other to rotate the winner amongst them, and soon every sub wore breast clamps.

Her Señor made the fifth point.

A tremor ran through Andrea when he smiled and motioned to her. Still, she already got nipple stuff, so what could he decorate now? But she doubted he had a necklace in mind, not with the smile he wore. He rummaged through the basket and took out one package, then another, before pulling her over to the stone where Jessica had gotten spanked.

"What are—"

"Now, love, you just added three swats for talking."

She closed her eyes. *Idiota.*

His hand cupped her cheek, and she looked up. "You know, I'm starting to like turning that soft ass of yours pink." Without waiting for her response, he picked her up and put her, stomach down, over the rock. She'd barely had a chance to adjust the pinching breast clamps before his hand hit her bottom. Hard. The sting bit into her, then another and another. Her cheeks burned, and somehow it made her breasts actually ache more.

"Open your legs, pet."

Here? Oh, Dios. Hard hands clasped her thighs and pushed them apart, and he touched her, sliding his fingers between her folds, making her shiver. "You're already nice and wet," he murmured. His finger skated across her clit, and she wiggled at the uncontrollable pleasure. He traced tiny circles around the increasingly sensitive nub, over and over until it throbbed with need, and her body tensed. She bit the back of her hand as a moan tried to escape.

"I almost forgot; you're here to be decorated." He used his fingers to open her buttocks.

When cool lube squirted down into the crack, she gasped. He wouldn't. Surely he wouldn't.

"You haven't done this before. But it wasn't on your list of hard limits, now was it?" More paper tearing, and then something pressed against her anus.

She tightened, trying to close it against him.

"Won't work, sweetie," he said, sympathy thick in his gravelly voice. "I picked a really small one that would slide in easy. Like this." Pressure, then the hard object entered her.

"Aaah!" She didn't like the feel. Her squirming earned her a brisk slap on the bottom right over where the thing was.

"Lie still."

But, but, but… He hadn't asked her or anything.

His finger touched her clit and shocked the ball of nerves awake again, only this time the excitement twined together with the stinging of her bottom and the odd sensations in her anus. She moaned, unable to tell what was what.

"That's a good sound," he murmured. His powerful hands closed around her waist, and he set her on her feet.

She didn't move. That thing was wedged up inside her, and the outside of it rubbed against her inner cheeks. It all felt wrong, and taking a step made it worse.

He slapped her butt, the impact jarring the plug again, and she glared at him.

"Little sub, if you are still here in ten seconds, I'll find a bigger plug."

The pendejo. She hurried, as much as anyone with something jammed up her backside could hurry. It felt as if she waddled like a duck.

The game restarted, and oh, Dios, going after the ball now created a dance of sensations as the jewelry dragged at her nipples, the plug inside her rubbed, and the water splashed against her swollen clit and labia.

She breathed a sigh of total relief when they lost, and the game stopped.

Kari had lucked out and didn't have to get the anal plug; she looked incredibly pleased by that.

As everyone got out, Master Nolan hugged his sub, then tapped her cheek. "You're cold, sugar." He glanced over at Master Z. "All right if we use the Jacuzzi?"

"Of course."

Master Dan grinned at Z. "We're heading to the breakfast nook and that round table." He buckled Kari's cuffs on and took her wrist. "Come, little sub. I have some favors to collect."

As they left, Z raised his eyebrows at Señor.

"Contemplation Grove if you don't want it," Master Cullen said.

"All yours." Z threaded his fingers into Jessica's damp hair and tugged lightly. "I plan to string my mouthy little one up by the lanai. If you finish before we do, you can watch."

Jessica's head jerked around, and she stared at Z. "You—"

She broke off as Master Z's brows lowered. "Kitten, I'm going to enjoy hearing the noises you make when you climax with a gag in your mouth."

Ignoring Jessica's gasp of horror, Z pulled his reluctant sub after him.

Andrea looked at Cullen. *Gagged? Please, no.*

His cheek creased. "Look at all that worry. Not this time, love." He took her wrist. "You don't trust me enough yet. The trust for that takes a while longer." He picked up the wrist cuffs from the path and buckled them back on her wrists.

"Bend over."

When she did, he removed the small plug and tossed it into a receptacle hidden in the flowerbeds. Her bottom felt strange and sensitive without it.

Silently, Master Cullen led her deeper into the gardens. Looking like miniature lanterns, solar lights lit the winding stone path. A gurgling stream ran beside the walk and under a tiny bridge, ending where flowers sprawled over rocks at the base of a small waterfall. More flowers, glowing white and blue in the moonlight, edged the clearing, and the scent of sweet almond drifted through the air. *How beautiful.*

Anticipation fizzed through Andrea as Master Cullen drew her to a group of chairs and tables. He sat on one wide lounge chair and pulled her down beside him. Brushing her hair back with one hand, he bent and kissed her lightly. Her hands curled around his muscular biceps as the sudden surge of her blood in her ears drowned out the splashing fountain. Dios, she felt as if she'd been waiting for his touch forever.

To her dismay, he pulled back and ran a finger over her bottom lip. Then he teased her with tongue and teeth and lips despite her hands trying to pull him closer.

"Please," she whispered.

His fist tightened in her hair, and he took full possession of her mouth. The hard demand of his lips melted her spine and wakened every wanton urge in her body.

He slid a hand under a nipple clamp and caressed the tender skin beneath her breast. With each movement the jewelry wobbled and tugged on her nipple. The sensation of his hard hand and the pinching clamps made her moan. She laced her hands behind his neck and tried to pull him closer. *More, more, more.*

He rumbled a laugh. "Demanding little sub." He swung her around and pushed her flat on the lounge. When he leaned over her, his wide shoulders and broad chest blotted out the sky. "Give me both wrists, pet."

Her breathing hitched. He planned to restrain her. Out here. Unlike inside the club, no dungeon monitor stood ready to rescue her. His hand open, his gaze level, he waited for her to master her qualms.

She trusted him, oh, she did, and she wanted this. She laid her hands in his, and his approving smile sent warmth through her.

He snapped her wrist cuffs to a chain at the top of the lounge, and the clicks of the snap hooks seemed awfully loud…and ominous…in the quiet clearing.

"Are there restraints on everything around here?"

Rather than reprimanding her for talking, he chuckled. "Z enjoys bondage." Grasping her thighs, he dragged her downward on the lounge until the chains pulled her arms straight above her head. Her buttocks rested near the bottom edge of the flat chair, and her legs hung off the end with her feet in the cool grass.

Master Cullen moved her knees outward, and the night air touched her wet pussy. "I don't want you to move. Not at all." His fingers wrapped around her thighs, and the feeling of his strong hands sent heat straight to her clit. "Do you understand me, Andrea?"

Her heart skipped a beat. "Yes, Señor."

He smiled into her eyes and deliberately ran his finger down through her folds, the feeling so exquisite that she gasped. And her legs trembled with the need to move. His eyes stared into hers. When he touched her clit, the sensation raised her heels as the wave of arousal rushed through her. *Don't move.* She forced her feet back flat.

"That's a good girl," he said softly. As his gaze dropped to her pussy, she felt very, very exposed. Her whole body shook with anticipation, with needing him, and he wasn't doing anything. Anything.

She clamped her jaw against the rising demands. *Touch me.*

His eyes glinted as if she'd spoken, and then he smiled slowly. "I've wanted to put you in chains since the moment I saw you, and, sweetie, I intend to take my time and enjoy myself."

His words sent a tremor of excitement through her, and his smile increased. He moved to sit on the lounge beside her. With one finger, he toyed with her breast jewelry. The tiny shocks zipped through her nipples and downward until she squirmed.

"These have been on long enough, and I've been looking forward to sucking on your pretty breasts." He removed the first one.

Blood surged back into her nipple, and pain blossomed so suddenly she squeaked. Her hands jerked in the restraints as she tried to move and couldn't. She gritted her teeth against the whine trying to escape.

Cullen's smile flashed before he licked over her throbbing peak, increasing the erotic burn.

"Unh." She gasped when his lips closed over her nipple. His mouth was hot. Wet. He sucked and tongued the sensitive nub until she arched up uncontrollably, the pain and pleasure so mixed she couldn't tell where one started and the other finished.

He pulled back slightly.

Her breathing had turned ragged. As the air brushed her wet, aching areola with coolness, her breast felt tight and swollen. When he sat up, she gave a sigh and relaxed against the lounge, the exquisite torture over.

His eyes crinkled. "You might not have noticed," he said as if having a conversation in a coffee shop or something, "but last time I looked, women possess two breasts."

What did that mean? She frowned.

"Which means you have two clamps."

Before she could yell no, he unfastened the other.

"Oh, Dios!" The rush of returning blood hurt even worse this time, and her hands jerked uncontrollably, trying to get to the pain. When his mouth closed over the burn, she whined.

His tongue, wet and hot and unrelenting, lashed across the throbbing sensitive tip. But as the pain diminished, the sensation kept getting more and more erotic, and her swollen pussy started to pulse in time with her heartbeat.

He curved his big hands under her breasts and pushed up, tightening them, as he sucked one nipple, long and hard, and then the other.

Her head tilted back, and her toes curled. She needed to move, to touch, and her arms tightened, the chains clanking against the metal frame of the lounge chair. Nothing gave and heat raced through her.

"Like those chains, do you?" He smiled into her eyes and clasped her elbows, leaning his weight down, adding to her feeling of being restrained. Held in place. He took her lips, sucking on her tongue as he had on her breasts, and she could almost feel his mouth on her nipples with each pull.

His control removed her ability to do anything, leaving her only sensation. And he was deliberately overloading her senses.

Abandoning her mouth, he moved down. He nipped her waist, circled her belly button with his tongue, and kissed the top of her mound. Each touch of his lips zinged straight to her pussy. When he knelt at the end of the lounge, she tensed. The V between her legs ached with need.

He ran warm hands over her ankles, squeezing calves, her thighs. One finger traced up, over increasingly sensitive skin and finally paused at the crease between her pussy and her leg.

She started to strain upward, and barely remembered he'd told her not to move. A shudder ran through her.

"Such soft thighs," he murmured, "with all those muscles hidden beneath."

He bent, and his lips touched her inner thigh. His shaggy hair brushed against her labia for a tantalizing second before he nipped the tender skin just below the crease. She yelped, then moaned as the sting ran straight to her pussy.

"I can see you're not going to last long," he murmured and licked her clit. A buzz filled her head as her whole body tensed. When her hips lifted, he curled his hands over her legs, pressing her into the pad, adding one more restraint, keeping her right where he wanted while he did whatever he wanted. And everything he did made her need worse.

She moaned as his tongue rubbed one side of her clit, then the other, until the nub felt too tight. Engorged and throbbing. *Oh, please...* She was going to explode in a second, and nothing would stop that. The nerves in her pussy seemed to bunch together in preparation as his tongue slid over the top of her clit, so slick, so hot.

He moved one hand so his finger could tease the outside of her labia, circling her entrance. She quivered, trying to press up, to urge him inside what was becoming an aching emptiness.

His tongue flicked over her clit, and his fingers circled until both sensations merged into one exquisitely sensitive whole, and anywhere—*anywhere*—he touched drove her nearer to the verge. The pressure became unbearable. She couldn't suppress the long whines that escaped her.

When he stopped, she moaned. *More. Oh, please.* She felt him move. A crinkling noise—a condom? He tongued her again, right over her clit, until she rose, closer and closer, hovering on the peak, waiting just for...

He clasped her waist and slid her up on the lounge. And then he came down on her, his body heavy and so hard. Her hands jerked at the chains, wanting, needing to touch him. "Let me go. Please, Señor."

He studied her for a long moment. Then his cheek creased as he set his hand on her breast, moving his fingers deliberately over her, rolling the nipple until her back arched.

"Please..."

"No." He moved fully on top of her, his size startling, adding to her sense of being controlled. His erection pressed against her opening. He swirled the head of his cock in her wetness, then pushed a bit inside, just enough to tighten the skin around her clit, wakening new nerves with the fullness at the entrance. He teased her, sliding in and out through her sensitive labia.

Then his finger touched her clit, lightly. A tiny stroke, two. Her hips raised as everything tightened again, her vagina trying to close around his cock. Dios, just a little...

"Come for me now, Andrea," he murmured, and rubbed a firm finger right over her slick clit—that one touch she'd needed to shove her over the cliff—and at the same time, he pushed farther inside her, huge and hard.

"Oh, oh, oh!" An indescribable explosion of pleasure burst through her, raging outward until even her fingers jerked. Her hips bucked uncontrollably against the startling thickness pushing into her entrance.

As the aftershocks died, Cullen kissed her. "Good girl. God, you're gorgeous when you come." He'd braced his forearms on each side of her head, and now he pressed his erection in, easing her open, inch by inch.

"Slow?" she asked, not even sure what she meant, and gasped as his cock went deeper into her.

"You haven't done this in a while, pet. Fast can wait." But his cock hadn't stopped advancing, and now she was starting to feel impaled. She wanted to retreat, but his legs between hers kept her open. His weight didn't let her budge.

His eyes had never left her face. "Right now, Andrea, you should be saying 'Yellow.'"

She could take it. She could. She panted. *He's too big.*

"Say it, Andrea." His gaze captured hers as he slid in farther, painfully. "Now."

"Y-yellow."

And he stopped. "There now. The world didn't end because you told your Dom you were getting overwhelmed." He braced himself on one arm and cupped her face. "I need to know, sweetie, and you need to be able to tell me. Do you understand?"

She swallowed and whispered, "Yes, Señor."

"Very nice." Now he pulled back slightly, and she shuddered in relief. His cock moved inside her, in and out in small thrusts, until she relaxed, and then he pressed forward again. She moaned, the fullness and sense of complete possession shocking in a way it had never before.

The little sub had definitely not made love in a long time, Cullen thought, his hands clenching the metal frame as he held himself back. She felt so fucking tight that the urge to shove into her grew almost unbearable. He felt her vaginal walls stretch to accommodate his size, and he slowed further, but continued in small increments until he was buried deep in her. His balls thudded against her poor bottom which was undoubtedly a bit tender from the anal plug.

She gave a muted squeak.

God, he loved the sounds she made. What would she sound like when he took her ass?

He studied her for a long, slow moment. Her breath came in tiny pants; her eyes were wide, her arm muscles taut and still pulling on the restraints. She needed more time.

So he leaned on one arm and diverted himself with a breast. Full and solid, it filled his big hand perfectly. The nipple jutted hard into his palm, and when he pinched it, her pussy clenched.

He kissed her soft lips, thrusting his tongue in and out to illustrate what he planned to do with his cock in the next minute. She shuddered.

Bracing his hands on the lounge frame, he started to move, pulling out a tad, moving forward, until he could pull almost all the way out and push all the way in. Her body eased and grew even more slick and hot. God help him.

Her eyes had closed, and her flushed face showed only the strain of increasing desire.

His fingers clamped around the frame, and he tried a hard thrust.

Her eyes shot open, and she gasped.

Two more thrusts and she moaned, a satisfyingly carnal sound. Looked like his little sub was primed and ready. And fuck, so was he. He set up a steady rhythm, one that would satisfy them both. Not that he could keep it up all night. He'd been erect all evening, and she was exquisitely tight.

He reached down and slid one finger over her slick tiny nub; she gave a choked cry. A few rubs and her clit hardened again and jutted out, begging him for more.

A plea that a Dom loved to satisfy. He caught her clit gently between two fingers. Thrusting his cock deep, he lifted the sensitive nub slightly as he withdrew. Her hips tried to follow, and he drove in hard. As he continued, her legs quivered beneath him, and her head tilted back. Almost there.

He changed to a hammering rhythm, and her vagina closed around him like a hot fist. Her body tightened into a rigid line, bowing upward.

He definitely heard when she hit the peak. Her high scream broke into the quiet night—the finest music in the world, and the milking convulsions of her pussy—the finest sensation.

As he released his own control, the pressure exploded from the base of his spine, rammed into his balls, and jetted out in God-I-may-die jerks of his cock. He roared, the sound drowning out her cries and the hammering of blood in his ears.

When his eyes eventually uncrossed, he rested on his forearms. The soft body under his shuddered every few seconds, her pussy clenching with each tiny tremor. He hauled in a couple deep breaths and smiled down at her. "You're beautiful, sweetheart," he murmured.

She looked up with dazed eyes, her lips swollen and so compelling he took them again for a long, slow kiss. He could feel her heart thudding in her chest.

With one hand, he unsnapped her wrists.

She wrapped her arms around him with a sigh of happiness. Strong arms and a strong woman. He moved inside her, just to please himself, and her vagina spasmed, buffeting him with aftershocks of pleasure. Very nice.

He bit her chin and smiled into golden eyes. "I wouldn't mind staying here, inside you, for a long, long time."

Her lips curved. "Okay."

The answer squeezed his chest, and her mouth softened under his as he took another kiss. How could this little Amazon punch through his defenses with a single word?

After a minute, he withdrew, smiling at her unhappy moan. He disposed of the condom, refastened his shorts, then picked her up and settled back on the lounge chair with her sprawled on top. The burn on his shoulder ached like a son of a bitch from the exercise, but he didn't give a damn. He'd waited to have her here in his arms, and he intended to savor every moment.

She wiggled until her full curves fit over him like a fluffy blanket. Her skin was still damp from their exercise, and her breath puffed warm against his chest.

With both hands, he cupped her ass cheeks, enjoying the combination of soft female skin and firm muscle. Much like her personality—determined and strong, yet so vulnerable.

And if he was thinking like this, then he was in a fucking lot of trouble.

She set her forearms against his chest and propped herself up so she could look down at him. Still slightly damp, her hair bounced around her face, curling wildly in the humid air. "Um, didn't you…? I thought…"

He caressed her cheek, smiling at her confusion. He hadn't felt this content in years. "Go on, sweetie."

"Uh, never mind."

Uh-huh. He studied her face, the averted eyes. All right, what worries had that twisty brain fastened on now?

As he ran his hand up and down her back, he mulled it over. After sex, most females wanted to establish a connection, which was one reason he indulged in sex only during scene play in the club or with women uninterested in a serious relationship. He'd broken that rule tonight. How many more would fall?

"Ask, Andrea."

Chapter Thirteen

Master Cullen had given the order in his deeper voice, the one that didn't let her evade an answer. Why had she asked such a stupid question? How could she ask this without sounding as if she wanted something? Well, okay she did. Oh, she really, really did, but not if he—

He snorted in exasperation. "Stop thinking, pet, and just spit it out."

"They said you never take trainees out of the club. Or date them."

"Looks like I broke my rule, doesn't it?" He had a faint smile on his face, but in the dim light, she couldn't read his eyes. Apparently he wasn't going to help her out here.

She sighed and laid her head back down, enjoying the even rhythm of his heart. Really, she didn't want to pursue this line of questioning anyway. She had him now, and that was enough. Her arms wrapped around him, and she hugged him, holding him tightly, not wanting to let go. Ever.

Change the subject. "Weren't you supposed to collect a favor from me since you guys won?"

Under her ear, his laugh rumbled through his chest. "True. Don't worry, love. I'll collect."

He undoubtedly meant it to sound like a threat. Instead it sent heat swirling through her until her toes curled.

And he laughed again.

Just then a woman's voice rose in a series of high wails, and Andrea grimaced, burying her head deeper into Cullen's shoulder. She didn't remember, but surely she hadn't sounded that noisy...had she?

With a low chuckle, he stroked her hair and answered the question she hadn't asked. "I enjoy hearing you scream, little tiger. Next time you'll be even louder."

Dios help her. She shivered.

"We should head in." Cullen pushed her up and off, then rose. "That was Jessica; Z must have ungagged her."

By the time they'd threaded their way back to the house, Nolan and Beth had also returned. Jessica, swathed in a long terrycloth robe the color of her eyes, handed out more robes.

Señor bundled Andrea into one as if she were a baby, refused one for himself, and unselfconsciously switched his wet shorts for his leathers.

When he turned his back, she saw the white bandages against his tanned skin, and her eyes widened. How could she have forgotten?

"Andrea"—Master Z paused beside her—"there's a first-aid box on the table over there for your master."

Andrea nodded then froze. *Master?* When she looked up at Cullen, she saw Nolan had asked him about building a dungeon in the beach house, and he hadn't heard Z.

She clasped her hands in front of her, Z's comment swirling through her head. "*Your master.*" Tilting her head to one side, she tried to think of him that way and kept getting diverted by his looks. Definitely not a gorgeous master. Way not a boy-toy, but so dangerously masculine that she could almost see the testosterone radiating from him. Big nose, strong jaw. His eyebrows were thick, darker than his brown hair, and the beginnings of a beard darkened his jawline. Boromir in the wilderness. All he needed was a sword and a few orcs to kill.

He glanced down at her then, caught her staring, and rather than making her feel dumb, simply put an arm around her and pulled her against his side. Like she belonged there. And why that felt so wonderful, she didn't even want to know.

As his conversation slowed, she patted his arm. "Señor. I'm supposed to change your bandage."

"It's fine, sweetie." Cullen smiled at her and turned back to Nolan. "But if we don't—"

"No, it's not," Andrea interrupted. "The gauze is wet and needs to be changed."

Yes, his dark eyebrows appeared even darker as they drew together. "Little sub…"

Her chin went up, and she stood her ground although everything inside her shivered.

To her surprise, he shook his head and grinned. "My sweet Amazon." He held his hand out, waited until she placed her hand in his. She heard Nolan's barked laugh as her Señor hauled her over to the first-aid kit.

She started to peel the tape off, but when he moved, his muscles rippled under his skin like waves, and it took her a second to focus on her task. The dressing finally came off, revealing that the skin underneath had been seared raw; bright red alternated with ugly blackness.

"Madre de Dios, what did you do?"

"Something hot fell on me," he said as if burning objects dropped on people every day.

"Doesn't it hurt?" Each time he moved his arm or shoulder, the skin tightened. "You carried me. Played volleyball. *Estúpido baboso*, what were you thinking?"

He turned far enough to tug her hair and growl, "I'm thinking that I am quite capable of yanking you over my knee and spanking your ass. Change the dressing, sub."

Ooops.

She heard a chuckle from behind her, and Z dropped a jar beside the kit. "Use this on it."

She dabbed on the white, creamy ointment, covered the burn with a nonstick pad, and taped everything in place. Cullen moved his arm and nodded. "Nice job, love. It does feel better. Thank you."

The glow warmed her as she slipped away to join the other subs.

Kari soon appeared, still flushed, and Jessica asked what she wanted to drink.

"Just water, thanks."

"You had *just water* all night," Beth said in her soft voice. "Are you pregnant or something?"

Kari jerked. "How did—"

"Oh, my God," Jessica exclaimed. "You are!" With a squeal, she hugged the schoolteacher. Then Beth did.

Andrea smiled, standing off to one side and wishing she knew them better.

Kari winked at her, holding her arms out. "It's lucky to hug a pregnant woman. C'mon."

And Andrea got a hug that made her feel like she belonged.

When she stepped back, the silence on the lanai was overwhelming. The Doms had stopped talking and turned their attention to the subs.

"Oh, God," Kari said under her breath.

Jessica's eyes widened. "He doesn't—"

"I was going to tell him later. In private, darn it."

"Kari." Master Dan stalked over, and Dios, he looked big as he stared down at his short, curvy sub. He tucked a finger under her chin. "Why was everyone hugging you?"

"Uh, strictly speaking, only the women hugged—"

"Little sub," he snapped. "Answer me."

"Jeez. Fine!" She stepped back out of his reach, shoved her long hair out of her face, and frowned at him. "We're going to have a baby."

A tender smile softened his lean face, and he pulled her into his arms, rocking her. "Now that's the right answer."

She stepped back. "Wait a minute. You knew?"

"Of course." He chuckled and reached inside her robe to cup a breast. "This is my body, little sub, and I know every inch of it. I'm not liable to miss when some of my favorite parts get bigger and more tender."

"Oh." Her lips curved, and she flung herself against him. "A baby. Isn't that cool?"

Andrea saw the mist in his eyes before he buried his face in her hair, murmuring in her ear.

He wasn't the only one puddling up. Tears ran down Jessica's cheeks, Beth's eyes gleamed, and Z and Master Cullen shook hands as if they'd personally arranged for a baby. Master Nolan actually grinned.

Well. Andrea leaned a hip against the table and wondered if Kari would like a baby blanket.

Everyone eventually moved toward the sitting area on the lanai. Nolan plucked his sub up and settled into a chair. Z put his drink on the table beside him and held his hand out for Jessica. Cullen took Andrea's wrist and pulled her down onto his lap. Startled at first, Andrea snuggled against her Señor's chest and sighed. Dios, she liked being held more than she'd ever thought. And how nice they didn't insist on having the subs kneel all the time.

The small group bandied about ideas for submissive costumes, and then Dan and Kari rejoined them.

Master Z raised his glass. "A memorable St. Patrick's Day. Here's to Daniel and Kari."

Glasses lifted as Kari beamed at everyone from Dan's lap.

Andrea tried to ignore the lump of envy in her chest.

"How many are you planning?" Jessica asked Kari.

"At least two." Kari patted her Dom's hand that curled protectively over her stomach. "I'm going to stretch this overprotectiveness out over a few more bodies."

"Sounds nice." Beth sighed. "I've always been envious of people with big families. Nolan has a half dozen brothers and sisters, and don't you have a bunch, Cullen?"

"Enough for a baseball team in just my family. And when the entire O'Keefe clan gathers for Sunday dinners, the neighbors hide." He tugged Andrea's hair. "How about you, love? Do you have brothers and sisters? Are your parents nearby?"

The pang of loss squeezed for a second. "There's just me. My parents are both dead."

"That's rough, baby." Señor rubbed his chin on her head. "How about cousins and all that?"

The question stole her breath. Dios, she could just see him showing up at Aunt Rosa's and finding out that drug money had bought the house. She sucked in some air. "Here and there. Kari, do you have family to dote over the new baby?"

As Kari answered, Andrea glanced up to see Master Cullen frowning at her. Obviously, she'd failed in diverting his question.

"So how's the arson business, Cullen?" Nolan asked. "Is that how you got scorched?"

"Yeah. I was careless."

Arson? He's a criminal! Andrea turned and looked at him. "You burn down buildings?" Even as she asked, she knew he'd never do such a thing.

"No, sweetie, I arrest the ones that do. I'm an arson investigator."

Every single muscle in her body tightened, and her throat closed so tightly that her voice came out hoarse. "A cop?"

His eyes narrowed. "Basically, yes."

She put her arms around herself, chilling despite the warm robe. "I thought you were a bartender. You act like a bartender." Not a cop. This couldn't be happening.

"I had helped my gramps at his Irish pub in Chicago, so Z asked me to tend the bar at the club." He grinned. "He knew if Nolan or Dan handled the bar, he'd lose half his membership."

"Hey," Dan said as Nolan snorted a laugh.

Andrea flinched. She'd forgotten the others.

Master Z studied her for a moment, then turned to Nolan, "Speaking of occupations, how is the landscaping going? Has Beth given you a rose garden yet?"

As Nolan growled something about herbs, Master Cullen put a finger under Andrea's chin and lifted. "Why does my being a cop bother you?" he asked softly.

Bother her? It terrified her. Nice, plain, normal people reacted badly to her background. But a cop? Oh, she knew what cops thought of her. The sense of despair sent coldness deep into her bones. "I need to be going."

His arm flexed, keeping her in his lap. "Not yet."

"Señor. Please."

His eyes had darkened like a pine forest in the twilight. His hand cupped her cheek, holding her so she couldn't look away, but the gentleness made tears prickle in her eyes. "Now tell me. Is your cleaning business a front for the mob?"

She blinked at the unexpected question. "No."

"Well, that's a start." His cheek creased. "Are you wanted for any crime?"

"No."

"No, what?"

She stared at him. How could he demand a title now? Couldn't he see her life shattering around her?

"Andrea…"

"No, Señor, I'm not wanted for anything." She took hold of his wrist, tried to push his hand away. "I don't want to talk about this; I want to leave."

"I'll give you what you need, not always what you want. And you *need* to get this out of your system." His jaw tightened, but his thumb caressed her chin. "Explain to me. Now."

She'd set herself up for this, wanting a man who could tell her what to do and make it stick. Now he demanded more, for her to open to him, and he was the enemy. One of them who had—

"What is my name, Andrea?" He broke into her thoughts with the question.

"Master Cullen." *Mi Señor.*

"Good. Now tell me."

"I have a…a background. And I come from the slums, so my family has a…background."

He chuckled, the sound vibrating through his chest and into her body. "Background is a good word. Is everything in the background and nothing current?"

He wasn't reacting right. What was wrong with him? She could feel her heart pounding as she nodded.

"Oh, little sub," he murmured. "There're very few people who haven't done something—or many things—they regret later. I don't hold a past against a person. Or their relatives." He grinned. "We have a large number of law enforcement types in my family, true, but my uncle used to be a bookie, a cousin dealt drugs, and my great-grandfather never would say where the money for the pub and other businesses came from."

"Really?" He wouldn't mind?

"I like who you are now, Andrea. I like your intelligence, your courage, the way you are willing to risk punishment to care for me, and your sense of humor, which is as warped as mine." He brushed a kiss over her lips. "But all that wariness obviously comes from a hurt in your past. I intend to find out what."

She stiffened again. She never wanted to talk about her past. Not to him. She started to undo the belt of the robe. "I need to go. Where should I leave the robe?"

He closed his fingers over hers. "We'll bring it back tomorrow and get your purse then."

"Tomorrow?"

Running a finger down her cheek, he smiled. "Oh, yes. Tomorrow."

"But I told you…" She tried to pull back. She needed to go home and think. "But… No."

"You may use a room upstairs if you wish," Z interrupted. He stood nearby, and Andrea realized the others had left.

"Thank you; we will." Master Cullen jerked his head for Z to move on.

As Z complied with a chuckle, Señor said, "You'll stay here with me tonight."

"I can't. I have work that I need to do."

"Your cleaning business?"

"Yes. I haven't found a replacement for one of my employees, so I'm picking up the businesses she did. I have two places to do by seven."

"Are you sure? I was looking forward to burying myself inside you again."

A quiver ran through her, and he smiled before his eyes turned serious. "And talking about this."

He just didn't make sense. "Master Cullen, I'm a trainee. For the club. Why are you doing this?"

He took her face between his hands. "I want to see if we have more than just trainee and trainer going for us." His thumbs stroked over her cheekbones, and her breathing paused.

Oh, please, she wanted that so much. She swallowed. "I… Can we discuss that later, maybe?" Would he still feel this way tomorrow?

He frowned but nodded. "I can't command your trust. But, Andrea, there will come a time when both your body *and* your emotions will be open to me."

She shivered, undone by the dark promise in his eyes.

Chapter Fourteen

As she entered the dressing room, Andrea hesitated at the sound of Heather's voice and choice of subject.

"He was still holding her when I left. And Jessica said Z was giving a party after closing for some of the Masters."

"You're mistaken. Master Cullen wouldn't be interested in her," Vanessa said. "That's insane. She's a maid, for God's sake."

"Yeah?" Sally spotted Andrea and rolled her eyes cheerfully. "So what?"

"So she doesn't belong here with us. She's—"

"Andrea, you'd better change quickly, or you'll be late," Heather called out.

Vanessa glanced over her shoulder and grimaced. "Look what the cat dragged in."

Andrea's chin went up. She'd run into this attitude before and undoubtedly would again. Damned if she'd let it drive her off. Especially now.

She opened her locker, her fingers trembling a bit. She'd see Cullen in a minute. Would he treat her differently after last night? He'd said her background didn't matter, but he'd had time to think. Had he changed his mind?

And she'd also thought about it and come to an uncomfortable decision. If he really wanted to continue with her, then she needed to tell him about her past. About Enrique Marchado, about her cousins. About her. Her stomach did a slow roll. But maybe he wouldn't care. Maybe he'd meant what he said. Her hopes blended with her anxieties until it seemed as if each heartbeat switched her emotions on and off like a light switch.

She'd find out all too soon. After hanging her long coat in the locker, she checked her attire. Señor had requested it last night during their discussion on submissive clothing, and between jobs, she'd gone costume hunting.

"Hey, that's cute," Dara said. The tough-looking Goth had a surprisingly high giggle. "I like the cat ears."

Andrea grinned. Most of the cat outfits for sale either looked silly or like a maid's outfit with ears. She'd found a couple of complete catsuits. But Señor didn't appreciate his subs wearing too many clothes, and she wanted to please him. She hadn't really understood when he'd talked about the difference in following the rules versus pleasing him. Now she knew. As she'd dressed tonight, she'd imagined how his eyes would light up and get that hot look into them, the look that made her want to feel his hands on her. Oh Dios, she had it bad.

Vanessa looked over and sniffed. "Sleazy."

"I don't think so." Sally hooked her fishnet stocking to a garter. "That's incredibly sexy. Do you mind if I copy it next week?"

Andrea laughed. "Feel free. In fact, maybe we should have a cat night sometime."

"A pussy night." Dara examined her fingernails. "I bet I can find a glove with claws."

"Shouldn't your outfit have a tail?" Heather asked.

"Master Cullen said he had one for me."

"He did, huh? Oh, man." Sally gave Andrea a sympathetic look that set off every anxious nerve in her body.

Cullen found the trainees already kneeling. He walked around the line, keeping his mind strictly on business. Austin got a nod of approval.

He tightened Heather's corset, enjoying her tremor as the constriction increased. Sally, as always, looked adorable. She had a child's delight in dressing up.

Vanessa. Cullen's mouth thinned. Last night, she'd mouthed off to a newer Dom who didn't meet her high standards. "When Gary arrives, you'll beg his forgiveness for your rudeness and ask him to discipline you."

The brunette glowered for a second before catching herself and turning sweet. "Please, Master Cullen, won't you punish me yourself?"

This sub wasn't working out well. Too self-involved. Too competitive. He stepped back and crossed his arms over his chest. "If Gary isn't pleased with your submission, I will strap you to the spanking bench and let every Dom in the place take a turn with a cane. Am I clear, Vanessa?"

Her eyes dropped. "Yes, Sir."

"Go."

Only Andrea remained. He lifted her to her feet and grinned. She wore a matching bra and thong with tiger stripes and black fur edging. He ran a finger across the top of the thong—very soft fur—and watched the muscles in her stomach contract. She'd gone all out with black fur cuffs and legwarmers. Black cat ears poked out from her mop of curly hair. "Now that is a very nice outfit, sweetie," he said softly

Her golden eyes lit up like the sun.

His little tiger. He ran a hand down her arm, wanting nothing more than to haul her upstairs and take her over and over until she wailed her release like a cat on a dark night, clawing his back as she came. *Later, buddy; it'll have to be later.*

Still… With the trainees gone and only Ben in the room, Cullen could at least have himself an appetizer. He clamped a hand on her slender nape. Putting a leg between hers and a hand under her ass, he slid her up his thigh until her lips met his. He ravaged her mouth, barely controlling the urge to shove her up against a wall and ravage everything else. When he pulled back, her arms loosened from around his neck slowly, her eyes dazed, her lips swollen and wet.

He let her slide down his leg, knowing the effect the friction would have on her sensitive little clit.

"You're an evil man." Her whisper was almost a whine.

He tucked his fingers under her thong. Very, very wet. God, he loved that. "What do you call me?"

"You're an evil man, *Señor.*"

"Did you clear your schedule for tonight?" He slid a finger over her clit.

Her breath hitched as he rubbed back and forth, and she only managed a nod. He pushed a finger inside her, enjoying the way her hands clamped on his arms, the fingernails digging in like tiny claws. Responsive little tiger.

"Good." He grinned and bent to kiss her again when a noise from the other side of the room drew his attention.

Vanessa stood just inside the clubroom door, her knuckles pressed to her mouth. Slowly she took a step back and disappeared into the bar without a word.

Andrea looked up, her eyes worried. "She heard you. Will you get in trouble? I mean, as the trainer—"

"No, little tiger." Regretfully, Cullen pulled back. "My rules are my own, not Z's." And according to those rules he'd made, he couldn't continue as a trainer if he got involved. He and Z needed to talk. "Go on in. And be at the bar in five minutes. I have a present for you that you might or might not like."

She swallowed hard.

Vanessa had been furious to see her with Master Cullen, Andrea knew. Would the other trainees care? The thought of their anger sat uneasily in her stomach. She enjoyed belonging to a group. Making friends. She hadn't had female friends before. As a child, the brief periods when her father hadn't needed her, she'd hung out with Antonio. Later, when she lived in Drew Park, no one wanted a friend associated with the dealer Enrique Marchado. After that, she'd buried herself in making a living and starting her business.

Now she had time for friends, but she'd discovered they were hard to find. But in the Shadowlands, maybe that would change.

She walked across the barroom and tried to ignore the dampness of her thong. Damn the man, he knew exactly what he'd done to her. Then again, she'd felt his massive erection pressing against her stomach. She wouldn't suffer alone tonight.

But what if Master Z assigned her to another Dom? She bit her lip as dismay ran through her. Would her Señor say anything?

Music started at the dance floor. Sounded like Adam and the Antz. At the buffet tables, Heather was arranging the munchies. Austin went down the back hallway, and lights flickered on in the theme rooms. The usual setting up for the night. Andrea headed for the bar.

Oh. Arms crossed over his chest, Master Cullen watched her, his expression unreadable. Back in trainer mode. She eyed him nervously. Why had Sally looked so sympathetic?

The members had started straggling in already. Masters Nolan, Dan, and Marcus sat at the bar along with Mistress Olivia.

"I believe my little tiger needs a tail," Señor said, his voice echoing in the underpopulated room. He rummaged under the bar, then ducked out and over to her with a long, furry tail in his hand. She frowned, looking for pins or belts. How would he keep it in place?

He smiled slowly, lifted her, and placed her stomach-down on the bar.

"Hey!" She started to push back and earned a sharp swat on her bottom and a hard hand pushing her down.

"Lie still." His voice deepened, and she stopped struggling. *The tail.* Relax. He'd fasten the tail to something and—

She felt the thong between her buttocks being moved, and then his big hand spread her cheeks. Her eyes widened, and she kicked out, but his hard body leaned against her legs.

"You can't be a tiger without a tail, sweetheart," Master Cullen said, amusement in his voice. "It's just not done."

Something pressed against her anus, cold and slick. She wiggled, trying to escape, her hands tightening on the bartop, but the pressure continued, and then, with a plop, it went into her and stayed in. Her muscles closed around the smaller part. Dios, he'd done it to her again.

"There we go, all set," Cullen murmured, patting her bottom. He moved the tail slightly sideways so her thong pressed tightly against the plug.

She gritted her teeth, trying not to whimper, and then couldn't help it when his fingers slid farther forward and over her pussy. She squirmed as he stroked her clit, turning it to an aching nub. He slowly pushed a finger into her vagina, and she could feel every inch going in. His finger in one place, the plug in the other... The sensations were too much.

He leaned forward, finger still in her, his chest hard against her back, as he whispered, "Later tonight, that will be me inside you, taking my little tiger from behind like this." His finger slid in and out of her, and every bone in her body melted.

"And then someday—soon—my cock will be where that plug is." He wiggled it, and she inhaled sharply at the sensation. It felt...different now with her clit throbbing. Erotic. Exciting. But to have *him* inside her? Put his huge cock...there? Madre de Dios.

He stepped back and set her on her feet. Her bottom closed over the anal plug, and she winced. His finger lifted her chin. "That's a very, very small plug," he said, "so you can wear it longer without a problem. But if it starts to hurt, I expect you to tell me, am I clear?"

"Yes, Señor."

"Good." He pressed a hard kiss to her lips, turned her around, and slapped her bottom, making the thing inside move. She glared at him and walked away to the roar of his laughter. The tail flicked against her legs with every step she took.

* * *

Cullen washed up and returned to bartending. Off and on, he checked the room for Andrea. She hadn't come up to the bar for quite a while, and he didn't see her in the room. Face it, he enjoyed watching her; she brightened his whole night. He shook his head and finished making a raspberry mojito for Maxie and handed it over.

How long since he'd felt like this?

Not since Siobhan had been alive. Yes, he remembered those first heady days of falling in love. His hand paused at that phrase, and his gut tightened. Love?

Maybe so. But there was no hurry. He enjoyed his unfettered life too long to jump into another relationship.

"Master Cullen?"

His eyes focused, and he realized he'd just poured tequila all over the counter. "Damn!" Slamming the bottle down, he heard Andrea's throaty laugh.

His chest squeezed at the sound. He shook his head. *Pitiful, Cullen.* He held his hand out for her drink order.

When she handed it over, he frowned at her wrists. "Even if you're wearing fur cuffs, you still need the trainee ones on, sweetie."

"Oh. Okay."

The urge to buckle his own cuffs on her ran through him. *No.* "Where have you been anyway? The members in your section have been coming up to the bar for their drinks."

"I-I'm sorry." She flushed, then paled. "I... A sub was upset after a scene, and the Dom who'd been with her just walked away. When she started crying, I stayed with her."

Testing her, he said, "We usually flog trainees who abandon their duties."

She flinched, but from the set of her shoulders and chin, she'd do the same thing again and take the punishment. The little sub had a soft heart, did she? And his was in fucking trouble. He walked out from behind the bar.

Her hands tightened at her sides. Damn. She fully expected him to drag her off to a cross and beat on her.

He shook his head, grasped her upper arms, and raised her onto tiptoes to get the kiss he'd been looking forward to since just after the last one. After one second, her lips softened under his; after two, he'd taken possession of her mouth. And there he stayed, savoring the give-and-take, the hot and wet. When he let her back down, her breasts jiggled from the intensity of her breathing, and her nipples poked out beneath the tiger striping.

Still holding one arm, he cupped a breast to thumb one peak and saw her flush increase. Leaning down, he murmured into her ear, "Little, softhearted sub, if I strung you up to a cross right now, it wouldn't be a beating you'd get."

His fingers on her breast, he felt her heart rate increase. A glint of laughter appeared in her eyes, and her lips curved. "I'm yours to command, Master."

Master. God, he liked the sound of that from her lips. Hauling in a breath, he set temptation aside. "This is true. So go put your cuffs on. And you've worn that tail long enough, so remove it, and get your ass back out here." He noticed Vanessa waiting at the waitress station, a dark frown on her face as she tapped her fingers on the bar. "Your partner is overworked."

Andrea gave a disappointed sigh. "Yes, Señor."

As he watched her walk away, hips swaying gently, his beeper went off.

* * *

Later than night, Andrea waited at the bar with a drink order and a grumpy attitude. Sometime in the last hour, Master Cullen had disappeared, leaving Master Raoul in his place. Had her Señor gone home sick? She bit her lip, wondering if Raoul would tell her. Compared to some of the other Masters, he was pretty approachable.

Or maybe she should call Señor. He'd given her his cell phone number last night when he walked her to her car. The thought of calling him, hearing his voice—

"Andrea."

She turned and saw Master Dan. Talk about approachable. *Not.* Unlike at the party, his face held no expression at all, and she shivered at the look in his eyes. "Yes, sir?"

"Please come with me." His fingers closed around her arm. Tight and hard. Too much like a cop's grip. The memory of being handled that way made her stiffen.

He led her past the dance floor to heavy oak doors that matched the ones at the entry and escorted her into a huge office with plush brown carpeting and creamy white walls. An antique desk sat in front of the wide windows.

Near the desk, Vanessa stood beside Master Marcus. Andrea saw a tiny smile appear on the trainee's face before changing to one of concern.

What was going on? Andrea stumbled, and Dan's hand tightened on her arm. She looked up. He had an expression he'd use on a cockroach that crawled into his kitchen, right before he stepped on it. Her ribs felt like someone had squeezed them in an iron fist.

"Wh—" Her voice cracked, and she swallowed. "What's wrong?" *Why are you looking at me like this?*

Dan said, "What's wrong is that Vanessa left her locker open earlier, and her money was stolen."

And he'd marched Andrea here like a criminal. Ice chilled her legs, creeping upward. "I don't know anything about that. I've been in the clubroom all night."

"Actually," Marcus said softly, "you went to the locker room to put on cuffs. Vanessa discovered the theft soon after."

The coldness reached her stomach and sent tendrils into her chest. "I didn't take her money. I don't steal."

"Apparently you do," Dan said. "We found the money in your locker."

No. That couldn't be.

Dan picked up a paper from the desk. "It's not the first time either, is it? Does breaking into a liquor store sound familiar?"

She recognized the look now. The same one worn by teachers or parents of the friends she'd tried to make and boys she'd tried to date. The ice on her chest weighed so much she had to fight to get a breath. "How did you get that? Those records were sealed."

"Not to cops."

I didn't steal anything. Believe me. Please. Her throat closed over the words. Futile. Saying anything to that hard-faced man—that cop—would be futile. Only Antonio and her family had ever believed her, certainly not rich people who looked on her as the scum of the earth.

I'm not scum. Anger rose, burning away the numbness. She'd try one more time. "I've never stolen anything in my life."

The disbelief in the men's faces showed as plain as the gloating in Vanessa's.

Vanessa had planned this. Andrea's lip curled, and she glared at the sub. "You lying puta. Just because Master Cullen spent time with me." Her gaze took in the two men. "*Desgraciados*, you deserve her."

Marcus hesitated. "Do you want to call Cullen and—"

"*Vete al Diablo.* I don't want anything to do with any of you people." Master Cullen wouldn't believe her any more than Master Dan had; he was a cop too. Her hands clenched. To see a look of scorn in her Señor's green eyes would hurt her worse than anything she could think of.

So much for this place. She kept her back straight, kept the anger high and hot against the despair seeping into her.

Master Dan looked at Vanessa. "The Shadowlands owes you an apology. It was our mistake in judgment that let a thief into our midst."

"Oh, well, everyone makes mistakes," Vanessa said lightly, looking oh-so-sweet.

The need to knock the smugness right off the trainee's face almost overpowered Andrea, and her fisted hand rose. But then the cop would arrest her. Not worth it. Instead she unbuckled her trainee cuffs and dropped them on the floor. *Thud. Thud.* Air brushed against the damp skin of her newly bared wrists. Yesterday she'd hoped to replace the golden cuffs with real ones; instead she had none. She stared at the cuffs on the floor and blinked back tears.

Master Dan picked up a pile of clothing from the desk, and Andrea recognized the contents of her locker. They had tried and convicted her before she even walked into the office.

He jerked his chin toward the door. "I'll walk you out."

* * *

She made it back to her apartment complex. Barely. The scene in the office had played in her head over and over on the horrible drive. *"Does breaking into a liquor store sound familiar?"* She'd gripped the steering wheel so tightly that her fingers now cramped as she unlocked her apartment door. *Don't think. Breathe. Take keys out of lock. Enter apartment. Lock door.*

Her purse dropped, followed by her keys. She'd left everything else in the van. *"In case you didn't get the point, Andrea. You're not welcome here."* Master Dan had thrown her clothing into the car like it was trash to dispose of...like her.

The table lamp that she always left on lit her wavering path to the bedroom. Her home, her comfort. All hers. Rented with her own money. Money she'd earned, not stolen. *"Don't ever come back,"* Master Dan had said.

She crawled onto her bed, feeling ninety years old, creaking like Abuelita. She curled into a ball, pulling her fluffy quilt over her, breathing in the clean scent. Even when camping in the snowy Rockies, she'd never felt this cold; she didn't think she'd ever get warm again.

The first sob. More of a whimper. *Only wimps cry.* The second worked up through her tight throat. Last night, she'd laid her head on her Señor's shoulder, kissed him, made love with him. The need to be held right now shook her. She pulled her pillow over and wrapped her arms around it. The hollow feeling didn't leave.

Not my Señor. Not any longer. The next sob ripped through her so hard she couldn't breathe.

Had they already called him?

She could call him herself. And say what? Vanessa lied? *Yes, the money was in my locker, and yes, I have a record, but Vanessa lied. Really.* Sure, he'd believe that. He was a cop, just like Master Dan. Maybe, maybe, he could have overlooked her background but not an accusation of stealing.

Why? Why did this happen to me? Why now when she'd just started to think it might work?

And then she cried.

Chapter Fifteen

Thursday afternoon, Cullen looked up at a tap on his office door to see Z and Dan. He leaned back in his chair, taking in the serious expressions. "What's up?"

"When I got back into Tampa last night, Daniel called me about a problem that came up on Saturday." Uninvited, Z sat in the chair in front of the desk. "I hear you've been out of town."

"I got yanked over to Miami on a related case. Just flew back in an hour ago." Cullen's eyes narrowed as an ugly sensation crawled into his gut. He nodded at the other chair by the desk, but Dan shook his head and remained standing. "You want to tell me what's going on?"

"It's about Andrea," Z said.

Cullen had given her a call when he returned to town, but no one had answered. "Go on."

His legs braced in a defensive stance, Dan said, "Vanessa hadn't shut her padlock in the dressing room. Andrea stole the money out of her wallet."

Cullen rose, a growl erupting from his throat. "No way. She wouldn't."

"There's more, Cullen. She has a record—sealed. Attempted robbery." Dan tossed a paper on Cullen's desk.

She had an actual record? Is that what she'd been so worried about? He leaned forward, hands flat on his desk, and glared at Dan. "I'm still not buying it."

"Dammit, Cullen, get your head out of... I found the money in Andrea's locker. Open- and-shut case."

Cullen forced his anger down and tried to think logically. Didn't work. His gut said this was all wrong. "Did she say she'd taken it? You're a fucking Dom—did she act guilty?"

"Of course she's..." Dan broke off, and his brows drew together. "And yet, she said, '*I don't steal,*' with no hedging or hesitation. The look on her face..." He scowled. "Hell, I was so damned furious at her taking you for a ride that I never tried to read her."

"And now?"

"Cullen...I don't know."

"I do. She told me she had some sort of nasty background. And the little Amazon has problems, no doubt about that, but I've never questioned her integrity. I can't see her stealing, no matter how much money you found." Cullen's jaw tightened. "Vanessa, however... She's a sneaky piece of work. One who shouldn't be in the program."

Z nodded. "I agree in both cases. I'm sorry I wasn't there to help determine what happened. But finding the money in Andrea's locker..."

Dan crossed the floor and stood at the window, his shoulders tight. The cop liked to think things to death, Cullen knew, but at least his brain had switched on. After a minute, he turned back to the room. "Her reactions were... I didn't see any guilt in her body language. Shock—definitely shock—especially when I showed her the rap sheet, and then she acted as if she expected everything that followed. But when she said, '*I didn't take her money*,' I saw no lie in her face."

Dan's face darkened. "Did I get taken for a sucker? Why the hell didn't she stand up for herself? Argue. Cry?"

"She wouldn't have argued," Cullen muttered. All the stubborn pride and independence that made her submission so intoxicating also made her downright difficult to deal with. Fuck, what must she be feeling right now? "Too much pride."

Z steepled his fingers, regarding Cullen with a frown. "I want to pursue this further."

Cullen stared up at the ceiling, trying to think, seeing instead a spider web swaying in the air from the vent. A good cleaning service wouldn't overlook cobwebs. Andrea probably wouldn't.

He picked up the information Dan had tossed on his desk and skimmed it. "She'd just turned eighteen and was arrested. Once. She hasn't even had a parking ticket since."

"Shit. Fuck." Dan paced across the office. "If she's not guilty... Hell, I feel like I ran over a puppy."

Cullen growled. "I think it's time to talk with Vanessa."

And then with a little sub. The pain running through him was partly at the hell she'd experienced.

The rest was the knowledge that she hadn't called him.

* * *

Z volunteered his office. That night, Cullen leaned against the oversize desk, his anger buried under a layer of icy control. Dan stood nearby, wearing the same expression. A chance existed that they'd come to the wrong conclusion, but he didn't think so.

Vanessa walked into the office, glanced at Dan, and gave Cullen a sweet smile. "You wanted to see me about last Saturday?"

He didn't speak.

Her smile faltered, and she clasped her hands together. "What's wrong? Oh, God, you blame me for Andrea being thrown out, don't you? Maybe I shouldn't have said anything. But…"

Ah-huh. Wanting him to reassure her that she'd done the right thing and so convince himself. *Not happening, sweetheart.* "Strip."

Her head snapped up, eyes widening.

He raised his chin slightly.

She glanced at Dan. With her lips tight, she peeled off the tailored blue dress and her undergarments, piling everything on a nearby chair. She might have a nice, shapely body, but he found her lack of character a total turn-off. After she finished, she stood in the center of the room, hands at her sides, breathing slightly harder, cheeks flushed. Uncertain.

Good. He didn't order her to kneel; he could read her body language better with her standing.

Dan moved closer. Vanessa took a tiny step back.

"Now, sub, let's talk about when Andrea was accused of stealing," Cullen said, pulling her attention to him. The lights they'd arranged spotlighted her as nicely as in any interview room. Interrogation 101. "What were you wearing that night?"

As she tried to remember, her eyes focused up and to the left. "Oh, well, I had on my blue bustier, and a blue vinyl skirt.

So eyes up and left might indicate the act of accessing a memory. Cullen noted it and picked another question she would answer truthfully. "And who was working the theme rooms?"

She blinked. Then her gaze went up and to the left again. "Dara was in the..." She listed each position.

"Now tell me about your missing money. How much and where was it when the evening started?"

Up and to the left. "Over a hundred dollars and in my purse. In my locker."

A definite memory. He glanced at Dan, got a slight nod. On to the real interview. "Now tell me everything about that night."

"Where...where do you want me to start?"

Stalling for time. "When you first got to the Shadowlands."

She rambled through the beginning of the night, nice factual statements of "I did this" and "I did that." Then she came to her visit to the dressing room. Her weight shifted, and one hand came up to cover her mouth in a you-can't-see-me-lie move. Her eyes went up and to the right this time—making up a story. "Well, I think that I remembered the lock wasn't snapped, so I went in. My locker door was ajar."

Nice shift of language also. "*I think*." Passive statements. *Lie, lie, and lie.* Cullen's satisfaction that the interview vindicated his belief in Andrea was overshadowed by the anger at what the little tiger had been forced to endure.

"And the money was gone," she finished.

"*The money*," not "my money," to distance herself.

"She stole your money and didn't bother to close the door or lock the padlock?" Dan asked, his voice grating. Vanessa jumped, her gaze jerking to him. "That seems stupid, don't you think?" he asked.

"I-I don't know. How do I know what she was thinking?" She toyed with her diamond ring, no longer looking at them.

"So then what did you do, Vanessa?" Cullen asked.

"I left the room. Since you weren't here, Master Cullen, I told Marcus, and he got Master Dan." Back to the facts.

Dan took a step closer to her. "Look at me."

She looked up, and he asked, "You left the room right away? Didn't do anything else?"

"What would I do? There was no money in my locker."

Cullen moved closer, forcing her to divide her attention between him and Dan. "When I talked to Sally, she definitely remembers that you locked your locker."

Vanessa's mouth dropped for a second, and she took a step back. "No. I think she's mistaken."

"You were there when I told Andrea to go put on cuffs. You knew she'd be in the locker room," Cullen said, keeping his voice level and cold. "The other trainees say you're always sniping at her. Saying she doesn't belong in the group."

Vanessa's hands clenched. "Well, she doesn't. Look what she did. She's just a thief."

"And you're a liar," Dan said. "A petty, vindictive liar. Why did you lie?"

Her hands clenched, and red splotches stood out on her cheeks. "I'm a respected person. I have money, and I don't have to steal. For anyone to believe I could do something like that—it doesn't make sense."

Not answering the question, was she? "I don't like liars," Cullen said. He considered her the worst kind of viper, one that bites without warning. "How did you get into Andrea's locker?"

"I had—" Her breath sucked in. "I didn't. Why—"

"Of course you did," Dan said. "We know that already. Don't be stupider than you already are."

"I'm not—"

Good. Frightened, distracted...ready. Cullen grasped her chin in a punishing grip. "How did you open her lock? Tell me, sub. Right now."

Too confused to hold out against his will, she started to cry. "She left the combination on the bench. The first day. Master, she doesn't deserve—"

"Stop." Cullen stepped back, disgusted. He glanced at Dan. "More?"

"No, I think that's clear enough."

"I believe so," Z said from the doorway. The mind reader shrink could have undoubtedly obtained the truth faster, but he'd graciously relinquished control to Cullen and Dan.

Vanessa whirled. She saw Z, and her face turned white. She wasn't totally stupid after all.

Z's voice sounded like smooth ice as he said, "Thank you, masters." His head tilted. "I believe Vanessa and I should talk."

Dan nodded. "We're through here." His gaze ran down Vanessa, and his mouth twisted as if he tasted something foul before he walked out of the room.

"Please, Master Cullen, I'm sorry." Vanessa held her hands out.

"So am I." Cullen glanced at Z. "All yours, boss." He closed the door on the sound of her increasing sobs.

As he stepped outside, Cullen breathed in the fresh air. First problem down. The next would be harder. The little tiger was probably in a very bad mood.

* * *

Cullen didn't particularly like the Hogshead Tavern, but at least it was close to the station and not filled with yuppies enjoying happy hour. His temper rode on a thin edge. Andrea still hadn't answered her phone.

The peanut shells covering the floor crunched under his feet as he got a beer and chose a corner booth where he could watch the door.

Antonio came in and spotted him immediately. He stopped at the bar for a cup of coffee, then joined Cullen. "Make it fast; I have a deadline to make." He slid into the seat and added, "You look like shit, *amigo*."

Fuck the amenities. "Where's Andrea? She's not answering her phone."

Antonio gave Cullen a level look over the rim of the glass. "She said she's done with the club, so that's something you don't need to know."

"And did she say she was done with me also?"

Antonio choked, coughing hard enough to turn his face red. He tried to talk, coughed again. "Mierda, you don't screw around with the trainees. Ever."

Well, this was where Andrea had received her information. Cullen leaned forward, resting his forearms on the table. "Apparently I do."

"With Andrea?"

"Yes."

"No." Antonio thumped his head against the back of the booth. "Fuck, no. You can't hook up with her. You're in law enforcement."

He remembered the way her face had changed when he said he was a cop. His voice came out rough. "True. I also know she was caught breaking into a liquor store."

"Damn you," Antonio said slowly. "The records were sealed."

"I have trouble seeing her as a thief. Talk to me, Antonio."

"You are such a fucking asshole." Antonio took a deep drink. "Fine. You might as well know. Her cousins had just gotten into robbing liquor stores, thought it was a fun deal, and dragged her along." Antonio closed his eyes for a second. "She...she wasn't used to having friends other than me, so for her the thrill was in being included. Being part of the family. Her first and only night of crime."

"But she's the one who got caught."

"Yeah. Tomás—" Antonio stopped, counted on his fingers, stopping when he reached seven. Obviously making sure the time of prosecution had passed. "Tomás said she deliberately turned back when it looked like the cops would get them all. She diverted them into arresting her."

Now that sounded like his little sub. "She resisted arrest too."

"Originally just to keep their attention on her." Antonio gave a bitter smile. "But apparently one of the cops groped her...and you've seen how she reacts to that."

"I saw that she decked him." Cullen snorted. "Good for her. She might not know it, but it's one of the reasons the prosecutor declined to adjudicate. Internal affairs was already looking into the cop's behavior."

"'Bout time she caught a break."

"Her cousins sure didn't give her one." The roil of anger changed to one directed at the family.

"They were nineteen and twenty. Although their mother managed to instill a conscience, they're also Enrique Marchado's kids."

Cullen frowned. Marchado had been a big-time drug dealer. Definitely a "background."

Antonio sighed. "The boys were so freaked at screwing Andrea up that they went straight. A marine captain and a lawyer. The whole family helped her with startup expenses for her business—against her protests—when the bank turned her down."

The bank turned her down. Had it rough, hadn't she? "She protested getting help?"

"Is there a word for being past independent?" Antonio pulled out his pack of cigarettes, frowned, and put it back in his pocket.

"She definitely goes overboard." Like why the hell hadn't she called him? "Is there a reason?"

"Her father made promises, then ended up too drunk to keep them." Antonio's face tightened. "Even I let her down, dammit."

Cullen raised his eyebrows.

"She was…fourteen? Gang activity was up, so she asked me to go with her after school to pick something up. Safety in numbers, right? But I caught a detention and was sitting in the principal's office when she almost got raped." He scrubbed his face. "God, I don't think she's asked me—or anyone else—for anything since."

She'd mentioned the assault. But the trust issue—that was worse than he'd thought. *Bad little sub, not sharing everything with your Dom.* Cullen leaned back. "A vindictive sub at the Shadowlands gave Andrea grief. It's resolved, but I need to see her for the club. And for me."

Antonio scowled. "She left town, went backpacking into some wilderness area. But she's due back today for a party that I'm going to miss. You think she wants to see you?"

"She will…eventually."

Chapter Sixteen

"Your mouth is smiling, but your eyes are sad, mija." Andrea's grandmother set her knitting in her lap.

Andrea sighed. Her abuela could read people even better than a Dom. The vision of her tiny, stooped grandmother in latex and holding a flogger lightened her thoughts, at least until Master Cullen stepped over and took the flogger. *The pendejo.* "I had a disappointment, Abuelita. The man who I liked turned out to be…unavailable."

She'd wanted to stay buried in the forest for a few more days, until her emotions didn't bounce around, but today was her grandmother's birthday which the whole family always celebrated together.

"Unavailable? Ah, this is the one we spoke of. Did he turn out to be so fainthearted?" Her grandmother had, at one time, been a social power in the ghetto, despite having a daughter foolish enough to marry a drug dealer. And she hadn't reached the top by fearing to ask questions.

Fainthearted? Cullen? "No, he's not fainthearted." Andrea stared down at the pile of yarn in her lap. When it transformed into a pretty blanket, how many people would look at it and think about the strands of yarn that had made it?

Unfortunately for her, people just couldn't look past the strands that had made up her life. She'd waited for two days for him to call, and he hadn't. How many times had she picked up the phone wanting to contact him? Finally she had put Selena in charge of the business, left her cell phone at home, and gone backpacking in the Ocala. "But he's a cop. And I have a record." And now everyone thought she'd stolen Vanessa's money.

Her grandmother's lips tightened. "Then your cop is a fool. He does not deserve my beautiful granddaughter."

Tears burned Andrea's eyes.

"Come to dinner, you two," Rosa called from the back door. "Everyone else is already seated."

Blinking away the weakness, Andrea helped her grandmother rise, then followed the tiny figure into the crowded dining room.

* * *

Not the greatest of neighborhoods, Cullen thought, as he drove down the street. Cracked concrete, minuscule weed-eaten lawns, houses with broken windows. Not a safe place to grow up either. The idea of a young Andrea walking to school in this area tightened his gut. The red-light district was only a few blocks away.

He checked the numbers—at least a few houses had them—and frowned. Cars were parked bumper to bumper up and down the entire block. Antonio had mentioned a party, hadn't he?

After parking the next block over, he walked back in the growing twilight. The aunt's place had a well-tended lawn of St. Augustine grass, and pots of pink pansies or petunias—damned if he could tell the difference—decorated the edges of the steps. A vine climbed a trellis on the side of the house. Pretty respectable looking for Enrique Marchado's home.

Cullen vaguely remembered the notorious dealer's death a few years back—shot when a buy went bad. No one at the station had mourned him.

He didn't spot a doorbell, so he tapped on the front door and knocked louder when the murmur of voices told him no one had heard. A party was definitely going on at this house, damn the luck. But his patience had limits. If the little sub wouldn't answer her phone or reply to her messages, then she'd get her Dom on her doorstep, up close and personal.

A tiny Hispanic woman frowned up at him through the screen. "Yes?"

"I'm here to see Andrea."

"But... Well, come in."

He followed her through a living room, spotless except for a scattering of children's toys. A picture of Jesus reigned above a table crowded with figurines of saints. In the dining area, people packed the small room so full that a fire inspector would have been screaming about exits and maximum capacity.

Cullen smiled. The party looked just like an O'Keefe gathering. As his hostess bent to whisper in the ear of a tiny old woman at the head of the table, he spotted Andrea disappearing into the kitchen with an empty jug of milk.

Satisfaction coursed through his veins. *You've been run to ground, little tiger.*

He took one step in that direction, but the lady who'd let him in grabbed his arm. "My mother wishes to speak to you."

The old woman in the place of honor was so tiny that when he knelt beside her, his head was still level with hers. She studied him without speaking for a minute. "Are you the man who hurt my baby?"

He winced. The thought of his sub, someone who he'd defend with his life, being hurt, cut deep. He hadn't done it, but he hadn't been there to save her. And that fact surely pissed him off. "Others did the hurting, ma'am. And your baby should have called me to defend her."

She pursed her lips. "Then why are you here?"

"To apologize for them and have it out with her over not calling me." He didn't evade questions, and this woman probably preferred blunt. He nodded toward the kitchen. "May I—"

"You may sit beside me and enjoy my birthday dinner. After, I might let you see her." The fragile shoulders straightened, and her chin rose.

Cullen grinned, recognizing the same spitting attitude in her as in his sub. "I would be honored, ma'am. My name is Cullen O'Keefe."

The daughter standing nearby sent one of the young boys off to fetch another chair.

A minute later, Cullen sat down next to the matriarch of the family. She reminded him a hell of a lot of his grandmother as she pointed a fork, naming off her children and their children. The great-grandchildren scrambling around with the enthusiasm of puppies moved too fast for her to name.

Cullen watched as Andrea carried out food, chatting with everyone, laughing at jokes, roughhousing with the youngsters. She wore cutoffs and a bright red shirt that showed her figure, and damn, she was gorgeous. Eventually, she took a seat at the other end of the long white-clothed table, and looked up, calling, "Abuelita, we have…"

Her voice trailed off, and Cullen met her wide-eyed gaze, caught the flash of joy, and then pain. Her face lost all expression, and she started to rise. To boot him out, no doubt.

The old woman pointed a fork at Andrea. "*Sientete.*" Her voice rose. "This is Cullen, who has come to be with Andrea. They have had a fight, so I am keeping them apart until dessert sweetens their tempers." Laughter rolled up and down the table.

The furious look Andrea sent him should have had a flammable sticker applied to it. He definitely had his work cut out for him.

What was he doing here? Sitting between her cousin and Aunt Rosa, Andrea tried not to look at him, but she couldn't help herself, especially when he laughed, the sound so distinctive and infectious. He'd already charmed her grandmother, the damned bartender who wasn't a bartender, and had half the table leaning forward as he described an arson investigation. He certainly wasn't hiding his occupation now, was he?

He looked up then and caught her gaze, holding it with his intent green eyes until she flushed. Until he deliberately let her go.

"He's hot," Jasmine, one of her teenaged cousins, whispered, fanning herself. "And he looks like he could really kick ass, even yours. Where did you meet him?"

"At a club. I thought he was a bartender." Not a damned cop. She deliberately met his gaze this time, keeping her expression hard. It didn't help. He smiled at her, and the sun lines around his eyes crinkled, and she had to avert her eyes. Too many memories came with that smile, ones of how he had looked after they'd made love.

"Madre de Dios, the way he looks at you, like he's just waiting to get you into bed," Rosa whispered.

"Aunt Rosa!"

Rosa gave her a sunny smile and patted her hand. "I have four children, and they didn't arrive by stork. I have seen that look on a man's face before."

The dinner lasted forever, and then the desserts came out of the kitchen. Even the thick chocolate brownie seemed tasteless, although Cullen ate enough and gave enough compliments to please every woman there.

As people finished eating and started clearing the table, Abuelita whispered into Cullen's ear.

He rose, strode directly to Andrea, and held out his hand. "We have been dismissed to make our peace. Come."

When she ignored him, he merely smiled and pulled her up. He placed a hand low on her back, pushing gently each time her feet stopped. The cabrón knew she wouldn't make a scene at her grandmother's party.

The heat of his hand and the intimacy of his touch there, right above her bottom, sent a simmer of need through her. She shoved it away. The Shadowlands had called her a thief and kicked her out. Her anger surged up again.

"Where can we talk?" he asked as they left the dining room.

"I don't want to speak with you." Why had he come here? Everything in her wanted to snuggle into his side, feel him pull her closer, and at the same time, she wanted to hit him very hard.

"That's a shame, since we're going to be talking now." He looked around and guided her out the front door.

On the steps, she planted her feet and stared up at him.

"I'll put you over my shoulder, little sub," he said softly.

"I'm a thief. You shouldn't be talking to me."

"You're not a thief. You never were. And Dan admits he acted like an asshole." His arm came around her waist, forcing her down the steps, holding her so closely that her hip rubbed against his leg with every step. "However, I didn't. You should have called me."

She stared up at him, her mind gone blank, and his eyes crinkled. His finger touched her bottom lip. "Don't look at me like that. We have some talking to do before I kiss you."

Her breath hitched and started again as he kept walking. The streetlight on the corner provided a faint amount of illumination as they reached the next block, and he stopped beside a truck. After lowering the tailgate, he plucked

Andrea up and sat her on it. He set one booted foot next to her on the metal and leaned both arms on his knee, staring down at her.

How could she fight him in this position? She started to slide off the tailgate, and he snapped, "Stay there."

"Fine," she huffed, trying to ignore the melting sensation inside. She looked down at her hands, saw her fingers trembling, so she crossed her arms over her chest. Dios, he was here. How could she hate him and want him so much all at the same time?

A big hand cupped her cheek. His thumb pressed her chin up and forced her to meet his eyes. "Why didn't you call me?" he asked.

What? How dare he try to give her the blame? "Why didn't you call *me?* I waited—" She choked on how much she'd wanted to hear from him.

"I didn't know, sweetie. I flew to Miami Saturday night and just got back yesterday, and then heard about you and Vanessa." His mouth tightened. "And I've tried to reach you ever since."

Oh. "I was backpacking." Fizzles of happiness bubbled through her. He'd called her. "I haven't even been home yet."

"Andrea, why didn't you call me?"

She closed her eyes. Damn Dom went straight to the point. She wasn't ready to answer that question. "So who was the thief at the Shadowlands?"

"Vanessa lied, and you know it. Don't play games with me, pet."

Caught. She stopped herself from leaning toward him and settled back. "But how did the money get into my locker?"

"You, sweetie, left your combination on the bench that first day."

"No way." The first day. Walking into the dressing room. Setting the padlock and paper on the bench. Choosing a locker and putting the padlock on. Storing her stuff—and being sidetracked by the other trainees' shock at her pants. *And never picking the paper up.* "Idiota. I made it so easy for her."

She felt like banging her head against a wall. A bit late for that. "What are you going to do with her?"

"After I questioned her, I gave her to Z to deal with. She's his problem now." Cullen moved closer; she could feel the heat radiating off his body. "Z plans to make an announcement and apology on both Friday and Saturday nights, so the members know what happened." Hard hands pushed her knees apart, and he stepped between her legs. "So we're back to the problem of you and me."

"Why don't we just leave it as it is? We don't live in the same worlds." The part of her that had stayed coldly angry shoved those words out, and another part wailed that she didn't want to give him up.

"That's not an option. Try again."

Her eyes burned at the flood of relief.

"Look at you. You don't want to call it quits any more than I do." Before she could answer, his hand clamped over her nape, and his mouth covered hers, opening her lips, and taking possession. Deep and furious. He pulled back long enough to put his hands under her thighs, lifting her, and reversing their positions so he sat on the tailgate. He wrapped her legs around his waist, pulling her tighter until her pussy pressed against a huge erection.

This time when he kissed her, her arms curled around his neck. Dios, she'd missed him.

"Looks like they made up. What do you think, Julio?"

Andrea stiffened at the sound of Rafael's voice. Her cousins had undoubtedly wandered down the block just to check on her.

Cullen merely chuckled and glanced over at the two men, standing with their hands in their pockets, grinning like fools. "I'm taking her with me before she has time to change her mind." Cullen's arm tightened, defeating her effort to pull away. "Please thank the ladies for a wonderful meal and for letting me share in the birthday dinner."

Her cousins laughed and headed back to the house.

How dare he tell her cousins what to do? And make plans for her. "No, I don't—" she started.

"Little sub"—the darkness of his voice froze her tongue—"you no longer have permission to speak."

As everything inside her turned liquid, he lifted her in his arms, put her in the passenger side of his truck, fastened her seat belt, and closed the door.

* * *

What had she done? Andrea toyed with the belt of her shorts and scowled as the truck headed down the empty country road toward the west. The moist scent of the swamp, the palmettos, and the orange groves drifted through the half-open windows. She'd said no. Why hadn't she made it stick? Why had he pushed her?

Because he was a damned Dom and could tell that she wanted to go with him. And oh, she did. This was just so confusing. Did he really want her?

And yet, everyone said he didn't take anyone home. Or maybe he did and no one knew.

"So much thinking." Cullen's hand closed over her cold fingers. "Did you get any answers?"

"No." She sighed. Just that she wanted to go with him more than anything she'd wanted in a long, long time. Her hands curled around his big fingers. Callused and warm.

The car slowed, and the headlights illuminated the end of the road and a sprawling one-story house, white with dark green trim. Cullen pulled the car into the garage.

Andrea opened her door and slid out as the lights came on. The coolness of the garage wrapped around her, smelling of exhaust and oil, sawdust and paint. The back wall held tools hanging over an old battered workbench. She studied it for a second. Yes, she could see his capable hands doing carpentry.

He led her into a rustic-looking kitchen with oak cupboards, dark green tile counters, and a big table. Comfortable. Friendly.

"What would you like to drink? Juice, alcohol, water?"

"Nothing, thank you." She stood in the center of his kitchen and wrapped her arms around herself, feeling as awkward and inadequate as at some job interview. The excitement she'd felt at seeing him again had drained away with the drive. What would happen now? Did he plan to pull her into the bedroom for sex?

He studied her face for a minute. "Come, pet." He pulled her to him. "I'll introduce you to Hector."

On the other side of a dark living room, he opened French doors and stepped out on a wide wooden deck.

A large dog came out of nowhere, jumped up, and knocked Cullen back against the rail. Oh, Dios. Andrea froze, then heard the deep rumble of Cullen's laughter. "Down, you idiot. Show some manners. We have a guest."

Andrea put her hand on her chest, feeling the furious beating of her heart. The cabrón had almost given her a heart attack.

The dog sat, his tongue lolling out. Scruffy gray hair. A long, long nose. The tips of its upright ears flopped over.

"What kind of dog is he?"

Cullen chuckled, and ruffled the dog's fur. "Some of this and that, but mostly Airedale. He was a pound puppy."

The dog cocked his head, obviously checking her out.

"Andrea, this is Hector. Hector, be polite and meet Andrea."

When the dog raised a paw, Andrea grinned and squatted down to be at the right level. Someday she would have a house and a dog too. She shook the dog's paw, and as if formalities handled, Hector shoved his head into her stomach, knocking her on her butt.

"Hell." Cullen grabbed the Hector's collar and dragged him back. "I'm sorry, Andrea."

She giggled and held a hand out to the dog. Stumpy tail wagging, the dog pulled forward until she could pet him. When Cullen let go, she ended up with an armful of dog.

"Likes you, apparently."

Obviously of the opinion that he was poodle-sized, Hector sprawled across her lap, his butt hanging off one side. Andrea grinned up at Cullen. "He's adorable. I bet he likes everybody."

"Hardly. He's very fussy about his friends."

She hugged the dog, collected a few snuffles, laughed when he nudged her hand to obtain more petting. His wiry mustache and whiskers reminded her of her history professor.

"Hector, time to play fetch."

The dog bounced off her lap, ran to the other side of the deck, and returned with a foot-long, barkless stick. Cullen held a hand down to Andrea and hefted her to her feet, then motioned to the dog. "Go on, buddy."

Andrea started to follow, but Cullen tucked a finger under her belt to stop her. "What?"

"Strip," he said.

"Excuse me?"

"It's warm enough." After pushing her hands away, he pulled her T-shirt over her head, undid her belt, and dropped her shorts. Bra and thong followed. She stood, stunned. "I like seeing you without clothing." He pushed her toward the steps.

She looked over the railing, expecting to see a backyard. Instead a path led down a tall bank to a beach, the sand white under the light of a half-moon. A beach? She turned. "I'm not going out there naked."

He gave her a level look that melted her bones. "Yes. You are."

"But—"

His hands cupped her breasts, and his thumbs circled her nipples. Sizzling shot through her, and she caught her breath.

"This is my body, Andrea. Mine to command." He pinched one peak, and her knees wobbled. "Isn't it?"

Dios, this was different from the club. Just him and her, yet it only made her reaction to his control headier. Crowding her back against the railing, he tilted her chin up. "Answer me, sub. Isn't it?"

"Yes," she whispered, helpless against the demand in his eyes. "Yes, Señor."

"Very good." He kissed her, hard and possessive and thorough, until her nipples ached and her pussy dampened. "Some Doms only exert control in the bedroom or clubs, some all the time. I'm halfway between the two."

He expected control...more than just for sex. Excitement vied with anxiety inside her, and her hands curled around his forearms. She wanted this, but she was a professional woman, a—

"I don't need a slave, Andrea. I can take care of myself. But I do want a naked sub in my lap when I watch the news at night." His eyes crinkled.

The image of sitting in his lap, having his hands wander over her without any clothing to limit access made her hot despite the breeze from the beach.

He nudged her toward the steps again. "Now go."

A tiny path wound through sea oats and sedges, across beach dunes, and down to the white-sand-covered beach. Hector trotted up and down the sand, his stick held high.

"Bring it here," Cullen said. The dog pranced closer and dropped the toy. Master Cullen threw it straight into the ocean; Hector darted after it. The dog splashed through the waves, and a minute later, returned with the prize.

After several tosses, Cullen sent the stick flying back toward the house. It landed in what looked like a jungle-gym setup of bars and logs and small platforms. A giant-sized playland. Metal poles with a high bar across them. Rings like a gymnast would use.

"What is all that?" Andrea asked.

Señor's warm hand covered her breast, and his hand on her bottom held her still while he pinched her nipple gently. "I use it for working out...and to string up insubordinate submissives."

"Oh, well." Her words came out disgustingly breathy. "It's good that I'm so obedient."

His grin flashed in the moonlight, his rough-hewn face dark with shadows. "Isn't it."

Eventually Hector returned, his head held high as if bringing the crown jewels. He dropped the stick at Cullen's feet and flopped down on the ground, his sides heaving.

The sand chilled Andrea's bare feet as she moved closer to the water. The waves washed onto the shore, hissing as they receded again. Moonlight glimmered off the water and turned the froth an iridescent white. "This is really beautiful. And so quiet."

In fact, she could barely see the lights of the nearest house. A private beach. How did a cop afford a beach house? She frowned.

He must have registered the suspicious look, and he chuckled. "I'm not taking bribes. My great-grandparents bought this place, and it came to me instead of money or property in Chicago. Everyone knows I hate the cold." He grinned. "I see my family every winter after the first few snows."

The affectionate way he spoke of his family made her smile. Maybe they had more in common than she thought. He'd certainly seemed at home with her horde of relatives.

Once back on the deck, Cullen leaned on the railing to watch the water. She stood next to him, enjoying the peace of the night. But as the moist breeze cooled, she shivered and wrapped her arms around herself. Would he yell if she put her clothes back on? She looked up and met his gaze.

He frowned. "Andrea, it goes like this: 'I'm cold, Sir—' no, 'I'm cold, Señor. May I have something to wear?' Say exactly that." His voice was soft as the murmur of the waves.

Her hands fisted, and she stared at him. Why did he insist on making her do this? "I'm cold, Señor. M-may I have something to wear?" Why was it so hard to admit a weakness? That she needed help?

"Good girl." His smile of approval set a glow inside her that helped ease the unsettling emotions. He disappeared into the house and returned with a long, fluffy robe and two drinks. After helping her into the robe, he picked her up and settled into an oversize Adirondack chair. His body radiated heat like a Tampa sidewalk under a hot sun, and she sighed and snuggled closer.

"Amazing you could get cold in Florida." He handed her a glass. "Ever seen snow, little beach bunny?"

She thumped his shoulder for the nasty term, then curled an arm around his big chest. Expecting water, she took a hefty gulp of the drink and choked. A very, very strong Seven and Seven. The alcohol burned all the way down and spread outward. "I go skiing in Colorado every winter."

"Do you now? Skiing is good. What else?"

"Well, backpacking here and there: Yosemite, Banff, the Rockies. Scuba diving sometimes."

He huffed a laugh. "You're a macho little sub, aren't you?" She might have taken offense except for the pleased tone in his voice.

"So what do you do on your vacations?"

"Exactly the same things and visit my folks in Chicago." He tugged on her hair. "I'm sorry your parents are gone, although Antonio didn't sound like he liked your father."

"He didn't know my father before—" She lifted her glass for a drink. Empty. Had she drunk it all already?

"Before what?" He plucked the glass from her fingers and set it on the table.

"Before an IED exploded near him."

"Right, military. How badly was he hurt?"

Andrea watched a cloud drift in front of the moon. "Arm and leg. The doctors amputated his leg above the knee. He had a prosthesis so he could walk with a cane. Not very well, since he had a hook instead of a hand on that side. He joked about being Captain Hook." But in a way that said he didn't find it funny, although he expected people to laugh. Every time Papa made fun of himself in that bitter, bitter voice, her stomach would twist.

Cullen studied her, then asked, "What happened to your mom?"

"She died of an aneurism when I was nine." So sudden. Complaining of a headache, then gone.

"I'm sorry, sweetie." He pulled her closer, kissed her temple, and the unexpected sympathy made her eyes burn. "How did your father handle it? Didn't he need a fair amount of help?"

"Oh, I learned to do whatever he couldn't. And he was pretty competent with just one hand." Until he started living in the bottle. Then his good hand would shake so hard, he couldn't fasten the buckles on his artificial leg or the buttons on his clothing. His temper would explode and... She'd had her first lessons in dodging by the time she'd turned ten.

"Shhh," Señor murmured and raised her fisted hand to his mouth, opening and kissing each finger. His breath blew warmth over her cold skin. "You were just a puppy, weren't you? Jessica said you learned to fight at ten. He taught you?"

"After Mama died, we moved to a cheaper...nastier...neighborhood. When I got roughed up, it really upset him that he couldn't do anything." "*Can't work, can't protect my own. Worthless. I should have died over there.*" One afternoon, he'd taken his rage out on the kitchen until all Mama's wedding plates lay in shatters.

"Anyway," she continued, "he decided I'd have to defend myself. He wasn't an easy teacher. I swear, he gave me more bruises and bloody noses than—" What was she saying? She put her hand over her mouth.

"Did he?" The clipped words didn't sound like Master Cullen at all. "Couldn't anyone there help you?"

She stiffened. "We did fine."

"I see. Just you and him, making do. And from what you said at the club, your father wouldn't have accepted help anyway, right?"

"Of course not. And it wasn't that bad. We had fun together." Sometimes. Especially in the earlier days before he was drunk all the time. They'd watch TV, like *The Incredible Journey*, and he'd talk about the dog he'd had as a kid. One day they'd run out of almost everything, so she made peanut butter and jelly sandwiches for breakfast, and he'd laughed. He'd once bought her an ice cream cone to celebrate a good report card.

"You loved him, eh?"

"Uh-huh." Loved him and hated him and cursed him for being too weak to stop drinking, for being a mean drunk, for never, ever doing what he promised. Not even staying alive. She blinked when Cullen ran his finger over her wet cheek.

"Oh, baby," Cullen murmured, his voice coming out hoarse. "You didn't have it easy, did you?" Alcoholic father, and those training sessions of hers sounded like a regular bloodfest. Yeah, the man had definitely run into some bad luck, but, rather than pulling it together, he'd made his little girl into his caregiver and punching bag. Fucking asshole.

"But you have family to help you now, right?" Cullen asked.

"I don't need help," she answered, so automatically that he knew this was a normal response for her.

His eyes narrowed. "We all need help sometimes."

"It's better to just count on yourself. Other people..."

Will let you down, he finished in his head. Like her father always had. Good thing the guy had gone toes-up, or he and Cullen would have a short discussion. "You think your grandmother would let you down?"

She blinked. "Well, no. But I like being able to do things for myself. I don't want to bother anyone."

"'*I don't want to bother anyone*,'" Cullen repeated slowly, the words scraping his nerves like a shard of glass. "My mother said that a lot."

He knew he'd growled from the way Andrea's expression grew wary. "Why does that make you mad?" she asked.

"Mom had been having stomach pains. Her eyes were too bad to drive, but she didn't want to bother anyone to take her to the doctor's office. Not for something that was probably nothing."

Andrea's fingers curled around his hand. "What happened?"

"The nothing was ovarian cancer. By the time the pain got to be too much to ignore, it was way too late." All that energy and fire slowly snuffing out, leaving only a heartbreaking husk behind. He opened his hand before he crushed Andrea's fingers.

"I'm sorry, Señor."

"We all were. My father still blames himself." He stroked a finger down her soft cheek. "He shouldn't. He would have done anything for her, but she never accepted that. She wanted to give, but wouldn't accept the same."

"Well..."

"A relationship needs both giving and taking. *I* need both, sweetie." He looked down into her amber eyes. "When you don't ask me for help—that bothers me as a Dom and as your lover."

She stiffened in his arms. "I like being independent."

"You don't have to always stand on your feet; sometimes it's all right to lean a bit." He tilted her face up. "I want to know that you'll lean on me when you need help. Can you do that?"

"I'll try."

"Good." He rose to his feet, holding her against him. "I just realized we've never enjoyed a bed together. I think the deficiency needs to be corrected."

* * *

Later that night, Cullen returned from disposing of a condom. The candlelight flickered in the breeze from the open windows and glowed on the little Amazon tangled in his covers. Her soft lips had felt as good around his cock as he'd imagined, and then he'd finally had the chance to bind and take her in his own bed. And she looked just right, he thought, smiling down at her.

Her face and breasts were slightly beard-burned, her lips swollen, her arms still fastened over her head. She gazed up at him with heavy-lidded eyes as he unbuckled the ankle cuffs and freed her legs.

"Is it bedtime?" she asked, her voice husky.

"Almost, pet, almost."

Her gaze dropped to his groin, and she blinked. "Again?"

"Yes." He turned her over, pulled her ass up in the air, and slid into her. The feeling that shivered through him felt oddly like coming home.

Chapter Seventeen

Night had already fallen when Cullen drove up his dirt road and frowned at the white cargo van parked in front of the house. Hell. He'd forgotten all about asking his little sub to dinner. After pulling into the garage, he slid out of the truck. Taking a minute, he braced his hands on the hood. Not a good day. Ash gritted on his skin, coated his mouth, darkened his mind. The knowledge—the sight—of what people could do to others sickened him right to the marrow of his bones.

She shouldn't have to see him like this; he needed to send her home.

With a sigh, he straightened up and looked around.

He hadn't given her a key, so she must have walked down to the beach. He went through the house and onto the deck. Near the water, Hector pranced across the sand. In cutoffs and a bright blue tank top, Andrea looked perfectly at home as she admired the dog's tricks. Cullen set a hip on the railing and simply watched.

The cool, salty breeze from the gulf ruffled his shirt, blowing away the smell of smoke. The sound of the lapping waves mingled with Andrea's laughter and cries of the sea gulls hoping for food. Normal sounds. Happy ones.

After few minutes, Hector spotted him and dashed up for an enthusiastic greeting that splattered Cullen with sand. Barefooted, Andrea followed more slowly. As she reached the deck, she paused. "Did I get the wrong evening?"

"No. I'm running late. I got caught in"— *a nightmare*— "an investigation and couldn't get away."

When she moved closer, he stepped back. He was filthy, stinking of smoke.

A flash of hurt showed in her eyes, and then her gaze searched his face. "You look horrible."

He sighed. "It was a...bad...fire. You know, sweetheart, I really need a hug." Stinking or not, he really did.

She didn't hesitate, just wrapped her arms tightly around him and held him. Her body pressed against him, soft and warm, but strong—strong enough to offer comfort as well as receive it. Slowly the blackness retreated from his soul.

When he pulled back, she lifted a hand to his cheek. "You want to talk about it?"

Never. But she deserved an explanation. "Someone tossed a Molotov cocktail into a pawnshop. The owner made it out, but two people renting rooms upstairs got trapped. A firefighter died too, trying to get them out." His mouth tightened. He'd arrived in time to hear the screams as the roof caved in.

"Oh, Señor, I'm sorry." She hugged him again, harder, as if the strength in her arms could squeeze the sadness and horror out of him.

He buried his face in soft curls that held the fragrance of flowers and felt his world start to balance.

"Thank you, sweetie." He straightened. "I should shower." The need to get rid of the grit of the ash almost shook him.

"Go. Hector and I will be here."

When he came back out, he found she'd fixed him chicken noodle soup. He sat at the kitchen table, his stomach still queasy, but the stuff went down smooth and finished the job of restoring his equilibrium.

Normally after a day like this, he and Hector would take to the beach, walking for hours and miles, until the nightmare images lost their grip. When he'd chosen law enforcement, his brothers and cousins had warned him about the dangers of ending bad days with alcohol, and recommended women. But he didn't like subjecting his dates to his dark moods after a bad fire.

The few times he had, the coldness inside him had only grown worse.

Not tonight. Cullen leaned back in his chair and watched Andrea wipe the counters. Her curly hair bounced against her shoulders, and her feet were still bare from the beach. She looked over her shoulder and smiled at him. Aside from having the same height as his mother, the resemblance halted there, but the warmth in their smiles was the very same.

"All done? Do you want more?" Andrea started to pick up his bowl, and he pulled her on to his lap, holding her firmly until she stopped squirming and settled. His little sub.

"Thank you, sweetie. I didn't realize how much I needed you." The pleasure in her eyes squeezed his heart. He lowered his head and kissed her soft lips. As he traced his fingers over her full breast, his body shifted into a new need. "Perhaps now you might provide me with something else."

"Oh?" A glint of mischief lit her eyes. "What if I'm not in the mood to provide anything but food?"

Interesting answer, considering, even through her clothing, he felt her nipple harden. "Since I'm the master and you're the sub, seems like you get to provide it anyway."

"Pfft. Who died and left you in charge?" She jumped off his lap and darted across the room before the surprise left his system.

Shaking his head, he pushed to his feet, amusement filling him. Had a brat on his hands, did he? The anticipation of battle lightened his mood.

When she retreated to the deck, he positioned himself between her and the stairs down to the beach, cutting off her escape.

Her eyes narrowed.

"I think we have a problem here." He moved closer, gradually backing her into a corner. "Little subs need to be respectful and obedient."

She stuck her fingers in her ears, adding a singsong, "Poo and poo. I can't hear you."

Well, damn. He charged. Ignoring the punches that bounced off his chest and arms, he set his shoulder in her stomach and hauled her up. Adorably hard fists hammered on his back, and her shriek made him laugh.

His cock had hardened like a rock. So. Beach or bedroom or... His eyes lit on Hector's igloo-shaped doghouse.

Balancing his squirming sub on his shoulder, he shoved the doghouse over to the railing.

Perfect.

Well, she'd sure vanquished his black mood. Andrea pounded on his wide back, but her fists got as much notice as if she'd hammered on a tank. Defying him had been as stupid as poking a stick at a cranky bear; she'd definitely roused more than anticipated.

And why the heck had he moved that doghouse?

Ruthless hands closed around her waist, and he dropped her on her butt next to the railing. "Give me your wrist."

She kicked him instead.

His laugh, deep and rich and infectious, made her grin. She repeated the kick anyway. She might be wet and excited already, knowing how hard he undoubtedly planned to take her, but that was no reason to make it easy for him.

He grunted when her foot caught him in the thigh, and she hesitated. She'd ruin the fun completely if she damaged his essentials; her next kick landed on his shin and made him wince.

"You little brat." He grabbed her ankles and yanked, tipping her onto her back. Before she could move, he set his knee on her stomach and pressed the air and fight right out of her, even though he kept most of his weight on his other leg.

He pulled her shirt over her head, then her bra. By the time she caught her breath, he'd chained her wrists to the railing. Ignoring her struggles, he unfastened her cutoffs.

Dios, he was good at this. She kicked futilely as he grabbed the hem of her shorts and dragged them right off. Her thong followed. She scowled. Outside. Naked. Did she see a pattern forming here?

When she glanced up at him, the heat in his eyes made her body melt. Dios, the way he made her feel...

"If you kneel and beg my forgiveness, I'll go easy on you, little tiger," he said.

The authoritative look on his face, the sternness of his jaw, made her insides quiver, but no, something in her just didn't want to give in. She'd started this as a joke, but now...now she'd gone too far to chicken out. Too stubborn for her own good, her grandmother would say. "Dream on, estúpido baboso."

The merciless smile he gave her made her shove back a few inches. Oh, Dios. Perhaps she shouldn't have called him a slobbering idiot? When he spun on a heel and stalked away, anxiety welled up in her.

He returned with his toy bag over his shoulder, and she eyed the oversize bag nervously. Dios only knew what he had in there. *Courage. Never show your fear.* She shook her head and put a wealth of sarcasm into her voice. "Boys and their toys."

"That's us. And I have a lot of them. Isn't that nice?" With one foot, he pushed Hector's dome-shaped doghouse closer and dropped the toy bag behind it.

She tried to kick him again when he approached, but with her wrists hooked to the railing, her aim sucked.

He grabbed her waist and thighs, flipped her, and laid her, stomach down, over the damn doghouse. The pebbled plastic was cold, and the position humiliating. She wiggled furiously, trying to slide off.

"Be still." He slapped her butt, and the sting ran right through her, straight to her pussy.

A strong hand gripped her foot. He buckled a cuff around her ankle and chained it to the back of the doghouse. Her toes rested on the plastic ridge at the bottom of the igloo.

With an implacable grip, he pulled her legs apart, then chained the other ankle.

Excitement and anxiety struggled inside her. A second later, she felt his fingers touching her intimately. "For someone playing hard to get, you're damn wet, sweetie," he murmured.

Hard to get? He had her spread open over an igloo! She tried to look back, but her head and shoulders lay halfway down the curved side.

He fingered her and pushed something long and cold into her vagina. Her body jerked with first surprise, then a surprising pleasure. Oh, she'd wanted this.

Lubricant squirted between her butt cheeks. *Oh, no, not that again.* She struggled, jerking against her restraints, knowing there was nothing she could do. "Hijo de puta. *Chíngate!*"

"No, I intend to fuck *you*, little sub." With a low chuckle, he pushed one of his damn plugs into her butt.

Slick, stretch, burn. She gritted her teeth. He'd obviously chosen a bigger size this time.

"You kicked me, called me names, and cursed me. I'd say you earned a reprimand, wouldn't you?" She heard him rummage in his bag. "Let's go for ten."

"*Pinche idioto*, let's not." Oh, she was the idiota, letting her mouth get—

Something smacked her bottom, and her hands clenched. Not hard, he hadn't hit her hard. His hand stroked gently over the spot, taking the tiny sting away.

Another smack. What he used was flat, not as solid as a paddle or cane. She craned her neck, trying to see.

He noticed and held up the long piece of leather, twice as wide as a belt.

Whack. She jumped at the hard blow, her arms jerking against the chains holding them down. That one hurt more.

"You may count the strokes, pet. Don't lose track or I'll start over."

That…cabrón. He'd already hit her three times. Pendejo. "I don't think so. With my hands tied, I can't see my fingers to count." Oh, bad, bad mouth. She'd just doomed herself.

A huff of laughter, then the sound of rummaging in the bag. "You, mouthy little sub, have earned this tonight. And the beating that you're going to get."

She could feel her muscles tighten even as her nipples got so hard they scraped against the rough plastic.

He knelt beside her, holding something in his hand. "Open your mouth."

Madre de Dios, no! She clenched her jaw and tried to turn her head away.

His thumb and fingers pressed on the joints of her jaw, forcing it open, until he could push in a hard rubber ball. He fastened straps behind her head as she glared at him.

Gagged? He'd gagged her?

"Hooting three times together or"—his grin flashed—"*screaming* three times in a row. That's your safe word." The caress on her cheek was disconcertingly gentle considering he planned to beat her. As he walked back, she yanked on her arms. Her legs. Nothing moved.

His fingers grazed up the inside of her thigh, warm and firm, straight up to her pussy. Suddenly the dildo came to life, buzzing softly, shooting currents of excitement through her.

When he touched her clit, she was so wet that she knew she'd been very aroused before he even touched her.

Hard hands kneaded her bottom. And then he stepped back. "Since you didn't want to count, I'll just continue till my arm gets tired."

Madre de Dios. She laid her cheek on the cold plastic, not letting the groan escape.

The leather snapped against her bottom. Soft, then harder, the sting never overwhelmingly painful. The vibrations from the dildo kept her body distracted as pleasure ran through her, meeting the stinging pain until the two merged. Until pressure started to tighten her insides.

He stopped and ran his hands over her bottom, his hands cool against the burning. His touch hurt, and yet more excitement soared through her. His fingers slid between her legs, and then he stroked over her slick clit. Her hips lifted involuntarily. *More, more, more.*

He pinched the nub lightly, and she jerked and whimpered.

"Yes, I think you can take some more," he said. And then the plug in her butt turned on too.

Her legs went rigid as the nerves in her bottom shocked to life. She moaned, unable to move, to do anything. Even to speak. Her brain fuzzed, leaving her nothing except the touch of his hands and the sensations running through her.

His fingers circled her vagina, then up and over her clit, spreading the slickness. Tightness coiled her insides, the pressure of need increasing with each circling movement. She panted around the ball in her mouth, her jaw clamping down on it as the humming increased and the vibrations sped up inside her. His fingers squeezed her clit between them, and she whined. *Please, please, please.*

Whack! The leather slapped her bottom. Her teeth dug into the ball at the burning sting, and her jerk shoved her clit even tighter between Señor's fingers. The stab of pleasure raised her to her tiptoes.

He hit her again, the pain shearing her brain from her feelings and pushing her against his hand. His fingers rubbed her clit. Her legs tightened as the vibrator seemed to shake her whole body.

Another blow, harder, stinging as he stroked over her clit, and the overwhelming sensations smashed into the vibrations inside her—every nerve exploded as her vagina convulsed, battering the hard dildo and plug with waves of exquisite satisfaction that shattered her. She strained against the restraints as her body shuddered.

He pinched her clit again, sending another spasm through her, and his hand caressed her sore bottom, mixing the pain and pleasure together. A tremor ran shook her. And another.

When her body finally stopped shuddering, she could feel her heart hammering out of control. She let herself go limp, stretched across the igloo like an exhausted sacrifice.

She looked like a virgin—well, maybe not *virgin*—sacrifice, draped on the gray dome, the moonlight streaming over her golden skin. Cullen grinned and removed the vibrators. Her moan sighed out as his fingers set off a few more aftershocks, and the scent of her arousal drifted around him. He tossed the toys into a receptacle, and just the noise made her quiver.

He grinned. The last trace of his black mood had disappeared with her noisy orgasm. God, seeing her bound, making her come—nothing equaled that feeling. Damned if he didn't need to get her off again, just to top off his evening. He ran a hand over the dark pink skin of her ass. She whimpered, her body no longer processing the sensation as enjoyment.

He didn't enjoy dealing out pain for pain's sake, but he loved using it to heighten a sub's pleasure until she went brainless. He ran his hand down her legs, spreading her even more open. Her pussy lips glistened, calling to his cock. He wanted to bury himself deep inside her, let her milk him dry, hear those high screams again as she got off.

But he wanted her louder next time. He knelt beside her shoulders and stroked her cheek. She stirred and looked at him with dazed eyes.

Smiling, he unfastened the ball gag and used the shirt at his feet to wipe her face.

The flushed cheeks from her orgasm diminished the effectiveness of her glare. "You gagged me!"

He tossed the red ball in his hand a couple of times. "Did you speak?"

Soft, sweet lips clamped shut. Her curved eyebrows drew together.

He ran a finger over one. "The attitude needs to go too, sweetie. I'd hate to have to pull out a cane. Your ass is already pink enough to satisfy me."

Oh, that one took more work, but the look disappeared. He barely managed to muffle his laugh. Damned if she wasn't even more contrary than Kari and Jessica. God, she pleased him.

She wet her lips. "Let me go. Please, mi Señor."

"Not yet, love. Did you know the doghouse is just the right height for me?"

She frowned, not getting it at first, not until he rose and unzipped his jeans, letting his cock spring out.

Her legs tensed as he walked back.

Her clit was still soft with the aftermath of orgasm, but no matter, he had just the thing to wake her up again. After sheathing himself in a condom, he pulled another toy from his bag and a packet of lube and set them on her back. Her muscles there flinched.

He ran his hands over her smooth skin, tracing down the small bumps of her spine, massaging her hot curvy ass until her muscles relaxed. Soft little sub. Swirling his cock against her pussy, he spread her slick juices around the head. She'd taken him enough times recently that her body could accept his size now, and his time of easing in was over. Gripping her hips, he drove into her in one hard thrust.

Wet heat enveloped him as her startled cry escaped, and her ass jerked, letting him even deeper.

Leaning forward, he cupped a breast in each hand to anchor himself, and started a hard-hitting rhythm, his body too eager to go slow this evening. The slope of the igloo tilted her hips downward just enough that he could thrust slightly upward, adding the power of his legs. Her ass was round and hot against his groin, her breasts soft and warm in his hands. When he felt her nipples pucker and tighten into hard nubs, he smiled.

She aroused so nicely and in so many ways. Now she could get off in another.

He pulled out, then opened her buttocks, and squirted the lube onto the pretty asshole.

Her back arched. "What are you doing?"

"I think you know, love. You've enjoyed the anal plugs; it's time to see if you also enjoy this." He pressed the head of his cock to the tightly puckered hole. Resistance. "Push back against me, sweetie, it'll be easier."

He pushed steadily past the entrance, and then with a cock-squeezing *plop*, he was in. Her ass squirmed under his hands, the muscles clenching. He held there, just inside, waiting for her shock to pass, and enjoying the hell out of the tightness.

Her whole backside felt impaled, pinned to the plastic, burning like fire. "Oh, Dios. Yellow—please, yellow."

"All right, sweetie, you let me know when you're ready."

She'd actually used a safe word. The world hadn't ended, and he hadn't called her a wimp or snorted in scorn. He didn't push into her any farther. She tried to catch her breath, her fingers scraping the plastic igloo for something to latch on to. There was nothing.

She started to move, but that just made it worse, and his hands tightened on her hips, holding her still. "No, love, give it a minute."

But he didn't shove in.

"O-okay." She closed her eyes. This wasn't fun or pleasant or anything, but if he liked it...she'd try. For him. "Go on."

"Brave little tiger." His hand stroked over her back, comforting her. "I'm proud of you for using your safe word. Use it again if you need to, pet." He withdrew slightly, not all the way out, and then pushed in more, over and over, a tiny bit each time until his hips rubbed against her bottom.

"There we go," he murmured.

"I don't like this," she whispered.

"Some do, some don't." His hands massaged her sore butt cheeks, making her nerves quiver, confusing her as the pain inside and outside slowly became...erotic.

I don't.

"I like it as a treat occasionally, and as your master, I want you to try it at least twice, and then if you still hate it, that's all right." Cold lube drizzled down between her cheeks again, slickening his cock as it slowly slid in and out. The burning decreased slightly. But it was still so uncomfortable.

"Some women can get off just from anal sex alone, others need more." He increased his pace, and a weird, exciting sensation joined the discomfort. "Either way, it adds a whole bunch of nerves to stimulate." She felt him pick something off her back and then reach around her leg.

Tiny, squishy nubs pressed into one side of her clit, and she jerked, making his cock slide inside her. *Don't move, stupid.* But the jellylike things hadn't added anything to get her off—they weren't even moving.

A hum sounded, and then every tiny jellylike nubbin sprang to life. A million tiny taps on the side of her clit. Oh, Dios, a vibrator. The sensation yanked her right out of indifference, into arousal, and into need.

He chuckled. "Enjoy that, do you?" He shifted the vibrator and placed it on the other side.

She actually felt her clit harden like a man's cock. *Oh, carajo, the feeling.* Her hips wiggled, and she squeaked when it moved his cock inside her.

"Looks like you're ready, love." With the vibrator pressed against her clit, he pulled his cock back and thrust into her. Fiery discomfort still, only now every nerve in her whole lower half had ignited. His withdrawal left burning in its wake, and his next thrust made her vagina clench, pushed her down against the vibrator. Brutal pleasure shot through her.

When he pulled back again, she caught her breath, waiting for the next shocking burst of sensation.

Her hips wiggled uncontrollably, trying to get more—more of something—more pressure against her clit, more sliding. His hand tightened on her hip, holding her down as he thrust back in.

Everything in her coiled together, waiting for just…just a teeny bit more. He slid in and out, and the nerves surrounding his cock seemed to merge with her clit, pushing her inexorably toward that moment.

He shifted the vibrator over until it lay right on top of her clit. A second later he thrust hard into her, raising her up on tiptoes, shoving her into the vibrator.

Her body gathered, drowning out everything else except what he was doing to her, coiling tighter, tighter—and then it all exploded into shocking, terrifying waves of pleasure. Her hips thrashed under his hands, as the storm of sensation surged outward until even her hair seemed to tingle.

She managed to catch one breath and another, and then his hands gripped her hips, and he hammered into her. He roared as he came, a thrilling sound, and the furious jerks so deep inside her set off more spasms.

Her head dropped down on the plastic as she gasped for air.

Dios, she'd never come so hard in her life. How many people died this way? How would he ever explain to the ambulance crews that he'd chained his girlfriend out on the deck and killed her with too many orgasms?

His big hands massaged her bottom, and the pain from the sore skin set her off into another rolling aftershock. She moaned and arched up as he slowly pulled out of her, leaving her empty and aching, quivering inside.

A minute later, he undid all the cuffs and lifted her against his hard body, holding her up as her knees buckled. Her hands grabbed his shoulders, feeling the iron-hard flex of his muscles, and she rested her forehead on his chest.

She'd never felt so small and helpless in her life. Not just helpless, but...different.

She'd started defying him as a fun way to take his mind off the day, but then she couldn't back down, and he'd not only mastered her, but he'd stolen more than she'd dreamed of giving.

The way he'd taken her and used her in such an intimate way—in so many ways—showing her that every part of her was his to use. And the way he'd forced her to respond... When he'd been inside her like that, she'd had absolutely no ability to control anything, to say anything, to do anything, except take what he gave her. To move where his big hands put her, to accept his cock, his fingers, to come when he wanted.

A shiver ran through her at how different his hands felt as they stroked her body now. Different, but the difference was in her.

* * *

In one of his huge, terrycloth robes, Andrea curled into a deck chair. The padding was soft, the chair oversize to fit

Cullen's tall frame. The moon hung low in the sky, glinting across the dark water, turning the sand to silver. As the waves washed quietly against the shore, she could hear Hector's low breathing from where the dog sprawled next to her chair.

The toys had been picked up and cleaned—her job, Señor had informed her with a grin—and the doghouse shoved back in the corner of the deck. Andrea frowned at it and huffed a laugh. He'd taken her on a doghouse. From behind. Did that make her a bitch?

He'd taken her damned hard too. Her insides felt battered, and the rest of her felt limp, like an undercooked tortilla.

The light from inside flicked off, and Master Cullen strolled out onto the deck, a bottle of water in each hand. He handed her one.

After setting his water on the small end table, he picked her up and sat down with a contented grunt.

Finding his legs even harder than concrete, Andrea squirmed. Her bottom hurt, inside and out. In addition, it still felt odd to sit on a man's lap. But nice. Somehow both safe and sexy.

Definitely sexy, she thought when his fingers, chilled from the cold bottles, slid under her robe and caressed her breast. She felt the nipple tighten. He shifted her slightly so she could rest her head against his shoulder. The sound of music spilled out through the open doors, soft and mellow, and the sensation of his chest moving with each breath was as comforting as the murmuring waves.

"Don't you have to work in the morning?" she asked.

"I do. But since I worked overtime today, I'll go in late tomorrow. After a good night's sleep." He brushed his knuckles over her chin with a smile. "Thanks to you, I *will* sleep."

Warmth filled her at knowing she'd helped. But, compliment or not, he shouldn't get off so lightly. She frowned up. "But you beat on me. Some thanks."

A finger under her chin nudged her face up, and he kissed her, taking his time. His lips were firm but velvety smooth, his tongue demanding. He withdrew only to nibble on her lips, sucking gently on the lower one, before plunging deep again. His arm around her waist tightened as he played with her breast, as he took her mouth, and the feeling of being held for his pleasure made her head spin.

He pulled back, relaxing his grip, still cupping her breast. "Little tiger, I thoroughly enjoyed beating on your cute, round ass, and I intend to do it as often as the occasion requires."

The tremor started in her stomach and radiated outward. Do it again? Have the pain twisting together with the pleasure; have him doing what he wanted with her body, giving her no say in what he did. "Well"—her voice came out breathy, and she cleared her throat—"maybe I've learned my lesson."

"Doubtful. You're a sassy sub." He tipped her back so her head lay against his arm rather than his chest. He studied her face for a moment before smiling. "You managed to use your safe word. I'm pleased, sweetie."

The memory of her panic and begging made her mouth tighten. She'd wussed out completely.

His eyes narrowed. "But I also saw how dizzy you were when you walked across the deck. And you didn't ask for help. You were cold before I brought you the robe, and you didn't ask for help. That displeases me."

She leaned her head against him. "Yes, mi Señor." She liked how he wanted to protect her, but she didn't need that protection. She could stand on her own two feet, dizzy or not.

Chapter Eighteen

Almost done with the cleaning, Andrea set her hands on her hips and surveyed the living room of her newest client. Everything sparkled from the windows down to the hardwood floors. Satisfaction welled inside her like a warm wave. She did damn good work.

She glanced at the high ceilings. No cobwebs. Her gaze snagged on the dust on the edges of the ceiling fan blades. *Carajo*, those definitely needed a good wiping down.

A glance at her watch made her wince. *Late.* She'd better get done quickly, shower, and change in order to arrive at the Shadowlands on time. Her heart gave a hard thump. This would be her first night back since Master Dan had thrown her out. She hadn't wanted to return last weekend, and her Señor had understood so completely that he'd told Master Z not to expect either of them.

Master Cullen's actions had surprised her. And scared her a bit too. What if Master Z blamed her because he'd had to scramble and find a bartender?

But oh, she'd loved having time alone with Master Cullen. They'd played at his house on the beach. Gone swimming, taken long walks. He'd even built a bonfire one night, and they'd made love beside it. He'd dragged her out of bed each morning to work out on his beach jungle gym. He'd also shown her the other way he used the workout area and chained her to the gymnast rings. It was appalling how much exercise a person could get just by coming over and over. And over.

He was so easy to be with—whether cooking or cleaning or playing—that he almost seemed like Antonio. A real partner.

Only then he'd look at her with those eyes—those Dom eyes—and command her. "*Strip.*" "*Kneel.*" "*Bend over.*" She pressed a hand to her stomach as her insides melted at the memory.

Of course, they'd had a few altercations, usually when he'd thought she should have asked for help and hadn't. Like when her van broke down and she didn't call him for a ride. He'd chewed her out good.

Unfortunately, the next day she'd bought a couch for her living room, and he'd come over early and found her trying to drag it inside.

His eyes had turned cold, and his jaw tightened, and oh, she'd known she'd screwed up big-time. He'd asked if she'd even thought of calling him, and she actually had, but somehow she hadn't. Damned if she knew why. Well, maybe because she didn't want to bother him.

And maybe because… Well, asking for something just made her feel funny. Unsettled. Nervous. So she didn't.

She turned around. If she hurried, she had enough time to clean those ceiling fan blades; she'd seen a stepladder right outside in the back.

* * *

Cullen worked his way through the myriad of drink orders. As always, at the beginning of the night, the scene and dance areas waited for the first few brave, I-don't-care-who-watches souls to venture out. A few others would follow, and once the magic number was reached, everyone else jumped in. Meantime, the members crowded the bar, catching up on news.

A Diet Coke went to one Domme, then a tequila sunrise to a new sub. Water only for Dan.

Dan nodded his thanks and asked, "Isn't Andrea returning?"

"She is. Tonight." And she was late.

"Good. I wanted to apologize. I treated her like shit that night." Dan frowned for a second before asking, "So, what are you going to do about her being a trainee?"

"She'll have to quit." Cullen turned away, ignoring the flashing grin on his friend's face. *Asshole.* And typical of him to go right to the point.

A trainee's body was available to the Masters, and to a certain extent, the other Doms. Damned if he wanted anyone touching his sub.

He knew she wouldn't want to stay a trainee, but he should have talked to her before she returned.

As he splashed some Glenlivet over rocks, he considered the last few days. Fun days as they learned all the small details about each other. She liked her coffee very sweet, cleaned up every spill, and preferred showers to baths.

In fact, he'd joined her in the shower this morning and startled her so badly that she'd punched him. He'd managed not to laugh, and in punishment for hitting her Dom, he bent her over and took her so hard and thoroughly that they'd both needed another shower afterward.

He frowned, remembering how she'd winced when he'd washed her pussy. He needed to give her a night off. And she needed to learn to speak up if she hurt.

He handed over the scotch, then smiled at a collared sub and waited for her master to order for her. Mineral water. He poured it into a glass, remembering how Andrea had refused a bottle, saying she wanted her water to taste like water. She loved Chinese food, adored Hector, liked total restraints. Her clit was sensitive at first, and once coaxed out, a nibble at the right time yielded explosive results.

A thin cane applied very lightly down there might be fun...

With uncomfortably tight leathers, he started on the next set of drinks. And where the hell was she anyway?

Jessica trotted up to the bar, wearing a pair of low-cut sheer pantaloons and nothing else. Either she'd annoyed Z, or the master was feeling generous enough to share his sub's assets. She did have gorgeous breasts even if she still turned pink with embarrassment.

Like Andrea on that first day when the top of her dress had finally slipped down. Her embarrassment and arousal had been one of the most appealing combinations he'd ever seen.

Stay on task, Cullen. "What can I get you, sweetie?"

"Oh, nothing," Jessica said. "Master Z sent me. Apparently Andrea left a message on the machine earlier that said she wouldn't be in tonight."

"Why?"

"Didn't say. Z says he'll give her a call while you talk someone into manning the bar."

Fuck that. Cullen spotted Dan across the room. "Dan, the bar is yours."

Not waiting for an answer, he turned to Jessica. "Bar's manned. Tell Z not to call; I'm going to her apartment."

* * *

The emergency room crew had been surprisingly efficient, Andrea thought, considering they'd had the normal influx of heart attacks, bar fights, croupy babies, and pneumonia as well as a bunch of injured people from a pileup on Dale Mabry. The doctor had tsk-tsked over the gash on Andrea's forehead, shone lights in her eyes, x-rayed and wrapped her ankle, and written her a prescription for pain medication. The nurse had brought in crutches and adjusted them, then said her family could take her home.

What family? But she'd made it to her apartment all by herself, although she probably should have stopped to fill the prescription. Oh well, she'd had worse pain before. With a sigh, she leaned back on her new couch and tried to ignore the throbbing in her head and ankle.

A while later, somebody pounded on her apartment door. The noise slammed into her brain like a hammer, her startled jump jostled her leg, and stabbing pain ripped through her ankle. *Carajo! Hijo de puta.* As she rose with the help of the crutches, all her blood rushed downward, and her ankle swelled so tight it felt like the skin would crack and peel.

What kind of cabrón pounds on the door of a woman on her deathbed?

Only one person came to mind. Her cousins rarely visited her here, she usually met her employees at the client's or a restaurant nearby, and Antonio would never pound on anything. That left Señor.

She awkwardly worked her way to the door and checked the peephole. Broad shoulders, muscular chest, brown leather vest. Hadn't he gotten the message she'd left at the Shadowlands? She opened her door and maneuvered clumsily backward.

He stepped inside and looked her up and down. His jaw tightened.

Was he angry because she hadn't shown up? "I wasn't quite up to—"

"If you weren't obviously hurting, I'd haul you over my knee right here and now." His rough voice held enough menace that she shivered. What had made him so angry? He glanced at her wrapped ankle. "How bad is it?"

"Just a sprain."

He cupped her cheek, tilting her face, the gentleness of his hand at odds with the anger in his eyes. "And your head?"

"A gash."

"Anything else?"

"Bruises here and there. Hurt pride. I was cleaning a ceiling fan and stepped wrong on the ladder." She attempted a grin.

Rather than laughing, he growled and lifted her into his arms. The crutches dropped onto the carpet.

"Hey. I can walk."

When she wiggled, he freed up one hand long enough to lightly slap her bare thigh. "We can do this two ways. You can be quiet, and I will carry you over to your chair. Or you can annoy me further, and I will beat your ass for a while and then carry you over to your chair. Which is it, love?"

Compared to how her head and ankle felt, his swat had barely stung; his reprimand had been more for the shock than true pain. She looked up at him. Taut lines bracketed his mouth, another formed between his eyes.

Don't push the mean Dom, Andrea. She swallowed and leaned her head on his chest.

"Very good." He walked across the living room as surely and steadily as if he wasn't carrying a hundred seventy pounds of woman. He settled her on her couch and lifted her legs up so carefully the throbbing didn't increase at all. "You need pillows under this."

He fetched two pillows from her bedroom and put them under her lower legs. "No ice bag?"

"Ah. No." The ER nurse had mentioned that, but it had seemed like too much work and pain to bother.

He gave her another of those frowns and then headed into the kitchen. She heard the sound of drawers and cupboards opening and closing. Scooting down, she leaned her head back against the arm of the couch and tried to identify the weird feeling running through her. Contentment?

She had a pissed off Dom in her small apartment, her whole body hurt like hell, and she felt content?

Idiota. Happy idiota.

Señor returned, wrapping her dishtowel around a large plastic bag filled with ice. He settled it on her ankle.

"Thank you."

A grunt was her only acknowledgement. He prowled across the living room, his size dwarfing the furniture, making the ceiling feel low. Pulling her favorite armchair over to the couch, he sat down next to her. After examining the gash on her face again, he tapped the hospital ID band on her wrist. "You went to the emergency room. How did you get there, and how did you get home?"

The stubborn little tiger gave Cullen a look as if he lacked any brains whatsoever. "I drove."

As his anger increased, his teeth ground together so hard they should have shattered. *She drove.* And acted as if everyone drove themselves to the ER and back. "Wasn't it difficult to use the pedals?" Considering she'd sprained her right ankle.

"I used my left foot." She shifted on the couch to look at him better. The muscles in her face, neck, and shoulders were tight, her skin slightly damp, her jaw tensed. Definitely hurting. If she'd driven herself home, had she stopped? "Did you get something for pain?"

"They gave me a prescription."

"Where's the bottle?"

"I..." A few streaks of color appeared on her pale cheeks as she admitted, "I didn't stop to get it filled." She shrugged.

Cullen closed his eyes and worked on breathing out the rage, although it didn't help worth shit. He asked, "Do you feel like I can't be trusted to help?"

Her eyes widened. "No. Of course not."

But that was definitely part of it. That and she saw herself as taking care of people and never the reverse. An ache settled into his guts, damping his temper, but hurting worse. "Andrea, would you like it if I was hurt and didn't call you?"

She blinked, and then said slowly, "Well, no."

"Exactly." Cullen ran a finger down her cheek and rose. "Does your apartment have rules about pets visiting?"

"Huh? I don't think so."

"Good. Where's the prescription?"

Señor returned an hour later with both the pain pills and Hector. Hector dashed over to greet her, and Andrea cringed, bracing herself, but the dog halted instantly and eased up to her as slowly as a snail.

She petted him, and he sighed in bliss, leaning against the side of the couch. "How did he know to be careful?" she asked, remembering how he'd knocked her on her butt the first day.

"Not long after I got him, I got busted up," Master Cullen said from the kitchen, "and when he rammed me, it doubled me over in pain. He's never done it since." He returned, bringing some toast and orange juice. "I don't know if he recognizes the smell of a hospital or pain."

She ate most of the toast, handing the crusts to Hector who accepted them with as much dignity as a stuffy butler. Since he'd brought Hector here, did he plan to spend the night?

Señor handed her a couple of the pain pills. "Let's get you to bed," he said, his anger gone as if it hadn't occurred, but no smile lit his eyes either. Something inside her stirred uneasily.

"If you hand me my crutches up, I'll be fine," she said and only earned herself an expressionless look.

"Do you need the bathroom?" he asked.

Why did that question feel so personal? But she did and very badly. She sighed. "Yes."

He actually carried her into the bathroom. After he set her on her feet in front of the toilet, she balanced herself with a hand on the sink counter. "I can manage now," she said.

He only snorted and had her shorts down around her ankles before she could protest. "Now you can manage, sweetie. Call me when you're done." He brushed his knuckles over her cheek and left her.

The relief of an empty bladder momentarily wiped out the throbbing in her ankle, but it came back soon enough. She managed to pull up her shorts, only having to catch herself once, washed her hands and face, and brushed her teeth.

He'd obviously heard the sink, for he opened the door—without knocking, the cabrón—and picked her up. Was it petty of her to hope he had a sore back in the morning?

In the bedroom, he stripped her impersonally and tucked her in bed with her ankle elevated on pillows.

"I wear pajamas." She pointed to the dresser.

"Not when you sleep with me." He bent to give her a hard kiss, then left the room, snapping the light out on the way out.

The television came on in the living room, a low murmur of sound, and Andrea stared up at the dark ceiling. Okay, he definitely planned to spend the night. She snuggled down under the covers, and smiled.

* * *

In the morning, she felt much better. The headache had disappeared, and the pain in her ankle had decreased to a minor ache.

In fact, sometime during the night, she'd sprawled on top of her Señor. Now her arms and legs dangled off his body, making her feel like a deflated starfish. After pushing her hair out of her eyes, she rested her forearms on his chest. The dark stubble on his jawline gave him a dangerous appearance, and she smiled at him.

He smiled back…or his mouth did. His eyes didn't.

"How long have you been awake?" she asked.

"A while." His big hands ran up and down her arms.

The somber note in his voice matched his gaze, and apprehension crawled inside her and lodged under her ribs. "What's wrong?"

His hand cupped her cheek. "I've been thinking about you and me."

She swallowed. "And?"

"And I can't continue like this, Andrea."

"Like what?" She wanted to be angry—hadn't the sex been great and all that?—but unease siphoned the anger away. His eyes stayed too serious, and he had on his Dom face.

"You didn't tell me about your injury."

Dios, that again? "I know. But I handled it all right and—"

"No, that's not the point." He didn't release her face, holding her so she couldn't look away. "When a sub has problems, a Dom wants to solve them. You pulled me out of a blue funk, remember? Did you enjoy it?"

She nodded.

"Doms enjoy helping too. It's part of what makes a Dom-sub relationship. Actually, any relationship at all requires give-and-take. Especially one that I'm in. Do you understand what I'm saying?"

"But I did fine."

"No. You didn't. You drove when you shouldn't have and were in pain " His eyes seemed too dark to be green. "We talked about this before, and you said you'd try."

"But…"

"I haven't seen you trying at all, and I can see that you still don't understand. You don't think you did anything wrong. This won't work, Andrea." Even as his mouth tightened, his eyes showed his pain. He'd looked like this after the fire, only this time rather than helping, she'd caused his hurt.

His voice was rough, uneven as he said, "I can't force you to change, but I know now, after yesterday, that I can't live with such a one-sided relationship."

She couldn't find any words; her brain seemed encased in ice, every thought frozen in place. "But…maybe…"

He sighed. "No, Andrea. It's over. We have nothing to discuss, and we won't draw this out any longer. I won't call you again; don't call me." He rolled her off of him and rose to his feet. His fingertips touched her cheek, featherlight. Then after gathering his clothing, he walked out of the bedroom. A minute later, she heard a low command and a whine from Hector. Her apartment door opened and closed, leaving her in silence. And emptiness.

A glimmer of dawn shone through the curtains, and the increasing noise of traffic said rush hour had begun.

He left me. "Don't go," she whispered as the frozen feeling started to melt, leaving pain behind. "I need you."

He'd probably say that she didn't act like it. Why hadn't she called him? Because she hadn't. That was all.

Her fists closed, wadding up the bedcovers. Why couldn't he take her as she was? Most guys complained about their clingy, needy girlfriends and wives, saying they demanded too much. He should have appreciated her independence, not rejected her.

Rejected. She sat up and hunched over her stomach, feeling as if he'd carved out her insides, leaving only a hollow behind. He'd left her apartment...her life. They hadn't been together that long, so why did she hurt as if she'd lost a part of herself?

Cabrón. He shouldn't want to change her. *I'm just fine the way I am.*

She slid out of bed and limped to the bathroom, the carpet muffling the sound of her feet. The mirror showed her pale face, eyes hollowed with pain. She leaned her hands against the counter, holding herself upright, wanting only to sink down on the floor in a miserable ball. She should have known any relationship she started wouldn't last. But how could she have imagined he'd leave her for such a...a *stupid* reason.

Her head bowed as the emptiness swelled inside her until she could choke with it.

It hurt, hurt so bad.

Chapter Nineteen

Three hours later, she answered the door, joy surging through her—*he'd come back*—only to see Antonio and his new boyfriend, Steve. They carried large coffees and a bag of donuts. As she tried to disguise the letdown, the two men gathered plates, then set everything up outside on her tiny balcony in the morning sun. Antonio made her put her foot up on the extra chair.

She pushed down a few bites. Hopefully the guys would think that the pain in her ankle had caused her lack of appetite and reddened eyes.

Their company was a nice diversion. Of course it was. She wouldn't waste any more tears on Cullen. The culero, the desgraciado, the hijo de puta. He didn't deserve her.

He didn't.

Steve studied her. "Are you hurting, sweetie?"

Andrea winced. *Don't use mi Señor's word.* She managed a smile. "No. I'm fine." She picked up her coffee and took a sip.

More muscular than Antonio, Steve wore a T-shirt and jeans, and was definitely the dominant one in the relationship. She'd wanted Antonio to find someone nice, but today...today it hurt to watch.

Antonio set his coffee down and cleared his throat. "I swung by Rosa's last week and got an earful about your wonderful new boyfriend. Gorgeous and such a stud and really hot, according to Jasmine."

His recitation cut through her hard-won equanimity like a knife. Her breath caught for a second, and then she forced a matter-of-fact tone. "He came to Abuelita's birthday party. But he's not a boyfriend. We're n-not"—her voice cracked—"not seeing each other anymore."

Antonio scowled. "But you got back together after he straightened out the other sub, right?"

"How do you know anything about that?"

"Who do you think told him where Aunt Rosa lives?"

Her mouth dropped open. "I-I figured it was some police thing."

Antonio snorted. "Hardly. He was so pissed off when we talked that I thought he'd get out the thumbscrews. And now you look like hell, and it isn't because of your ankle. What happened?"

"He wanted..." Her eyes burned, and she turned her face away, blinking hard. Wussie, crying over a *bastardo*. "He didn't like me to be so independent. He said if I didn't look to him for help, then he didn't want to be with me."

Antonio set the fork down gently. "Hell."

"Yeah, well, *me importa un carajo*."

"Bullshit. You do give a damn."

"No, I don't. I stand on my own two feet. Where does he get off wanting to make me dependent on him?" She tried to bolster up the sense of righteousness and found only aching misery.

"Listen. It's not like that. You can be independent and still…"

Steve looked at her over the top of his coffee and set it down without drinking. "Did you know your uncaring boyfriend phoned Antonio this morning? Before the sun was even up?"

"What?"

"Yeah. All worried about you. He wanted to make sure Antonio kept an eye on you."

Señor had called Antonio after he left? Warmth ran through her, then receded, leaving her colder than before. "Well."

"That's not the point I'm making, though." Steve's brows drew together, and he squeezed Antonio's shoulder. "Your boyfriend said you'd been injured badly enough to go to the emergency room. And that you hadn't called anyone. Do you know how upset Antonio was?"

The verbal blow was totally unexpected, shocking as a slap across the face. Her coffee thumped on the table, sloshing brown liquid over her fingers. She stared at Antonio and saw the truth in his eyes. She'd hurt him. "But—"

"I know why you didn't, chica, but… How would you feel if I landed in the hospital and didn't call you?"

Hurt. Angry. Really hurt. She shoved her chair back, limped over to the railing, and gripped the wood. Her vision blurry with tears, she watched as two young men jogged down the sidewalk, veering around an old lady walking her

Yorkie. A car door slammed, and a woman hurried into the building across the street, carrying a bag of groceries.

Normal sights and sounds of living. Only silence came from behind her. Silence from her Antonio because she'd wounded him. Just like she'd wounded Cullen because she hadn't called him. Because she'd wanted to do it all herself.

Her lip quivered, and she bit it, using the sharper pain to hold back her tears.

After a minute, she forced her fingers open, released the railing, and returned to the table. Steve had his hand on Antonio's shoulder, holding him in the chair.

She smiled, just a touch of amusement trickling through her at the fury on Antonio's face at being kept from her.

"Thank you," she said to Steve. "I needed a moment."

He nodded and dropped his hand. "I figured."

She bent to give her best friend a hard hug. "I'm sorry. I wouldn't hurt you for anything." But she had.

Because of Papa. She'd let her father mess her up more than she'd realized, let him shape her view of the world. She sat back down, saw Antonio's reddened eyes, and her heart squeezed. *Dios, I've screwed everything up.* How could she fix it?

"I'll try, Antonio." But she'd promised her Señor the same thing, and she hadn't tried at all. No wonder he'd washed his hands of her. "I really will."

He nodded. Then he scowled at Steve. "You and I are going to have a talk later, amigo."

"Bring it on."

Andrea thought for a second she'd caused a fight, but then Steve's hand slipped under the table, and Antonio flushed a dark red. No, they probably wouldn't fight later.

When Steve sat back and picked up his coffee, Antonio grinned at him before looking at her. "So what are you going to do about Cullen? You still want him?"

More than she could possibly say. "Yes."

Steve asked, "Maybe if you tell him you're sorry and—"

"He said, '*Don't call*.'" Just the memory of that made her want to cry.

Antonio winced. "Pretty harsh, chica, but I've never known you to give up without a fight."

"No." She stared at the table. *But I don't know if I can be what he wants; I don't know if I want to.*

* * *

The week limped on, much as her gait. But although her ankle improved, the pain of Master Cullen's rejection never eased, throbbing inside her like a deep gouge in her heart.

With her laid up, her employees took over her jobs, leaving her with too much time to think. Or maybe just enough time. By Friday afternoon, her anger had faded. Cullen and Antonio had a point. Her need to show her independence bordered on crazy.

Although Mama had liked people, Papa had been a loner, always preferring to do things himself. And after his discharge from the military, he'd grown even more reclusive. He'd despised having to ask for help, and she'd absorbed those feelings and made them her own.

Why hadn't she seen that before?

She snorted. *Because no one had ever cut me open inside and left me bleeding before.*

But people needed help now and then, and it didn't make them helpless or worthless.

And there was even more to it. When Papa asked for something, and she could fulfill that need, she'd felt good—responsible and caring. In a relationship, both people should feel responsible and caring, and she'd denied Cullen that satisfaction.

Now she knew what she'd done wrong, she'd fix it.

If he let her. "*Don't call,*" he'd said. *Fine. I won't call him.*

She punched buttons on her phone and waited, her lip between her teeth. Would a secretary answer? Could she tell a stranger what—

"Shadowlands." Master Z's voice. Oh, Madre de Dios, she'd far rather have spoken to a secretary.

"Hello. Um, I'd—" Would he remember her? Or maybe they'd already found a new trainee to take her place? If so, the guard wouldn't let her in, not even to see Cullen.

I want to come back. Nothing came out of her mouth even as she called herself names for the silence.

"Is this Andrea?"

"Yes."

"Are you returning to us, little one?"

Oh, he made it so easy, and his voice was so gentle. "I'd like to return."

"Of course. Tonight?"

The rush of anticipation at seeing her Señor made her hand shake. "Oh, yes."

"Excellent. We're having an auction, and the trainees will be needed to inspire the rest. Wear only fishnet stockings, a garter belt, and sexy shoes. I have extra clothing upstairs if you need it."

Auction? What kind of auction? And yet she knew exactly what kind. A thrill of excitement ran through her. Might Master Cullen bid for her? What if he didn't? "Ah...um. Okay. Yes, Sir."

She heard the amusement in his voice as he said, "I look forward to seeing you, little one."

* * *

That night, Andrea hung her long knit dress in her locker at the Shadowlands. After squeals of joy from Heather and Sally and a slap on the back from Dara, and babbling about what happened to Vanessa, the talk turned to the auction.

"We haven't had one for almost a year." Standing in front of the mirrors, Sally put her hands on her hips and shimmied. "Do you suppose I can get Master Marcus to bid on me?"

"What are you offering?" Dara asked.

"I'm still trying to make up my mind."

"What does that mean?" Andrea finger-combed her hair and checked her makeup. She'd worn more tonight than normal...just because. *Liar*—just because she'd see Master Cullen. "What offering?"

"Come, young Skywalker, and I'll explain." Sally linked arms with her. "First of all, there won't be an inspection tonight, and we won't be waitressing. Right now, we have to go get our cards."

"Cards?"

"They'll show what we're offering to auction off."

As they left the dressing room, Andrea smiled at Ben where he sat behind his desk.

The guard gave her a once-over and grinned, gifting her with a thumbs-up. As he turned away to help the first of the members sign in, Andrea and Sally entered the bar.

Andrea paused just inside the door, pulling in a breath redolent with the fragrance of leather and a hint of the bleach cleaning solution. In another hour, the room would smell of sweat and perfumes and sex. The light from the wall sconces flickered over gleaming brass and polished wood as the harsh electrobeat of Virtual Embrace assaulted her eardrums. Dios, she loved this place.

What would Master Cullen do when he saw her? "*Don't call.*" She couldn't get those words out of her head. She'd walked halfway across the room before she dared look at the bar. And she stopped dead.

Señor stood in front of his bar, his arms folded across his broad chest, and no expression on his rough-hewn face.

Last week, she'd touched that face, stroked her fingers over the craggy bones, and he'd smiled—that Master Cullen smile—just for her. What if he never gave her that again? *He must.* Somehow she'd make him see.

She crossed the rest of the way, a miracle considering she couldn't feel her legs. "I..."

His eyebrows rose.

"I-I'm here. I want to... I'll try. I want to try again." She swallowed against the tightness in her throat.

His expression remained set, and she saw the reserve in his eyes. He didn't believe her. She'd said exactly the same thing before. But how could she ever prove she'd change—really try to change—if he didn't give her a chance?

He tilted his head. "Go join the others, trainee."

Disappointment squeezed her insides. Had she thought he'd just grab her and kiss her and... She whispered, "Yes, Señor."

But hope flickered inside her and pushed some of the desolation aside. He hadn't kicked her out. She was still a trainee.

I don't want to be a trainee.

Before she could do something stupid, Sally grabbed her arm and pulled her away. "Geez, did you stare at him long enough? You're going to get yourself in trouble. Come on." At the far end of the room, the secluded sitting nooks had been merged into one big area, sheltered by the tall planters. "This is our cozy subbie home for tonight."

Only Kari and Jessica occupied the area. Attired in normal dungeon-wear, they apparently didn't plan to participate in the auction.

When Jessica saw Andrea, she bounced to her feet. "Andrea! You're back."

By the time she'd collected a hug from the two, Andrea was blinking back tears.

Jessica smiled and patted her shoulder. "Okay, we'll ease up on the emotional stuff. Why don't you guys tell me what you're offering before the hordes arrive?"

Andrea hauled in a breath. "Would someone explain this offering thing?"

"I haven't seen an auction before either, but according to Master Z, you're auctioning off your time and willingness to negotiate a scene—for here only." Jessica held up a heavy card about 5x5 inches. "I write what you're interested in doing for whoever buys you. It can be anything from waiting on someone by bringing them drinks, to a back or foot massage, and/or flogging and that kind of stuff, and/or blowjobs and sex."

"Madre de Dios."

Kari laughed. "That's what I thought. I think it'd be fun, but only if Dan bought me."

"And you need to remember that," Sally said. "The Dom who buys you might be one you don't especially like. So what you put on the card needs to be something you're okay giving to anyone." She shrugged her hair back over her shoulders. "Of course, you will talk with them before scening, and this isn't a club where any dude with the admission price can get in. Master Z screens the members."

Andrea nodded.

"And the idea that just anyone can buy you..." Sally giggled. "It's a rush, you know?"

"You're such a brat," Jessica said. "What should I write on your card?"

"Let's say a two-hour time limit. Sex—any kind. Flogging or canes to moderate pain." Sally tapped a finger on her chin and added, "More than one Dom is okay, or a Dom and his sub."

Andrea's mouth dropped open.

Sally grinned. "Hey, it's fun, adding in another female. And two guys can be really hot."

Jesús, María, y José! Andrea pressed a hand to her quivering stomach where a whole raft of uncomfortable sensations had taken residence. Maybe she should get out now while she could. The thought of letting someone other than her Señor touch her made her almost sick.

But if she left, they'd drop her from the trainee program, and she'd never see him again. If she stayed, maybe she could convince him she'd changed. Somehow.

But she'd have to let someone else play with her. Her lips thinned, and her shoulders straightened. Okay. She'd done it before, after all.

"Andrea?" Jessica held up a card. "What goes on yours?"

"Light pain: flogging or canes or a spanking." She bit her lip and stared at the green ribbon on her cuffs. *What about sex?*

Jessica added reluctantly, "For you guys—the trainees—Z said he'd be disappointed if you didn't do your part toward making this a success. A lot of the donations the Doms make to earn their fake dollars go to his favorite children's fund."

"All right. A blowjob." She didn't consider a blowjob all that intimate.

Jessica wrote that, and then looked up, her pen raised above the card.

Andrea shook her head. "I can't do more." Maybe she should leave. She took a step back.

Kari curled an arm around her waist. "That's enough. You don't have to do anything else."

Andrea nodded as Jessica strung a ribbon through the card and hung it over her head like a necklace so the card bounced between her breasts.

Chapter Twenty

She was here. His little sub—no, not his. Striving for control, Cullen worked his way down the bar, handing out drinks and waters, Cokes and iced tea. He tried to keep a mental tally of who had alcohol so he could cut them off after the second drink, but for the first time in his life, his brain had shut down. The only thing he could remember was the look on Andrea's face, the joy in her eyes when she saw him, the husky sound of her voice. The pain when he hadn't responded.

The hurt in her face had almost broken his resolve.

She was here at the Shadowlands. Pleasure surged up in him, and he stomped it down. Dammit, she'd promised to try before and hadn't done it.

He scrubbed his face. He'd walked around the last few days like an amputee. Perhaps he understood her father better now that he knew what it felt like to lose an essential part. His nightmares had gotten worse too. Her accident had hit too close to home, and now he not only dreamed of his mother's death, but Andrea's also.

Every night he'd wake and reach for his little sub and find only emptiness. He'd almost called her a couple of times just to make sure she really was alive. *You are so screwed up, buddy.*

But she'd returned to the Shadowlands; she wanted to try again. Should he relent? Or would that return them to the same unacceptable habits? He doubted he could walk away from her twice. Fuck, he might not survive *once.*

What should he do?

Buy her? Between the workshops he'd given and his donations to the local children's fund, he'd earned plenty of fake money.

If he only had a way to know if she meant what she said. "*I'll try.*" *Would she really?* Scowling, he looked over at the submissives in their special spot, now crowded with Doms interested in bidding. After reading a card, the Dom would talk to the sub and get an idea of how a scene might work. Every time a Dom picked up Andrea's card, brushing against her bare breasts, Cullen's jaw tightened until he could feel the muscles knotting.

He reached the end of the bar and found Jessica waiting, almost quivering with her need to talk to him.

After handing her a margarita, he lifted an eyebrow.

"She picked blowjobs and light flogging." Jessica grinned. "Even when I told her what Z had said about trainees doing their duty, she couldn't go further. And she said she didn't belong here anymore."

"What?"

"No, no, relax. Kari talked her into staying tonight, but she looks pretty unhappy." Jessica frowned. "I really like her. You be nice to her, or I'll wallop you."

Z's sub got a lot of leeway, but in the club, threatening a Dom, even as a joke, wasn't permitted. And she hadn't been joking. Cullen leaned a forearm on the bartop and looked down at the short blonde. "Jessica, I don't like your attitude."

Jessica stiffened as if someone had icicled her spine.

He noticed Z standing nearby. Z nodded.

Cullen reached across the bar, lifted Jessica by her upper arms, and yanked her facedown on the bartop.

She yelped.

He flipped up her skirt and swatted her ass hard enough that the sound of flesh against flesh rang through the room. Then he set her back on her feet.

"How—how dare—"

"Master Cullen." Z's smooth voice cut off the sub's sputtering. "If my pet gives you any more trouble, you have my permission to tie her up and keep her as a bar ornament." Z stroked a finger down Jessica's flushed cheek before glancing at Cullen. "You may strip her first if you wish."

And he walked away.

Cullen crossed his arms over his chest.

"Oh shit, oh shit, oh shit," Jessica muttered, before looking up. "I'm sorry."

God, she was cute when she went all submissive. But she didn't mean it. Not yet.

She stared at him, and then her face crumpled, tears glimmering in her eyes. "I really am sorry, Master Cullen."

Much better. "And you really are forgiven, sweetie."

He handed her the drink. "Thank you for helping with Andrea."

Her smile came out like a beam of sunlight. She took two steps back, putting herself out of reach before saying, "The poor girl has no idea of the nasty Dom she's getting."

As Jessica scurried away, Cullen barked a laugh. Nasty? Compared to some of the other Doms, he was sweetness and light. If Jessica smarted off to a real sadist, he'd cover her backside with welts, and she... His eyes narrowed. *Well, now, there was a thought.*

After the majority of the members had arrived, Cullen turned the bar over to Raoul and searched out Karl and Edward. Then he wandered around and talked with every Dom interested in the auction. If he missed any, hopefully they'd get the word.

Finally he and Z discussed the future of the trainee program.

At nine thirty, Jessica, Kari, and Beth herded the subs who'd volunteered to be auctioned-off over to the raised stage Z put up for special events. Members gathered, pulling couches and chairs into a semicircle.

Z walked across the stage and stopped in the middle. "Welcome to the Shadowlands' charity auction. We have a fine selection of submissives who have offered their time." He nodded to the subs lined up to the right of the stage. "Give them a hand, please, for their generosity."

After the clapping and cheering stopped, Z continued. "Remember, your win entitles you only to negotiate with the submissive for what she wrote on her card. Also, before you drag her off to a scene area, before you even touch her, you hand over your Dom Dollars to my sub." He pointed at Jessica who sat at a table to the left of the stage.

Unable to tolerate sitting, Cullen stood off to one side of the area. *Quite a nice variety of subs this year.* One curvy woman's breasts overflowed her corset—she'd be popular, he knew—and one had such a slender waist, she probably never ate more than three crackers at a meal. A couple of women were short enough that Cullen might step on them by accident.

Now with Andrea—her lovely height and curves balanced beautifully. He wanted to toss her over his shoulder and find a place—any place would do—to savor those curves, to cup her full breasts and tease her pink-brown nipples into hard peaks. Her fishnet stockings and hot pink garter belt perfectly framed her pussy, and she had nothing covering it.

As he watched, he saw the little Amazon's gaze flickering over the crowd. She rubbed her hands on her thighs and shifted her weight every few seconds, uncomfortable in a way she hadn't been since she first came to the Shadowlands. Unfortunately for her, he planned to make everything worse.

Guilt joined the worry in the back of his mind. But she needed a chance to prove herself to both of them, which meant neither of them would enjoy this auction. Shaking his head, Cullen leaned on a chair and prepared to endure the show he usually enjoyed.

A quiet sub with a sweet smile went first, offering herself for a light flogging by one Dom only. She was fairly new to the club, Cullen knew.

An auction at the Shadowlands served two purposes. Local charities benefited since members could earn the fake Dom Dollars from donating time or money.

Almost more important, the auction provided a way for the quieter or newer members to make friends. The Doms planning to bid would talk with all the subs as they checked their tags, and in turn, subs had a chance to evaluate potential Doms. If a Dom won, he and the sub would negotiate a scene. If he lost, the two could always hook up later.

"I'm opening the bidding at fifty Dom Dollars. Will anyone give me fifty for this pretty sub?" Z looked around. "Ah. I have fifty from Aaron. Will anyone give me more?"

And the auction took off. For the next two subs, Z kept the patter fairly quiet, easing both the crowd and the subs into the swing of things. Sally was the third in the line—a line that Z arranged every year according to some arcane logic of his own. The sub grinned as she climbed the steps to the stage.

"Here is Sally, one of our own Shadowlands trainees, and she is offering"—Z's eyebrows rose as he looked at the card—"Little one, perhaps you should have put down what you *won't* do."

The audience laughed as he read off the card, and brisk bidding ensued. When it slowed, Z tugged on the sub's hair. "Sally, I think the Doms should see the cute little bottom they get to cane or spank. Turn and bend."

Sally laughed, turned her back to the audience, and bent over. Z stroked his hand down her butt, and Cullen could almost see the Doms lean forward.

Then Z slapped Sally's ass hard enough to make her jerk, and the fair skin pinken. "The bidding stands at seven hundred twenty. Am I offered more for the chance to flog and fuck this soft little ass?"

Bidding continued upward for another hundred.

By the time Andrea reached the stage, about three-fourths of the subs had been auctioned off. The crowd thinned as Doms took their prizes off to the various stations. Stomach heavy with dread, she climbed the steps, hoping no one could see her legs shaking. Once there, she looked out over the audience, keeping her gaze away from the left side where she'd seen Master Cullen standing. If she saw the cold look in his eyes again, she'd probably burst into tears.

Z smiled at her, picked up her card from between her breasts, and read, "Andrea offers light flogging or spanking, and a blowjob. One Dom only. Time offered: now until closing."

Closing? Andrea's jaw dropped. *No. No way.* She hadn't specified any time at all; why would Jessica write that? One hour—she'd figured on only one hour. That was more than plenty. She turned to Master Z. "Mast—"

"Did I give you permission to speak, trainee?"

She shook her head. *But, but, but...*

A big, blond Dom with a military haircut opened the bidding.

Andrea took a step back. Oh, Dios, not him. Before the auction started, he'd read her tag and laughed. "A trainee and you only want *light* flogging?" He'd pinched her cheek hard enough to bring tears to her eyes. "Sure, I'll go *light* on you."

Someone else bid, please. A soft voice called, "Fifty."

Oh, thank you. Andrea looked at the bidder, and her vision blurred as horror washed through her. *Not him, please not him.*

Soft voiced, tall and thin, he looked like an escapee from a Dilbert cubicle. But every weekend she'd seen him with various subs; they all received horrible long welts across their butt and legs from his single-tail.

The first Dom growled and upped the bid, and then the two ran the numbers up. She should be pleased she was making money for charity, but, Madre de Dios, she didn't want to do it like this.

Another Dom entered the bidding—one of the hard-core sadists.

Why? Did she have some sort of sign that said HURT ME stamped on her forehead? The new Dom started an argument about whether a sub should be flogged first or suck off their Dom first. One pointed out that after a flogging the sub would still be crying and have a stopped-up nose, and the blowjob would suffer. None of them disagreed on the crying part.

Whoever won would have her until closing. Safe word. She could always use her safe word.

Why didn't she find that reassuring? Should she just leave now? Hands clenched, she closed her eyes. Wouldn't anyone else bid on her? She kept her gaze averted from where Señor stood. He wouldn't. Someone else must.

But these three had run up the total as high as Sally's. Her knees wobbled. *Walk away, estúpida. Go home.* But then she'd lose her Señor for certain.

Another Dom bid, a younger Hispanic one, and Andrea closed her eyes in relief. Maybe... But the big blond snapped out another bid, and when she checked the Hispanic, he was talking with Master Nolan.

Her gaze swept the audience, drawn to the side where Cullen had stood. He wasn't there. The feeling of abandonment hit her as if someone had punched her in the stomach. He hadn't stayed to see her auctioned off. Maybe, maybe he didn't care at all. Even a little.

The soft-voiced Dom raised another ten dollars and ran his fingers over the whip coiled on his belt. She cringed and pulled her gaze away. And saw Master Cullen sitting right there in the front row. Joy surged up through her as she stared down at him.

Long legs stretched out, arms folded over his chest, jaw stern. His jade-colored eyes met hers.

Buy me, buy me, buy me. She opened her mouth to ask, but nothing came out. What if he said no? Refused her?

Just the thought made her quail.

Oh Dios, was she *afraid* to ask? The realization hit her so hard she staggered back a step. She'd thought she had it all figured out, but her need to stand on her own feet had only been part of her problem. The rest was that she was afraid that once she did ask for help, that person would let her down.

Like her father had.

Her hands fisted at her sides as the memories swamped her. Disappointment after disappointment—"I'll come to your play...your confirmation...your parent-teacher conference..."—until she'd finally stopped asking to save herself the inevitable letdown and pain.

And now, because of her father, she didn't have the guts to ask for help from someone else. Especially from Master Cullen. If he let her down, it would hurt much, much worse than anything a sadist could do to her.

But her Señor wouldn't say no. The certainty welled up in her with the memory of his anger when she'd needed help and hadn't called him. All he'd ever wanted to do was to care for her.

Cullen's dark green eyes met hers. Steady. Level. Controlled. Her father'd possessed physical courage, but not the bravery to dare emotional fire. He'd retreated from everyone. Especially her. But Master Cullen would never crawl into a bottle to escape life. And she'd never seen him let anyone down, not his friends or the trainees or his family.

He wouldn't let *her* down. All she had to do was ask.

His gaze hadn't left hers.

Against the roaring in her ears, she couldn't hear her own voice as the words punched through the tightness in her throat, free at last, "Master, please buy me."

Pleasure and approval filled his eyes. "That's my girl," he said to her alone, his voice rough. Unsteady as she'd never heard it before. His big voice filled the room. "One thousand for my courageous sub."

The relief filling Andrea almost took her to her knees.

Z chuckled. "Going once, going twice... Sold to Master Cullen. *Finally.*" He put a hand under her arm, and helped her down the steps and off the stage.

And there she stood, holding the edge of the platform, feeling as if the floor undulated beneath her feet. Her breath shuddered through her chest as fear unhooked its claws. She'd asked him for help, and he'd given it. *Don't cry, don't cry, don't cry.*

Suddenly hard hands on her shoulders turned her, and Master Cullen yanked her into his arms. When her legs sagged, his grip tightened, molding her against his huge body.

Surrounded by his embrace and his scent of leather and man, the feeling of safety rose like a wave through her, crumbling all her resolve. A sob shook her ribs and broke free. And then she was crying, horrible, ugly sounds that she couldn't stop.

"You're safe, sweetie," he rumbled, rubbing his cheek on her hair. "Poor baby."

She cried until she felt empty inside, and his chest was wet with her tears. Her voice hitched as she whispered against his skin, "Thank you."

His arms tightened and even though her bones ached, it felt as if he'd pressed some of his strength back into her. When he released her, she could stand on her own.

His finger nudged her chin up. "Let's see the damage," he murmured.

Dios, she must look a mess. He handed her a paper towel. "Blow."

She blew her nose and dropped the makeshift handkerchief into the wastebasket by the stage. Then he used another to wipe her face, even under her eyes where the mascara had undoubtedly run. A man who knew how to clean a woman's makeup?

His eyes crinkled. "I've been a Dom a long time, sweetie." He turned her face, side to side, and grunted in approval. "All better."

With a shaky hand, she took another towel. As she wiped her tears from his chest, touching the crisp hair, the hard curve of his muscles, the hollow of his shoulder that had always seemed just designed for her, she let the small task fill her mind and push all her doubts aside for the moment.

When she finished, she looked up slowly, gazing up over the muscular corded neck, his jaw, the firm lips that held no smile. The lines beside his mouth had deepened, and her finger traced one. His cheekbones seemed more prominent as if he'd lost weight. Green eyes, darker than a forest at dusk, focused on her. Dom eyes.

Caught in his gaze, she stilled, and her heart started to pound. He leaned forward, one arm on each side of her, bracing his hands on the stage and trapping her inside. "Ready to talk?"

"Yes, Señor." She looked down.

He set a finger under her chin and lifted, studying her face for a long moment. "Did you wonder if I'd buy you?"

"No." She hesitated and revised, "No, Señor. Not once I managed to ask. You"—she swallowed hard—"you care too much to let me down like that."

"There we go," he murmured. The back of his fingers brushed her cheek. "I'm very proud of you, love. I know it wasn't easy."

Her chest felt tight, as if he was hugging her, although his arms hadn't moved.

"It will get easier." His gaze intensified. "If we continue. Do you want me as your Dom—your master?"

The question, the offer felt like a big wave under her, hurtling her toward the shore. "Oh, yes. Please, mi Señor." *Please, please, please.*

His mouth curved. "I'll make sure you get lots of practice in asking for help." His hand threaded through her hair, and he pulled her head back until he could capture her lips. A hard possessive kiss, not kind, and the very lack of gentleness told her how much her answer had meant. He bit her lips, sucked the lower one into his mouth. Then his tongue swept in again. Heat flared through her, burning her fears away. When he pulled back, her arms were around his neck and her body plastered against his.

He felt so good. So right.

"Come, sweetheart," he said, wrapping an arm around her waist. "You need some water, and I really need a beer."

The auction had apparently concluded, for the stage had emptied and people were moving chairs back to the usual places. Halfway across the room, the big blond who'd bid on her called out to Cullen. "Did she wipe out your Dom Dollars?"

Cullen laughed and said, "You ran that up pretty high, asshole."

The man smiled before looking at Andrea. "I'm rather sorry you won. I'd started to think I'd be enjoying myself." A look from eyes the color of blue ice made her shiver, and she edged closer to Cullen.

Her Master laughed and simply tightened his arm. Safe. Protected. "Dream on, Karl," Cullen said mildly. "But I appreciate the help."

Help?

At the bar, Raoul and Marcus were serving drinks. Raoul looked up, grinned. "Beer and water?"

"Definitely." Master Cullen pulled Andrea over to join Nolan and Beth.

Nolan nodded, then growled, "You almost lost her to that youngster. For a moment there, I thought I'd have to deck him, but he decided to see reason."

Andrea's mouth dropped open. Nolan had kept the young Dom from bidding? And the sadistic Dom had been...*helping* Cullen? Hijo de puta, he'd terrified her into begging him to buy her? She scowled.

"Look at that face." Cullen rubbed his knuckles over her cheek. "Yes, it was a set-up. But the choice was yours. You didn't have to ask for help."

"And if I hadn't?"

"Then Master Marcus would have bought you."

A warm feeling grew in her stomach. "Even if I hadn't done what you wanted, you'd still protect me?"

His thumb caressed her cheek. "A master protects his sub. Anytime and anywhere. Always."

His. The surge of joy almost hurt. *Am I really?*

As if in answer, he lifted her arm and unbuckled her gold leather trainee cuff.

The stab of disappointment took her breath. He didn't want her?

But then he looked up. "Nolan." He held his hand up and caught a pair of leather cuffs from out of the air. Unclipping them, he buckled them on in place of the trainee cuffs. She stared down at them. Incredibly soft fleece lining. The rich brown leather matched the color of Cullen's vest and each cuff was engraved with Cullen's initials.

Master Dan walked up. Kari, still wearing the auction apron, danced with excitement beside him. Her smile at Cullen and Andrea brimmed with pleasure…and satisfaction.

Well, carajo. Andrea's mouth dropped open. Both Kari and Jessica had taken part in the scheme. They'd pushed her to enter the auction and deliberately not set a time limit. *Those sneaky brats.* But her anger slid right away as her fingers ran over the cuffs. *Soft. His.*

Señor chuckled and squeezed her hand.

Dan nudged Nolan with a shoulder. "Why do I get the impression that he's not going to share his submissive?"

Cullen growled, "You touch her, buddy, and I'll break your face."

Nolan barked a laugh. "She doesn't get to play, and you do, oh, Master of the trainees?"

Andrea took a step away. As the trainer, Cullen touched the subs all the time. She smoothed her expression out so maybe he wouldn't see her unhappiness.

Cullen looked down. The pinched look around Andrea's mouth and the furrow between her eyes plainly showed her unhappiness. He almost laughed. The little tiger didn't want to share him; she considered him hers.

He'd spent years going from sub to sub, now he'd settled on one, and he felt damned pleased about it. She was his, problems and all. He'd have to make sure he stayed on top of that asking for help problem.

In fact... He pulled her back against his chest and cupped her breasts, enjoying her muffled gasp. "I think we'll practice having you ask for help some more," he murmured into her ear. "Tonight, I'll find out how prettily you can beg for release. Over and over and over."

In his palms, her nipples puckered, and he could feel her heart rate increase.

He pressed a kiss to her curly head, then called, "Master Marcus, I need you, buddy."

Marcus walked down to the end of the bar. His glance took in the location of Cullen's hands, flickered over Andrea's cuffs. He smiled. "I do congratulate you, Master Cullen. She is a prize."

"She is that," Cullen said. "But since I don't want to wake up with my throat cut some night, I think you'd better take charge of these." He nodded at the gold trainee cuffs lying on top of the bar.

His little sub looked back over her shoulder, her eyes wide and worried. Adorable. Cullen kissed her cheek.

"Can y'all elaborate on what '*take charge*' means, please?" Marcus asked.

"You're the new trainee master. It'll be good for them to have a new boss." Cullen waited for some sense of loss and felt only satisfaction. He'd done his job there; time to move on, and what he was moving toward filled him with anticipation.

Marcus studied the cuffs for a minute and then smiled slightly. "I am honored."

"And Marcus? I'm afraid you have another vacancy in your trainee list. This little sub is so much trouble that I'm going to give her my personal attention." Cullen caressed her velvety nipples, and Andrea made a hungry noise.

Marcus laughed and tipped his head before moving away.

Andrea's auction card kept bumping against Cullen's fingers as he fondled her breasts. Come to think of it, he'd bought her, hadn't he? He picked the paper up and read it, grinning when he saw the totally blank space after TIME OFFERED. Apparently Z had added the "Until closing" part all on his own, the lying bastard. He'd have to thank him later.

Cullen glanced at the offerings. "I see that I've won a volunteer for a blowjob. Perhaps we'll start there and work our way through each item on this very *short* list."

Those soft lips wrapped around his cock would be a fine way to start the evening. Then perhaps he'd chain her to the bondage table with her legs wide open and tease that sensitive pink clit of hers until—

His little sub turned in his arms, derailing his thoughts. Her eyes were already heavy-lidded, her cheeks flushed with arousal. After a second, her lips, swollen from his mouth, curved. "May I be excused for a moment, Master?"

Master. Did she know how that turned his heart to mush? He lifted an eyebrow at the mischief glinting in her big eyes. All right, let her run with it. "You may."

She joined Kari for a moment's conversation. After rummaging in her apron pocket, Kari pulled out a felt marker and handed it over. Andrea smiled at Kari and wrote something on her auction card.

Cullen exchanged glances with Dan who looked equally confused.

When Andrea walked back, the look she gave him was one he hadn't seen before—one he'd thought would be offered to another Dom someday. *Complete Surrender. Complete trust.*

Love.

A submissive's gift. She dropped to her knees in front of him, and he touched her face, hoping she could see his acceptance in return.

Her eyes gleamed with tears for a moment, and her lips quivered. Then she smiled and the mischief returned as she offered her auction card.

What was she up to now? Cullen put a hand on her shoulder, to keep her in place, enjoying the tiny tremor that went through her. He lifted the card, and his gaze dropped to where two lines had been added.

He chuckled at the first: *Sex. Lots and lots of sex.*

How had he been so lucky as to find someone whose sense of humor matched his?

He read the last line, then lifted her into his arms, his own sweet sub to cherish and protect and love.

TIME OFFERED: *Forever.*

 **THE END**

Cherise Sinclair

I met my dearheart when vacationing in the Caribbean. Now I won't say it was love at first sight. Actually since he was standing over me, enjoying the view down my swimsuit top, I might even have been a tad peeved—as well as attracted. But although our time together there was less than two days, and although we lived in opposite sides of the country, love can't be corralled by time or space.

We've now been married for many, many years. (And he still looks down my swimsuit tops.)

Nowadays, I live in the west with this obnoxious, beloved husband, two children, and various animals, including three cats who rule the household. I'm a gardener, and I love nurturing small plants until they're big and healthy and productive...and ripping defenseless weeds out by the roots when I'm angry. I enjoy thunderstorms, playing Scrabble and Risk and being a soccer mom. My favorite way to spend an evening is curled up on a couch next to the master of my heart, watching the fire, reading, and...well...if you're reading this book, you obviously know what else happens in front of fires.

Loose Id Titles by Cherise Sinclair

Master of the Mountain
The Dom's Dungeon
The Starlight Rite

The MASTERS OF THE SHADOWLANDS Series
Club Shadowlands
Dark Citadel
Breaking Free
Lean on Me

The above titles are available in e-book format at www.loose-id.com

Masters of the Shadowlands
(contains the titles *Club Shadowlands* and *Dark Citadel)*
Breaking Free
Lean on Me
The Dom's Dungeon
The above titles are available in print at your favorite bookstore

LaVergne, TN USA
28 October 2010
202554LV00003B/26/P